Sutter's Landing

Betty Thomason Owens

Write Integrity Press
Sutter's Landing
© 2017 Betty Thomason Owens

ISBN-13: 978-1-944120-31-3
ISBN-10: 1-944120-31-9
E-book ISBN: 978-1-944120-47-4

Published by Write Integrity Press, PO Box 702852, Dallas, TX 75370
Find out more about the author, Betty Thomason Owens, at her website: **BettyThomasonOwens.com**
www.WriteIntegrity.com
Printed in the United States of America.

Library of Congress Control Number: 2017941453

Dedication

For Aunt Jen, Aunt Fran, Aunt Edna, and Mom

I would have lost heart,
unless I had believed that
I would see the goodness of the LORD
in the land of the living.
Wait on the LORD;
be of good courage, and
He shall strengthen your heart;
wait, I say, on the LORD!

Psalm 27: 13-14 NKJV

What Readers are Saying about the Kinsman Redeemer Series ...

This beautiful story is told gently and thoughtfully-- trademark of Betty's writing. Readers of women's fiction will enjoy this one.

– Linda Yezak

I enjoyed the characters and the way they interacted. Also, she portrayed the prejudice that was so prevalent in the south during this period of time in a realistic manner. I can't wait to read her next novel. This book is well worth the read. I loved it!

– Jennifer Hallmark

There is a moment, with every great book, when you realize you are just a chapter or two from the end and you are conflicted. You don't want to finish it because that means the end of your 'relationship' with the characters. But you can't put it down because, even though you think you know how it will end, you HAVE to find out HOW. This author has a unique knack for weaving a story around Biblical stories, principles and truths that I absolutely love. I highly recommend this book.

– Sharon Coleman

The tone and atmosphere of this Appalachian-feel story was so realistic I felt like I was living in 1950's Tennessee. The dialect was perfect, the setting beautifully described, and the characters completely identifiable. I've read several of Owens' books, and I think this is the best.

– Ginny Smith

Chapter One

April 8, 1955
Trenton, Tennessee

Connie Cross sat straight up in bed. What was that sound? Slowly, her vision adjusted to the semidarkness of her room. Outside, but close—too close. A gunshot? She slipped out of bed, donned her robe and tiptoed through the next room where her mother-in-law Annabelle lay. A soft snore told her the woman still slept.

Quiet as possible, Connie opened the back door and stood looking through the screen. Chilled air curled around her ankles and sent a shiver up her spine. She pushed the screen door open. Outside, on the small back porch, she stood for a moment to get her bearings. A thick, white fog enveloped the surrounding area. She wrapped her arms around herself for warmth and peered into the mist.

One of the hens broke into a loud cackle, which wasn't unusual, though a bit early in the morning for such a racket. Connie was just about to retreat to the warmth of her bed when she caught movement out of the corner of her eye. She squinted in that direction, listening. Was someone approaching the house? An odd noise, like an animal snuffling, was the only sound. Her scalp prickled. She trembled, though not because of the cold. The sound moved closer.

Gradually, a shape emerged, advancing through the mist. Before she could make out what it was, there came a sharp whistle. Her back straightened as her nerves uncoiled. She recognized that whistle. The thing halted. Connie stepped forward. "Samson, is that you?"

The dog whined, and gave a soft yip. He trotted closer, nose to the ground, tail at attention.

A smile warming her insides, Connie peered into the mist. "Alton?" Their nearest neighbor, Alton Wade, was also her fiancé, though they hadn't publicly announced it yet. A moment later, she made out his lanky frame, moving toward her.

"Samson, sit," he said.

The dog sat.

Alton stopped below the porch, too far away for her to make out the face beneath the brim of his hat. Dressed in a loose jacket, he held a disjointed shotgun in the crook of his arm. "Did I wake you?" His voice was low, as though he was not yet fully awake.

Keenly aware of her state of undress, Connie kept both arms crossed over the front of her blue chenille robe as she crept closer to the edge of the porch. "You did. Was that a shot I heard?"

"Yes, it was. A fox was about to have herself a morning snack on Miss Annabelle's chickens."

Connie caught her breath. "Did you kill it?"

"Of course, I did."

Connie could hear the prideful grin on his face. She gave him an answering one. "Of course, you did."

Behind her, the screen door inched open and Momma spoke. "Killed what?"

Connie turned to look at her. "Alton killed a fox about to get your chickens."

"Land sakes. Well, thank you kindly, son. Will you come in and warm yourself?"

He gave a low chuckle as he shifted his stance. "No, thank you, Miss Annabelle. I've got to get back home and see to my animals. I'll take that vixen's carcass with me, if you don't mind."

She giggled. "Not in the least. You take it with my blessing."

Alton hesitated another moment, while his gaze burned into Connie's. He lifted one hand to tug the brim of his hat. "Good morning, ladies. I'll be back around later on."

"Good morning," Connie whispered. *I love you,* her heart sang, as a thrill chased up her spine.

Momma held the door for her. "You best get in here before you catch your death."

Death. As she turned toward the door, Connie glanced

over her shoulder to the place where Alton had disappeared into the mist. By now, he'd be back at the chicken coop, gathering his prey. Would death steal him away from her, too? She sucked in a jagged breath as the screen door eased shut behind her. She sincerely hoped not. But thoughts like these were a daily struggle. When did one overcome such a fear?

It was less than a year since she and Momma had been widowed. Ray Cross and both his sons had drowned in a boating accident. Three lives snuffed out in a moment's time. She rubbed her arms against another tremor that shook to the very core of her being. Forcing those thoughts aside, she moved purposefully toward her bedroom, to make the bed and get dressed before little Joseph David awoke. She hoped he'd sleep for another hour or so, since he'd been awake so much last night.

As she straightened the bedclothes, Momma shuffled in from the kitchen. "I've gotta get a peek at my grandbaby." She bent over the cradle for a moment. "Good morning, precious." Before leaving, she pressed a kiss against Connie's cheek. "Coffee's on."

Connie hoped she'd brewed it good and strong. Perhaps the grayness of the morning had set her on edge, she wasn't sure, but she'd need to pull herself up and out of this melancholy soon. She glanced at the snoozing baby and breathed a soft prayer.

She and Alton had sat together at church for the first time this past Sunday. Up until that time, they'd been discreetly separated by his mother and Momma. The rumor mill that had been a mere trickle, let loose like a flood. The looks cast her way after the service told her she was not a popular choice for this eligible bachelor.

Alton's older brother Jensen's gaze was the most brutal of all. She could easily understand why he was such a success as a lawyer. His wife, who had never said two words to Connie, looked down her regal nose before turning her back, feigning an interest in the altar bouquet.

Connie blew out a breath in an effort to cleanse her mind of the troubling memories. The only expression she should be remembering was the one on Alton's face. She smiled at that thought. His eyes had taken possession of hers, searched the depths, and left her weak in the knees. In church. She'd scurried down the aisle to join Momma who'd been busy showing off her precious bundle. Joseph David was the delight of the senior ladies' Sunday School class these days.

Momma was certainly humming a happy tune when Connie entered the kitchen a few minutes later. The sweet, spicy smell of cinnamon rolls filled the air. Connie breathed it in. "Oh, my, what's the occasion?" Momma usually saved cinnamon rolls for Christmas morning, or once in a while on Easter Sunday.

"Does it have to be an occasion?" She cast a grin over her shoulder as she drew out a pan of the fragrant pastries. "I just had a craving for cinnamon, and this is what came of it."

"I'm not complaining," Connie assured her. She crossed to the dish shelf, grabbed a cup and poured herself some coffee. While Momma iced the rolls, Connie stirred the eggs. Their hens weren't laying yet, so Mrs. Byrd, their neighbor across the road, kept them well supplied in return for a bit of help. Connie had learned to gather the eggs, clean out the chicken coop, milk the cows, and feed the horses. She enjoyed most of it, and Momma didn't mind watching the baby. It was a lot easier than picking cotton. She hoped her cotton-picking days were over.

Momma set a heaping plate of rolls in the middle of the table. "I expect to see Riley one of these mornings. He did promise to plow my garden."

Connie ladled a serving of scrambled eggs onto their plates. She set the skillet back on the stove. "Maybe he expects Alton to do it."

"Now why would he expect that? Y'all haven't announced anything." She settled into her chair and waited for Connie to join her.

"I imagine by now, it's probably all over town."

Momma giggled. "Only that he's interested. Interest doesn't obligate a man to take care of a widow's chores. Riley's one of my oldest friends. Besides, he promised."

Joseph David decided now might be a good time to wake. He let out a squall just as someone knocked on the front door.

Momma frowned as she pushed away from the table. "You get the baby, I'll get the door."

Curiosity drove Connie to peek out the window on the way to the bedroom. Why had she done that? A black sedan with an emblem on the door sat in the drive. A man in a dark suit stood on the porch. Not again. Please, God, not again.

Chapter Two

The air left Annabelle's lungs when she opened the door and found a stranger in a dark suit standing on the porch. Her gaze traveled instinctively to the drive, where sat a black sedan with an emblem on the door. Not again—but who could it be this time? She'd already lost her entire family. *Breathe—don't jump to conclusions.*

Her gaze on the stranger's face again, she collected herself enough to ask his pardon for the delay. "I'm so sorry, how can I help you?" With any luck, he needed directions to someone else's house.

He removed his hat. "Miz Annabelle Cross?"

She swallowed and nodded, forcing her lips to curve into a smile. "I'm Annabelle Cross."

He tucked his hat beneath his left arm, and stuck out his right hand.

She noticed he held a clipboard in the other.

"Walter Daley, with the Gibson County Department of

Agriculture."

A sensation somewhat like cool water spread from her head to the soles of her feet. Not a coroner. The Department of Agriculture. Thank God. She pushed her hand toward his. "Pleased to meet you, Mr. Daley. Won't you come in? I just now took a pan of fresh, hot cinnamon rolls out of the oven. We have hot coffee, too."

He let go of her hand and cleared his throat. "Er … no, thank you. I'm on the clock." He held up the clipboard. "I just stopped in to introduce myself. I'm going to walk your fields, to check on their condition. I talked to Alton Wade—I believe he's your cousin? He asked me to stop by."

Annabelle drew up at the mention of Alton's name. "Oh, I see. Of course. Alton's been concerned about the … condition … of the soil."

A truck passed by on the road. It slowed to a near stop before speeding up again. Annabelle watched as it disappeared over the hill toward Wade's Grocery. Probably someone curious about why the county agent was here.

Mr. Daley replaced his hat. "Well, I'll get at it. It won't take long to look at the fields and gather soil samples. It was a pleasure meeting you, Miz Cross."

She gave a nod, then let the screen door close as she stepped back, almost shaking with relief.

Tom Franklin drove his pickup into a lane that led to Mildred Parmenter's cabin. As the main local pharmacist, he seldom made a delivery, but Miss Mildred needed her pills. The rough-hewn cabin stood next to a pond, behind the farmhouse she'd given over to her son and his family. It was the original structure on this property. The Parmenters had kept it in good condition.

Pulling to a stop, Tom sat still a moment before shutting off the engine. Who was that man standing on Annabelle's front porch? It could be anyone at all. A neighbor, a passerby looking for directions. Surely, at this hour of the morning, it wouldn't be a caller. He leaned forward to grab a small prescription bag from the box in the seat beside him. He checked the label to verify it was Mildred's, pushed his door open, and climbed out. Twice in the past week, he'd heard someone mention Annabelle's name. Land, it hadn't even been a year since Ray Cross passed, and already, the vultures were gathering.

He stepped up onto the small wooden porch and rapped on Mildred's door.

"Come in," she called.

He turned the knob and pushed the door open. "Miss Mildred? It's Tom Franklin—with your prescription."

She squinted up at him from her rocker beside the fireplace. "I knowed it was. I recognized your truck." She sighed. "I hate you had to bring it out yourself. What happened to that nice delivery boy?"

Tom stepped nearer, leaving the door slightly ajar.

"He's back at school. He still makes afternoon deliveries, but Doctor said you needed this first thing, so I brought it on out."

"Well." She rocked twice and almost seemed to forget the direction of her thoughts. "I'm mighty glad you did. Won't you sit a spell?"

"No, thank you. I need to get back to town. Can I get you anything before I go? Do you need some water?"

"I'd be much obliged if you'd fill that dipper for me, so I can take one of those pills."

Tom handed her the bag. He stepped to a narrow table near the stove, and slid the lid off a bucket of water. He found a dipper beside the bucket, which he filled halfway. Keeping his palm beneath it to catch any drips, he held it out to her.

She accepted the water and took a drink.

Tom poured the remains in the wash pan and replaced the dipper. Brushing his hands together, he smiled at Miss Mildred. "Well, I'd best be on my way. Got to open the store this morning."

"I thank you again, Tom. Don't you be a stranger, now." She leaned her head back against the rocker and closed her eyes.

Tom suspected she'd go right to sleep.

Back out on the road, he slowed again in front of Annabelle's house. That black sedan still sat in the drive. Who could it be? There was one sure-fire way to find out. He peeked at his watch. There was time enough.

Annabelle thought her eyes must be playing tricks on her. She blinked twice to clear her vision before pushing the screen open and stepping onto the porch where Tom Franklin stood, a bright smile on his face. "Tom?"

"Mornin', Miss Annabelle. I hope I didn't alarm you, knocking on your door this early."

"Well, I reckon you did startle me a bit, but only because you're the second one to knock at my door today."

He stuck his hands in his pockets. "I had to deliver a prescription out this way. Thought I'd stop by and see how y'all are doing."

Annabelle folded her hands together. "We were just sitting down to breakfast. Won't you join us? We've got fresh-baked cinnamon rolls."

"Now that would be pretty hard to turn down. I can smell them clean out here. I've had breakfast, but I wouldn't mind one of those." He reached around Annabelle and pulled the screen door open.

Annabelle stepped inside and almost plowed into Connie, her arms filled with baby. "You remember Tom Franklin, don't you, Connie? He's out this way delivering medicine. I invited him to join us for a sweet roll."

A smile lit Connie's eyes before she turned and preceded them to the kitchen. She glanced over her shoulder. "Good morning, Mr. Franklin. Momma, I'll join you in a few minutes, as soon as I take care of Joseph." She crossed to the bedroom door, pulling it shut behind her, leaving Annabelle alone in the kitchen with Tom.

Tom frowned in the direction of the table. His gaze circled the room before landing on Annabelle's face. "I thought I saw a car in your drive."

Annabelle crossed to the shelf and retrieved a cup for Tom, which she filled with steaming coffee. "Have a seat, there, Tom." She pointed to a chair. "That car belongs to the county agent. He's checking on the fields for Alton. Testing the soil and whatnot."

Tom's expression brightened as he pulled out a chair and sank into it.

His change of countenance puzzled Annabelle somewhat. She set the cup in front of him. "You still drink it black?"

He nodded, his gaze fastened on the stack of cinnamon rolls. "Fog's about burnt off. I believe it's gonna be a lovely spring day."

"I reckon it is," Annabelle set a plate and a fork in front of him. She removed Connie's plate, placed it on the warmer, and covered it with a towel before taking her seat opposite Tom. She wanted to ask who he'd brought a prescription to, but she knew that was inappropriate. While he speared a cinnamon roll, she searched her mind for a safe topic. "Alton killed a fox early this morning. It was trying to get at my new setting hens."

Tom washed down a bite with his coffee. "Sure enough?"

"He said it was a vixen."

"It might have kits somewhere or other. I reckon that dog of his can find them. He's a right smart hound." He polished off the roll and sat back in his chair.

Annabelle smiled. Men did love to talk about their dogs.

Connie had overheard most of the conversation between Momma and Tom Franklin, and deemed it a bit dull, but she was curious to know why Tom had stopped by so early in the morning. She peeked around the corner before reentering the kitchen, and found his gaze fastened securely on Momma's face, as though fascinated with her responses to his questions. Could it be? Was Tom Franklin sweet on Momma?

She hid a smile behind Joseph's velvety head as she stepped through the doorway.

Tom rose from his chair. "Well, I hate to eat and run, but I need to get the store opened." He nodded to Connie before turning a warm smile on Momma.

Her chair scraped the floor as she pushed away from the table.

"Would you like to take a cinnamon roll or two with

you, Tom?"

He patted his rather flat abdomen and shook his head. "I wouldn't mind one bit, if you have another to spare."

Connie sincerely hoped there were plenty of those aromatic delicacies, since she hadn't even tasted one yet.

"Oh, there's enough to share with half the neighborhood."

Or one famished nursing mother.

Momma wrapped a couple sweet rolls in a sheet of waxed paper and folded the ends securely.

Connie patted Joseph on the back and stepped to her chair. "Well, it was nice to see you again, Tom."

"Thank you, Miss Connie. I hope to see you again, real soon." With a quick nod, he picked up his hat and followed Momma from the room.

Connie gave a soft chuckle as she forked a roll onto her plate. That man was most definitely interested in her mother-in-law. She'd suspected it last summer, when he'd bought them that new refrigerator. Momma had tried to smooth it over—said they had always been good friends—but Connie hadn't been convinced. She helped herself to a second cinnamon roll before Momma invited the rest of the neighbors in to partake.

Upon her return, Momma freshened their coffee. On the way back to her chair, she stopped to remove Joseph from Connie's shoulder. She smacked a kiss to his fat cheek. "This is the best feeling in the whole world. If ever one feels sad, just cuddle a little one."

Connie shot a look at her mother-in-law. "Are you feeling sad this morning, Momma?"

Momma shrugged, her gaze fastened on something outside the window. "I don't know why I would be. But sitting here with Tom ... I remembered ..." her lips trembled. She sucked in a slow breath and exhaled. The wisp of a smile lit her face when she turned back to Connie. "It was kind of nice, having breakfast with a man." She blew out a sigh. "You must think I'm a silly old woman."

"I don't think anything of the kind. You should have friends. I don't want you to be lonely." After a sip of coffee, she set her cup down and leveled her gaze at Momma. "I hope you'll remarry someday, too."

The change in Momma was immediate. She turned pink as *Pepto Bismol* and giggled like a schoolgirl. "Land sakes, I don't reckon I'll do that. Who in their right mind would marry an old widow like me?"

"Momma, you're not old. You've got plenty of years left. You're funny, and caring, and ... one of the best cooks around. And you're still a fine-looking woman."

Momma covered her mouth in mock surprise. "You're determined to make me laugh out loud and wake this baby."

"That wouldn't hurt a thing. He needs to be awake for a while."

Momma gave a slight frown. "I think what he needs is a clean diaper."

While Momma took care of Joseph, Connie cleaned up

the kitchen. Nice to have a morning off from chores at the Byrd's farm across the road. Their grandchildren were visiting. Mr. Byrd was a big believer in keeping young ones busy with chores, so he'd told Connie to take a couple days off. She'd miss the fresh milk and eggs, though.

After finishing the dishes, she stepped out onto the front porch where Ginger, their expert mouser, reclined in the morning sun. Connie bent to scratch behind the cat's ears. Ginger stretched and yawned. She rolled over on her back, exposing her belly. Moving to the edge of the porch, Connie wrapped an arm around the post and leaned against it.

The county agent's car was gone. She'd seen Alton out in the field with him earlier. What news had he, of the condition of the land?

Letting go of the post, she reached up to smooth her hair back, tucking loose strands into her braid. Though it wasn't in style, she always wore her long tresses in a single braid that reached almost to her waist. Most of the stylish young women cut their hair short and covered their heads with bobby pinned curls to create soft waves. Others wore their longer hair in pony tails. Her husband, Joseph, had loved her long hair. He'd begged her to wear it loose. She'd done it occasionally, just for him.

Would Alton love her hair? He'd never seen it out of its braid. She tingled at the memory of his hand stroking her hair, smoothing the wayward curls away from her face.

As if he'd read her thoughts, Alton stepped into her

line of vision.

"Hello, beautiful."

Chapter Three

Alton's heartbeat quickened each time he gazed at Connie. He closed the distance between them in two long strides. She stood still, her hands clasped at her waist, her complexion a soft rose, which was exactly why he liked to greet her in such a way. Calling her beautiful always produced a nice result, sweetly upturned lips, a sparkle in her dark eyes, and that lovely blush. He would never tire of it.

He still needed to pinch himself every now and then to see if he was dreaming. Had this exotic beauty truly accepted his proposal? Had she only done it so he'd take care of her and little Joseph? That's what his older brother, Jensen, took every opportunity to observe. Alton didn't care why she'd said yes. It was enough that she had, and the look on her face at this moment told him all he needed to know—she cared for him. Yes, it was enough.

He climbed two of the four front steps, which brought

their faces on a level. Removing his hat, he smiled as her blush deepened.

"Hello, Alton."

"I wondered if you might want to go for a stroll."

One lovely eyebrow arched. "A stroll? I'd think you'd be all strolled out, after walking the fields with that county agent."

He shook his head. "We didn't walk that far."

"Did he say anything about the fields—give you any idea of their health? Do you say 'health,' regarding dirt?"

He chuckled. "I'd normally use the word fertile, but healthy soil works just as well." He set his right foot on the third step and rested his hat on his thigh. Allowing his gaze to leave her face for a few seconds, he nodded toward the nearest cotton field. "Mr. Daley agreed with my plans for the land, but he won't know anything for a couple of weeks or so. He has to send the soil samples off to be tested. How about that walk? Are you busy right now?"

"I just need to check with Momma, make sure it's all right."

Alton suspected Miss Annabelle was probably nearby, listening to their conversation. He smiled when her shape materialized behind the screen of the kitchen door.

"Y'all go on and take your time. Little man is fast asleep."

Connie's amused expression told Alton she was not surprised by Annabelle's presence either.

"Thank you, Momma. We won't be long." As she

spoke those words, Connie removed her apron, folded it, and laid it over the back of the nearest rocking chair.

Annabelle stepped outside, a light blue sweater folded over her arm. "You'd best wear this. Early spring weather is changeable."

Connie slipped it on. When she turned toward Alton, he held out his hand to steady her descent on the steps.

Samson, his Bluetick coon-hound, chose that moment to zip around the corner of the house. He bee-lined for Connie, sniffed her shoes, and wagged his body like a fury.

"Heel," Alton commanded. The dog halted, his love-sick gaze glued firmly to Connie's face. Alton cleared his throat to keep from laughing out loud. "You ready?"

They set off across the yard toward the drive. A tractor chugged along in the neighbor's field. The scent of freshly-turned earth mingled with the aroma of lilacs blooming in Lettie Byrd's front yard.

Samson dove through the weeds at the road's edge, clearly on the trail of something huge.

Alton glanced at his companion, hoping to determine her mood. Whenever they'd had a moment to talk, she'd always turned the conversation to him. She knew pretty much everything there was about him, but he had scant knowledge of her. After starting the discussion several times in his head, he finally blurted out, "It occurred to me, I know very little about your family."

Her head down, Connie picked her way across the dusty gravel of the road.

Alton swallowed hard. Had he blundered? "Ahem—
I'm sorry if I've touched on a difficult subject—"

"No, it's all right." She raised her eyes to his. "I
suppose you would wonder about them. And rightly so."

"You don't have to tell me anything." He always
backed off, lest he offend someone. Why did he do that?

"I've considered telling you about them more than
once. I just didn't feel the time was right."

He mulled that over. What did she mean by that? What
kind of people were her family? At the sound of an
approaching car, he gently pulled her aside. He lifted a
hand in greeting as one of the young Parmenter boys drove
past, blaring his horn, but barely slowing down. Good thing
they'd had a recent rain, or they'd both be covered in silt
and dust. Young folks were just rude these days. He led the
way toward the plank bridge that connected the road to the
cotton field. Once they'd both reached the other side, he
stood for a moment, gazing down at her.

More than anything, he wanted to take her in his arms
and kiss her. But it wouldn't be right. Connie had only been
a widow for barely ten months. After his initial proposal,
he'd promised her they'd wait at least a year before
announcing their intentions. He didn't want to scare her off
by moving too quickly, or make her an object of scorn in
town. Folks were so judgmental.

Easing out a slow breath, he stepped past her. He
hooked his thumbs in his pockets in an effort to seem
nonchalant.

As though unmoved or maybe oblivious to his emotions, she crouched beside a low-growing clump of wildflowers. "What are these?"

He moved closer. "Spring beauties—that's what Mother calls them."

"They're lovely, so delicate." She rose up to follow his lead through the fallow field.

Of course, she would notice flowers, she'd grown up in paradise. At least that's how folks usually described the territory of Hawaii. He sighed, thinking of all she'd left behind, compared to what she'd have here.

A Kingfisher ran ahead of them, causing her to laugh. The bright sound of her laughter eased the tension in Alton's breast.

Finally, she paused and looked up at him with an expression he'd never seen. "My father met my mother while he was on leave in Hawaii. He was in the Navy, and she was a hula dancer at a bar."

Averting his gaze, Alton stood still. What did she say? He opened his mouth, hoping words would come, but before he could speak, she giggled. He turned to look at her. "You're joshing me, aren't you?"

Her eyes sparkled with mischief. "Sorry, I couldn't resist." She laughed again. "You should have seen your face."

There was something so tantalizing in her nature. He could get used to that. With a low chuckle, he offered his arm.

She moved closer, settling her hand into the crook. "The actual story is quite dull. They met at a luau hosted by her family. She was serving food. They fell in love, and he settled down on the island of Maui."

"Had he no family stateside?"

She shook her head. "None, to speak of. His parents were dead. He'd no wish to return."

Alton watched her face. "What of the war? I suppose you must've been right there when it happened?"

"I was only nine years old, but I remember the planes, the loud booms. Everyone was panicking. After the attack on Pearl Harbor, Dad went to see if there was anything he could do to help. He was reinstated. My mother took me and my sisters into the interior, to stay with her family until the war ended. When Dad returned, he bought an abandoned sugar cane plantation. We lived in a run-down manager's shack, since the main house had been destroyed by the Japanese. Eventually, he rebuilt the house."

"I've heard raising sugar cane is no easy feat."

"It's hard. We were expected to help, too. They'd work around the clock to harvest it. I remember my little sisters, sleeping in the field while the rest of us worked."

They walked along in silence for a time, drawing ever nearer the house and yard. Alton hated to see the walk come to an end. He had so many more questions, but he supposed there'd be time enough to search out the answers. As he was fast learning, it was not easy getting Connie to talk about herself.

"So, is your father still producing sugar cane?"

She nodded. "As far as I know. He's done very well." She paused her steps, lifted her eyes to his. "My mother died, a couple of years after I left. Dad said it was cancer."

No wonder she didn't talk about them. He placed his hand over hers, still resting in the crook of his arm. "I'm so sorry."

She paused to look up at him. "It's all right, really. I should have told you all this before. I'm not good at talking about me. Especially my life before I met Joseph. Momma took me in and treated me like one of her own. She's been more of a mother to me than mine ever was. But I don't have bad feelings toward my mother. She did the best she could." She turned forward and began walking again.

The sound of Annabelle's voice calling to them put an end to further conversation. Did the woman used to call pigs? That's exactly what it sounded like.

"Hoo-EEE! Connie! Alton! Hoo-EEE!"

Connie glanced up. "Joseph must be awake, and hungry."

Alton tried not to think of what that meant. He led her forward at a quicker pace, meaning to deposit her at the front porch and make his excuses. Time to be getting home, anyway.

After the service on Sunday evening, Connie and Momma were invited to go home with Alton and his mother.

Miss Lillian served coffee and apple pie while they watched *The Ed Sullivan Show*.

Connie savored the wonderful pie. If only she could bake something like this. Would Miss Lillian's cook part with the recipe? During the next commercial break, she turned to her future mother-in-law. "The pie was wonderful. Do you think Regina would share her recipe?"

Miss Lillian sniffed.

Alton chuckled. "Regina's a little tight-lipped with her recipes. But she likes you. Maybe she'll make an exception."

Little Joseph woke up toward the end of the program, so Connie had to retire upstairs to the new nursery to feed him. As she sat in a comfortable slider rocker, she giggled at the memory of Alton's expression whenever she excused herself to feed the baby. The man was prone to blush a deep russet at the mention. One would think, growing up on a farm, he'd be used to such things.

In the soft light of the lamp, she took in the changes to the small room. They'd painted the walls a powdery blue, the woodwork white. Blue gingham curtains hung at the window. Connie had had very little say in the decor, but she hadn't really minded. The attention embarrassed her. Though she was certain of Alton and their upcoming marriage, she had to wonder … what if the unthinkable happened?

She blew out a slow breath and rocked. What if their plans changed? She couldn't even imagine that, but she'd never thought of losing her first husband either. Alton was truly one of the nicest men she'd ever known—including her first husband—God rest his soul. She'd loved Joseph, but he could be so headstrong at times.

Closing her eyes, she tried to catch a moment's rest while the baby nursed, tried not to think about all that could possibly go wrong. "Don't borrow trouble," Momma would say when Connie tended toward worry. She focused on a framed verse over the crib. She didn't need better light to read the embroidered words, she knew the verse by heart. *For he shall give his angels charge over thee, to keep thee in all thy ways.*

Joseph stirred and gave a soft sigh. He had dozed off. And just in time. Footsteps sounded on the creaky stairs. No doubt, Annabelle was ready to head home. Tucking her blouse into place, Connie stood and tiptoed to the door, hoping to pull it open before anyone had to knock. She was relieved to find Miss Lillian instead of Alton.

"Alton's got the car ready, dear."

"Thank you, I was just about to return. He's finally asleep." Connie slipped past her and started down the stairs.

"I hope he sleeps a good while, so you can get some rest. I remember how it was to have an infant in the house."

As they approached the front door, lightning flashed in

the distance, illuminating the night sky.

"Looks like we're gonna get some rain," Momma draped a jacket over Connie's shoulders and addressed Miss Lillian. "Thank you for your wonderful hospitality. And tell Regina her pie was delicious, as always."

"I'll do that. And I hope to see you both again, later on this week."

Connie smiled into her future mother-in-law's face. "Goodnight."

"Goodnight, dear."

Thunder rumbled as they climbed in the car, both sitting in the front seat with Alton. He drove as if they carried eggs as cargo, taking the last turn so slowly, Connie thought the engine had died.

The wind whipped around them when they stepped out of the car. Annabelle snatched at her hat, which almost went airborne.

Alton laughed. "We're just in time." Once he'd helped them inside, and delivered the food his Mother had sent, he turned to Connie. "Guess I'd better not linger. Looks like a pretty big storm headed our way." He made eye contact with Connie. "I'll be by in the morning."

Connie soaked in the silent message of his gaze and tried to send one of her own in return.

Momma closed the door and faced Connie. "How long is that man gonna wait? Is he afraid I'll disapprove of a goodnight kiss?" She reached to remove Connie's jacket, to hang it on a hook near the door.

Connie sucked in a breath. "Momma, shame on you." Though she tried to keep her countenance, it was no use. She could barely keep from laughing out loud. "Please don't make me wake the baby."

Joseph snoozed on, through the thunder and lightning and metallic drumming of the rain on the roof. Maybe the droning noise helped him sleep, Connie wasn't certain. Hopefully, she'd sleep through it, too. She yawned and snuggled into her bed.

Near dawn, she awoke to complete silence. The rain had let up. But something else was missing.

As quietly as possible, she slipped out of bed and tiptoed into the kitchen to peer out the window. The rain was still coming down outside, but in more of a mist. In the front parlor, she reached to turn on the lamp, but nothing happened. Perhaps the bulb had burned out? Feeling for the back of the sofa, she crept behind it to the other lamp and pulled the string. Still nothing. At least now she knew why it was so quiet. No humming of the refrigerator motor. The electricity had gone off.

Chapter Four

Though it was nearly six-thirty in the morning, it was still too dark for Annabelle to see inside the house. Weird shadows danced in the glow of many candles as rain pelted the tin roof. What was happening outside? She'd never liked storms, especially this time of year when tornadoes could wipe out an entire town. That was one thing she'd especially loved about living in San Diego—no tornadoes. She'd not missed them. A sudden gust jarred the windows and increased her heart rate. She took a step back.

Connie padded into the room. "I wonder how long the electricity will be off?"

"Depends on the cause. Could be lines downed by a tree. That type of repair takes a while out here, especially if it continues to rain. Don't open the refrigerator any more than you have to."

"I won't. Good thing you were late defrosting it this month. All that extra ice should help."

Annabelle chuckled as she encircled Connie's waist and pulled her close. "You do have a way of looking at the bright side of things."

"I had a good teacher." Connie placed a kiss on Annabelle's cheek, then moved away to settle into the rocking chair. "I hope you slept well."

"I had a wakeful night." Annabelle sat across from her, but found it difficult to relax. She sat forward, hugging herself against the chill in the air. A cold front coming through was not a good thing. Sudden temperature changes brought severe weather. "Times like this, it would be nice to have a radio. Though I suppose it wouldn't make any difference if it was powered by electricity."

Connie giggled. "Good thing we have a gas stove. I'll put the coffee on."

"That sounds good." Annabelle got up and followed her into the kitchen. "You never did finish telling me about your talk with Alton the other day. Did y'all set a date?"

Connie moved a candle near the sink so she could see to fill the coffee pot. "We didn't talk about our plans. Alton's a man of his word. I believe he intends to delay until July to broach the subject."

"Ha! If he can wait that long. I've seen the way he gazes at you, every bit as love-sick as that hound of his."

Connie turned from lighting the burner. "Oh, Momma, you're so funny, though I believe you're right about Samson. He does seem to dote on me."

While they waited for the coffee to brew, Connie told

her how Alton had seemed so interested in hearing about her family in Hawaii.

Annabelle nearly laughed out loud when she shared the part about the hula dancer. It took some effort, but she managed to control herself. Neither of them wanted to wake the baby.

As thunder rumbled overhead, the coffee pot perked, lending a sense of comfort and peace to the homey kitchen. Annabelle let her weary gaze wander, taking in the humble furnishings that had been given them last summer. Folks had certainly thrown together to bring stability to their little family.

Finally, her eyes rested on her daughter-in-law as she smoothed her hair and braided it. There was no denying, the girl was a beauty. No wonder Alton was so taken with her. Annabelle was glad of it, though pain stabbed her heart at the thought. Soon, Connie and little Joseph would be leaving, and Annabelle would be alone. She blew out a soft breath, hoping Connie wouldn't notice. The girl deserved to be happy, and little Joseph David needed a daddy.

Tom Franklin stood in the drug store window, peering out at the near darkness, though it was not yet noon. Heavy rain fell in sheets. Downtown Trenton had emptied quickly. Only the occasional vehicle passed, moving slowly through the onslaught. It had rained for two days now. The radio announcers were calling it a hundred-year storm. They warned of flooding in low-lying areas.

Though service had been patchy, the phone had already rung half a dozen times this morning, folks asking for delivery of various necessities, unwilling to make the trek in this weather. He could hardly blame them.

Behind him, Bo Anderson laughed out loud at one of his own oft-told stories. He spent most mornings sitting on a stool at their counter. He'd down two or three cups of black coffee and entertain whoever happened to be in the store. This morning, it was just Freddie West—part-time soda jerk and delivery boy—though he'd left boyhood more than thirty years ago. He worked weekday mornings until Arnie Douglas came in from school.

Huffing out a breath, Tom turned away from the deluge outside. His hope of driving out to Miss Annabelle's dwindled. He'd no desire to plow through a flood, possibly ending up in a ditch.

"What's this I hear about you, Tom?" Bo asked. "Is it just tattle, or is it true?"

Tom sidled over to the counter and leaned against it, propping his elbow on the shiny surface of the dairy bar. "I don't know. Depends on what you've heard." He winked at Freddie. "Most likely tattle, though."

"Some say you've been sniffing around a certain widow's place out on the Milan Highway." He gave his usual hooting laugh, and swiped at the corners of his eyes.

Tom drummed his fingers on the counter. The rumor mill in a small town could be ruthless. "Now you know I have to make the occasional delivery out that way. I stopped to check in on the widows—both of them. After all, Miss Annabelle is one of my oldest friends. We've known each other since we were children."

Bo's face scrunched up like a monkey's. "He's making a powerful lot of excuses, Freddie."

The phone rang again. Tom was glad for the interruption. He'd no desire to be teased by Bo Anderson. But he knew it was coming. Sometimes it was a trial and a tribulation, living in a small community.

He picked up the receiver. "Trenton Pharmacy, how may I help you?"

"You been listening to the radio?" Tom could barely hear his cousin, Riley Franklin, on the other end.

"Riley—that you?"

"They're talking about it raining for days. Flood stage on the river. You need any help out there?"

Tom lived along the North Fork of the Forked Deer River, in the house where he'd grown up. Every few years, he'd be flooded out, but he always returned to clean up the mess, and move back in. One of these days, the old house would be declared a total loss. He'd considered selling the land and moving into one of those new tract houses, but he'd held off. In between the floods, it was easy to forget the hardship.

"I've already moved everything upstairs, Riley. I'll be

all right. Won't be any worse than three years ago, maybe not as bad."

"Hundred-year storm, they said! Me and Thelma want you to stay at the house tonight. She's got a really bad feeling about this one."

Tom knew about Thelma's "bad feelings." Sometimes they were on the mark, sometimes not. "We'll see how it's going around closing time. I may just take you up on that. Thanks for calling, Riley."

Tom hung up and brushed his hands together. Thelma and Riley didn't have a phone of their own. Riley would've run through the rain to make the call. No doubt he was looking like a drowned cat by now, skinny as he was. Tom chuckled as he slipped behind the pharmacy counter. He and Riley had been friends since their infancy. Looking out for each other was second nature.

"Was that Miss Annabelle inviting you over for tea?" Bo called out, snickering loudly.

Tom rolled his eyes and muttered, "Oh Lord, deliver me." But he knew it was no use to pray. If his hopes became reality, there'd be a lot more chatter before it was over. Only one thing worried him. Miss Annabelle was mighty fond of church. Would she keep time with a man who didn't attend?

Tom and most of his family had quit the church after that fiasco with Jensen Wade. And when the man was voted in as head deacon, well, Tom and Riley both vowed never to darken the doors. Except Riley did choose to attend

Christmas and Easter celebrations. Tom knew that was because of Thelma wanting him to set an example for the kids. Tom didn't have any kids, so no example to set, though Thelma still beat him down about it as the holidays approached.

Sunday was Tom's only full day off from the pharmacy, and he meant to enjoy it. He loved Thelma like a sister, but he'd developed a tin ear where her nagging was concerned.

Dressed in a black slicker and fishing boots, Alton stomped out to the creek bank. Swirling muddy water filled the usually dry creek and threatened to spill over the opposite side into the newly plowed cotton fields. Bad timing. Raging floodwaters could wash away valuable topsoil. They'd have to wait for the water to recede and the ground to dry. This could delay planting a couple of weeks or more. On top of all that, the weatherman was calling for more rain. Alton took off along the creek's edge, keeping a sharp eye on the roiling water. He checked for property damage and sinkholes.

This was the first major flood they'd had since Alton took over running Sutter's Landing. He'd hoped the dam they'd built would keep it from happening, and he supposed it had held back some of it. At least the house sat high enough that it wouldn't be affected. With that thought in mind, he swiveled around and squinted toward the road, where water had risen to within a foot of the bridge. Beyond the road, Miss Lucy's house sat dangerously close to the deluge. He strode toward his truck and grabbed the door handle, barely diverting Samson's muddy paws. "Up," Alton ordered, gesturing toward the truck's bed.

The dog obeyed, but kept his ears plastered to his head.

Alton chuckled. "I know you don't like it, but I'm not having you muddy my seats again." He patted the dog's head before he hopped in the truck and closed the door. It took only a couple of minutes to reach her place. Miss Lucy had lived in that old shack since long before Alton was born. She seemed ancient, but he didn't think she was much older than his mother. Her family had once lived as slaves of the Sutters. Now she earned a living working cotton for whoever would hire her.

He pulled the truck close to the front porch and hopped out. "Miss Lucy, you in there?"

The door swung inward, revealing several of Miss Lucy's family, and after only a moment had passed, their matriarch appeared. "What you doing out in this weather, Mr. Alton?"

"I've come to check on you. Water's getting a mite close to the house."

"It shore 'nuf is, and we is packing up to go to Brother's. He done been down to make sure we all right."

A deep masculine tone piped in. "You better get back

over that bridge afore the water come up over it, Mr. Alton. Looking mighty bad."

Alton recognized Lincoln's voice before the young man stepped forward. "I just wanted to be sure y'all were safe. I'm glad to know Avery invited you up to his place. You need any help getting your things up there?"

Miss Lucy shook her head. "Don't reckon so, Mr. Alton, though we thank ye kindly for your concern. Avery done carried a load with him and most everything else, we kin back-carry. You be careful now, crossin' that bridge. We'll see you in a few days, I reckon."

Alton returned to his truck. He sure hoped it was days and not weeks, before the water receded. The old wooden bridge was still dry when he crossed it, but the water had risen another few inches. He reckoned any minute now, it would completely disappear, leaving Sutter's Landing on one side, and the old Sterling Place on the other. He hated being cut off from Connie, but he dared not take a chance on getting stuck away from his house, the barn and the livestock. His mother would not like to be all alone over here.

Connie stood on her back porch at the old Sterling place, listening to the unmistakable sound of rushing water. "That's something I haven't heard in while." It reminded her of the waterfall near her home on Maui. After heavy rains, she could hear the cascade from her bedroom window.

But this was different. There was no waterfall, but a flood. It was a good ways from the porch, probably close to half a mile. The noise of the rain-swollen creek found its way to Connie's ears, along with the echo of voices. The neighbors must be out there, investigating the damage. Was that Alton's voice in the mix? Until now, not having a telephone hadn't bothered her. It would sure be nice to talk to him. She missed him so, and it had only been three days.

Joseph let out a wail. Connie turned from the scene in the field, opened the screen door, and stepped through.

Momma had gone across the road to the Byrd's farm to help with the morning chores. Connie hoped she returned with fresh milk and maybe even some cream. She craved it in her coffee. But could they manage to keep it cool? Oh well, they'd have to drink it up right away, or maybe Momma would make egg custard. Her mouth watered at the thought.

After changing Joseph's diaper, she carried him to the parlor and laid him in the cradle, let him kick freely for a few minutes. His face reflected pure joy. Though difficult to tear herself away, she had a couple of chores to finish before Momma returned. She cast a glance out the door on the way to the kitchen. The sun was out. A clear sky promised a break from the rain. Connie hummed as she prepared a couple of sandwiches for their lunch.

Sometime later, the screen door swung open and Momma entered, her arms weighed down with goods. She blew out a breath as she set a two-quart Mason jar of milk on the table, along with a paper sack. Her expression lit as she took in the table, already set for a meal.

"It's so thoughtful of you to make lunch. I'm plumb wore out. Lettie's chicken house was a mess from all that rain. It took us the entire morning to get it cleared out and new straw thrown down. And guess what?"

Connie arched her brows at the look on Momma's face. Was Lettie Byrd rubbing off on her? Was she about to repeat a juicy tidbit of gossip?

"They ain't going to be needing us anymore. Their son and his wife are moving in for a while. The boy's been laid off from that big factory he works for. He doesn't know how long the layoff will last, so thought it'd be best to come help his daddy on the farm."

Connie hefted the fresh milk with a healthy layer of cream on top. "Better be sparing with this—could be the last time for a while."

Annabelle pulled out her chair and sank into it with a loud sigh. "I doubt that. All I have to do is let your young man know how much you love cream in your coffee. We'll have all we need, you wait and see."

Connie glared at her. "Momma, don't you dare do that."

Momma's giggles ended abruptly at the sound of a car pulling into the drive. "Who could that be?"

They hadn't seen a soul pass by since the bridge flooded over. Her heart fluttering, Connie stopped to glimpse at her reflection in the mirror, just in case Alton had found a way around the water.

Chapter Five

Annabelle stepped out of the kitchen door, reaching the porch as Riley Franklin's car erupted with redheaded children. She looked for her cousin, Thelma, but only Riley got out and closed the door.

Connie joined Annabelle on the porch. "We've got company—lots of it."

Annabelle chuckled as the clan picked their way through the mud and muck to the porch steps, whilst Riley shouted orders.

"You kids wipe your feet! Better yet, kick your shoes off before you go inside."

Five-year-old Stevie and seven-year-old Raydeen, arrived first. Annabelle greeted them with open arms. Next came J.W., who had just turned eleven, and still needed to grow into his teeth. Seventeen-year-old Judith lagged behind, following their daddy onto the porch.

Connie directed them where to leave their muddy

shoes. "It's so good to see you all." She glanced past Riley to Judith. "Are we missing someone?"

"Drew's working today," Judith told her, as they entered the house through the kitchen door. At almost sixteen, Drew held the spot between J.W. and Judith.

Annabelle turned to greet Riley, who'd sat down to unlace his work boots.

"How are the roads?"

He shook his head. "Sakes alive, Miss Annabelle, it's sure enough a mess. We tried every back road in the area, I do believe. Had to turn around a couple of times. And it's fixing to rain some more, is what the weatherman says."

"That's what Lettie told me this morning."

"I've never seen the like." After removing his shoes, he followed Annabelle into the house. "Tom's done been washed clean out."

Connie's hand flew to her mouth. "Oh dear, is he all right?"

Riley nodded. "He's been a-staying at the house."

Annabelle poured a glass of tea and held it out to Riley. "Have a seat at the table. We were about to have lunch. Just sandwiches, if you don't mind that." Her thoughts dashed ahead, wondering what she'd put on those sandwiches to feed so many. Was there any peanut butter left?

Judith tiptoed in from the parlor. "Joseph's growing so big."

"I hope you didn't wake Miss Connie's baby," Riley lowered his wiry frame into the chair at the head of the table.

"I didn't, Daddy. I was real careful."

Connie gave her a hug and smoothed her hair. "I wouldn't mind if you did. He sleeps too much, so he's wakeful at night."

"I remember them days." Riley shook himself, "and I'm happy to be on this side of it."

Connie removed a jar of preserves from the pantry closet and reached for the bread. "Momma, I'll make some jelly sandwiches for the kids. You sit down with Riley and y'all eat the ones I made earlier."

Annabelle gave her a smile and mouthed a thank you. Connie to the rescue. She sat down beside Riley and handed him the sandwich Connie would have eaten.

"Thank you, Miss Annabelle, my tummy's plumb empty after that long ride." He took a large bite, savoring the taste. "I do love egg salad." After a long draw of tea, he set his glass down and took up his sandwich again. "I guess you're wondering why we're here."

"It doesn't matter why. I'm just happy you've come."

"That's mighty nice of you to say. Since y'all don't have a phone, Thelma can't check on you, so she sent us."

"I'm sorry she couldn't come."

Riley gulped down the remaining tea, and grinned. "She's doing some spring cleaning. Best for all of us to be somewhere's else."

Annabelle giggled as she refilled Riley's glass. "I reckon so."

Judith got the children seated around the room on whatever chairs, stools, and boxes she could find. She handed out the sandwiches as Connie made them. Once everyone had food and a beverage, she and Connie sat down at the table, opposite one another. "I'm about to graduate, Aunt Annabelle."

Annabelle loved that the children called her "Aunt," though she was their mother's first cousin. Thelma had always been her dearest friend, the closest to a sister Annabelle would ever know. She gripped Judith's hand and gave it a squeeze. "Oh, my goodness, I suppose you are. I'd lost track of time."

"She's tied with another girl for valedictorian," Riley added.

Connie clapped her hands. "Congratulations. I'm so proud of you."

Annabelle beamed at Judith. "Your momma told me about you being accepted to Union."

Judith nodded. "I'll start in the fall."

Finished with his sandwich, Riley leaned back in his chair. "She's hoping to find work of some sort this summer. She's got that scholarship to help with the tuition, but she needs some spending money, you know."

Connie leaned forward. "Are you going to live on campus?"

"I think so, but maybe come home on the weekends, if I can."

Annabelle finished the last of her sandwich, brushed

the crumbs from her hands, and picked up her glass, but held off taking a sip. "Jackson's a short bus ride away. You shouldn't have any problem."

"Well," Riley ran his fingers through his thinning hair. "I was thinking she could use my car. I found a sweet deal on a 1949 Chevy. It's in cherry condition. Old man Harper owned it. Took real good care of it. Now that he's gone, his widow's looking to sell. She asked me about it before she put it in the paper."

"That's good, Riley." Annabelle looked from Riley's face to Judith's, then back again. There was something going on. What were they not saying?

Now finished with their lunch, the children were getting antsy. Judith got up to see they were settled in the sitting room. "Y'all play checkers and stay quiet, okay?"

Annabelle glanced at Connie, who met her gaze with a slight shake of her head. Something was definitely up.

Riley drummed his fingers on the table and cast a sideways glance at Annabelle. "Judith's a real good girl. A hard worker. I wondered if maybe she could help Mr. Alton this summer. She can maybe chop cotton."

"She could, I reckon, but she'd run out all her money, driving back and forth."

"Yeah, so we thought she could stay out here with y'all," Riley nodded at Connie. "She could help out some with the baby, too."

When Connie rose to clear away the dishes, Judith followed.

Riley leaned close to Annabelle. "And from what I'm hearing, you're going to have a spare room before too long."

Of course, Thelma had told him about Alton and Connie. Annabelle met his gaze. "I hope no one else knows about that."

"Absolutely not. You know we're good for it. Well, except we did tell Tom. He's been staying with us and he overheard me and Thelma talking." He sat back, shaking his head. "He's one reason we were thinking Judith could come out here. Tom's house is done for. A complete loss."

Annabelle laid a hand to the base of her throat. "Oh, my goodness, Riley."

His mouth drooped. "It was shore a sight, Miss Annabelle. Nothing but water over there. I don't know when it will recede, but looks as though the entire house is plumb gone."

"What's he going to do?" Connie asked as she handed another washed plate to Judith.

"He's thinking to build, Miss Connie. We told him he could have Judith's room for the time being. It seemed like good timing, you know, with her going off to college. So, her staying out here would just be for the summer, if y'all could see your way through to allow it."

Armed with all the facts, Annabelle sat back in her chair. "I reckon it's all right with me, what do you think, Pumpkin?"

Judith's face lit. "I can sleep on the sofa, I don't mind."

Riley rubbed the back of his neck. "Or we could get you a cot. I reckon they's room for one somewhere."

"We can set one up in my room." Annabelle reached to pat Judith's arm. "There's plenty of space in there. It'll work out. And I can't answer for Alton, but I'm sure there's work to be had in the fields, as long as you don't mind that sort."

"She's chopped cotton near about every summer since she was old enough to handle a hoe."

Judith put the last plate in the cabinet and shook out the drying towel. "I prefer outdoor work, Aunt Annabelle."

"All right."

The rest of the visit, they talked about the graduation ceremony, where it was to be held, and what time. The words seemed to rush over Annabelle's head like the floodwaters outside. Her brain had snagged on the certainty of Connie's leaving her. Eventually, Judith would leave, too. Annabelle would be alone for the first time in her life.

Alton dragged a weary forearm across his brow to clear away the sweat after another day spent filling sandbags. They'd stacked the bags along the swollen creek to protect the barn and the livestock. Alton had never seen the water this high. He'd never known such rain. Willie had been making jokes about building an ark.

As he hefted the last bag onto the makeshift levee, Alton rested his tired arms on the top. His gaze traveled beyond the flooded field to the house on the far side. Thankfully, the Sterling house sat on high ground. But it also stood on the far side of the bridge, now completely submerged and possibly damaged by the violent current.

If the rain held off, he'd maybe venture out in the morning. He could wind around the back way to Wade's grocery. Check in on Judd, then head on over to visit Connie and Annabelle. He'd noticed Riley Franklin's car in their drive this morning, so figured they were all right. Surely Riley would have seen to it they had necessities. Of course, if an emergency arose, they could use the phone across the road at the Byrd's. If it was working. The electricity had finally come back on, so maybe the phones were working, too.

He pulled away from the sandbags and trudged across the muddy pasture toward the barn. He'd sent Willie over there after dinner to muck out the stalls. The animals needed plenty of fresh straw to keep their hooves dry. As he passed a blackberry thicket, Samson leaped out, shook himself and fell into step behind his master. Alton bent to pat the dog's soaking wet head. "I'll bet you're just as tired of all this rain as I am."

Samson raised large, serious orbs to Alton's face, as if in total agreement.

As Alton approached, Willie's bass voice rang out, singing *Onward Christian Soldiers*. He didn't miss a beat, but nodded his head. Alton returned the greeting, lifted a bale of straw, and carried it to the front stall. It looked like they'd need every bale he'd stored last fall. He sliced through the twine with his knife, folded the blade and dropped it in his pocket.

When he caught up with Willie, he grabbed a pitchfork and strode to the far side of the barn, intending to meet in the middle.

"You trying to keep up with me, Mista Alton?" Willie asked in his sing-song voice.

"No use in trying," Alton stopped to mop his brow. "I'd lose. I never could keep up with you."

Willie laughed, also wiping sweat from his face. He removed a floppy work hat and dried his head with a rag. "It's for the best, Mista Alton. You're good at many things I can't even imagine."

"We're a well-matched pair, aren't we?"

"Yes sir, I reckon we is."

Willie was not a tall man, but the muscles of his arms and shoulders strained against the pale blue cotton of his work shirt. He'd built those muscles working the farm alongside Alton. Day after day, he was there as long as he was needed. Alton thanked God for such a dedicated worker. But Willie was more than a laborer, he was a gifted carpenter as well. Alton had only to draw something on paper and Willie could make it. That kind of skill came in real handy.

They'd just finished up the last of the straw when the

supper bell rang. Alton could hardly believe the day was so far gone.

Rain pummeled the countryside throughout the next couple of days. Connie stood with her nose to the glass of the front window. Would it ever stop? She turned to find Momma fast asleep in the chair, Ginger curled up in her lap. They'd worked since dawn, cleaning every inch of the two bedrooms, making room for Judith. Though they had a few weeks yet, Momma said they'd best do it while trapped inside.

For Connie, the rain was an inconvenience, but she'd been through worse. The rainy season inland on Maui. The tropical storms, the occasional typhoon. An erupting volcano. At least they'd had no repeat of the violent storms of last week, with thunder that shook the little house's very frame and rattled the windows till Connie feared they'd shatter.

A shaft of light shone on the gravel road. Connie watched its progress. Soon a dark blue pickup truck slowed to make the turn into the drive. Her heart pounded like Pahu drums. Alton.

Her next thought was of her appearance. She must look a sight after working in the house all morning. She scurried to the nearest mirror, smoothed her hair back, and pinched her cheeks. As if they needed brightening. The very thought of Alton sent a warmth dancing up her neck. She reached the front door just as heavy footsteps sounded on the porch.

Rainwater dripped from the hood of his raincoat. Connie could see little of his face, except the bright white of his smile. In his arms, he carried a wooden crate draped with an oilcloth.

"I brought y'all some groceries."

She held the door open for him. "Oh, Alton, you're an angel."

He stepped through. "You may not think so when you're cleaning up this mess." His boots were muddy and water pooled on the floor, dripping from his coat.

Momma startled awake, sending Ginger for parts unknown. "Oh, my goodness, who's this?"

"Just me, Miss Annabelle. I've come bearing gifts, hoping to make up for my long absence." His gaze lingered on Connie's face, making her knees go weak.

"Don't worry about the mess, it'll clean up. Set the box on the kitchen table." She rushed ahead to clear space on one end.

Momma helped him out of his wet coat, which she hung on a hook beside the door. "Sit down and get those boots off. I'll get you a towel. We don't have any man-sized clothes you can change into."

"Miss Annabelle, I'm not worried about it. I've been wet for a week."

"How is it out there?"

"The levee's busted through. Water everywhere. You won't believe how far I had to go to get here. I'm going to leave the truck in your drive, if it's all right. Willie brought the boat over from the lake. He's going to meet me later at the old crossing."

"Well, I'll be," Momma clucked her tongue. "I don't remember it ever being so bad."

He used the towel to dry his hair. "Neither do I. Mother said she remembers it nearly this bad some years back, when she was a little girl, but not since."

Connie lifted the oilcloth from the top of the box he'd set on the table, eager to know what he'd brought. She found cheddar cheese, bologna, peanut butter, flour, sugar, cornmeal, coffee—even some cornflakes and oatmeal. She smiled at Alton. "What a treasure trove of delights."

He returned her smile. "That's not all." He pulled a small brown paper bag from his pocket, opened it and held it out for her to see.

"Is that what I think it is?"

He nodded. "One for you and," he drew another bag from his other pocket and handed it to Momma. "One for you."

Momma sucked in a breath. "Chocolate drops!"

Chapter Six

All sudden-like, that's how the rain stopped. Annabelle sat up in bed, listening. It was quiet. "The sun'll be out in the morning," she whispered, as she turned over and laid back down. Clear, blue skies. Her eyes ached for the sight. Sleep crept up and claimed her.

When she woke again, light streamed in at the window. The smell of brewing coffee tantalized her. Reaching up, she took hold of the bedpost and pulled herself upright. The floor was cold, but not like it had been. She shrugged into her robe as she pushed her toes into her pink house slippers. That coffee sure smelled good.

Connie stood at the stove, Joseph asleep on her shoulder. She turned and spoke as Annabelle entered. "Good morning, sleepyhead."

A chuckle rose in Annabelle's throat. "Good morning, Pumpkin." She fondled the baby's sweet head. "Is he fretful?"

"Just a little. He may lie down now, I'll try again. Coffee's ready." She slipped through the bedroom door.

Annabelle hummed as she mixed up the biscuit dough. There was something so relaxing about working it with her fingers, feeling the softness, the slight give of the dough. She pressed it into a flat disk, and rolled it out.

After cleaning up the mess from the biscuits, she stepped out the door onto the porch and brushed the crumbs from her palms. The sun lit the pale green branches of the quince apple bush and set it to shining like diamonds. She drew in a long, slow breath and exhaled.

"Momma? Are you all right?"

Annabelle looked up to see Connie standing just inside the door. "I'm fine, just enjoying the morning sun and it not raining."

Connie held the door open for her. "I know what you mean. I hope we can get out of this house today. Even if it's just to walk down the drive."

Annabelle, her feet protected by rubber boots, made her way slowly across the backyard. Connie followed, carrying Joseph, swaddled in a blanket, a knitted cap on his head.

Annabelle breathed in the scent of spring: unfurling leaves and damp earth. As they neared the barbed-wire fence that bounded the cotton field, she scanned the landscape. What should be empty fields—freshly-turned brown earth—instead looked very much like a large lake.

"Oh my."

"It's devastated. What will they do?"

Annabelle lifted her shoulders. "It'll dry quickly enough. The creek will empty out. The crop'll be late, for sure. But there's time."

Connie shaded her eyes. "I wonder how deep it is?"

"Not very."

"Hel-looo!"

Annabelle recognized Alton's voice and turned to see him striding over the crest of the slope. He'd probably paddled across the water and walked up the old wagon road from Sutter's Landing. Funny how she'd never thought about that name before, and how it came to be.

Once upon a time, a long time ago, the creek had run full all the time. There was no bridge on the main road, so the early residents of the big house had forded the creek at the landing. When had she ever been told the history of the place? Maybe Lillian had talked about it. They'd spent many a summer day together, growing up. Back when the shanties still stood behind the Sutter house. Miss Lucy's ma had lived in the least dilapidated one until she died. She'd been there since her days as a slave.

Annabelle breathed a sigh. "Miss Lucy's ma."

Connie glanced over. "What did you say?"

"Oh, just remembering the old days."

Alton swung one long leg then the other over the barbed-wire fence. "Good morning, ladies. Nice weather we're having." He stepped closer and peered into Joseph's bright-eyed gaze. "Hello there, young man. You're looking wide awake for once." His face relaxed into a slow grin as his gaze met up with Connie's.

Annabelle sniffed and turned aside. Let the two have a moment to themselves. Young love. She held back the sigh. Did she miss it? Sometimes.

For some odd reason, Tom's face drifted into her mind. She gave her head a quick shake. Best not to dwell on such things. Squeezing her eyelids shut, she forced her memory to conjure up Ray's countenance. Not that last picture—in his final repose—but one with the smile crinkles around his eyes. The wide smile on his face as he laughed out loud at something David said.

David—her beautiful baby boy. From her gut, a sob rose. She quick-stepped toward the hen house to disconnect her mind from its present moorings.

Tom drove his truck through the murky water covering the road as he approached the Milan Highway. Should he turn left, away from town? Swing by Annabelle's place? Riley said they'd fared well in the storm. No damage, and the water hadn't come near their house. A sudden thought slowed the truck's progress almost to a complete stop. Maybe now would be a good time to scout out a place to build a house. While water still stood in the low patches, and the streams and creeks were overrun. What a great idea. He looked both ways, before making a left turn. If he never had to deal with flooding again, that would suit him perfectly.

Sunlight filtered through the overhanging branches of an old oak tree as Tom approached the turnoff near the old Sterling place. He'd had to swing around the back way, because the bridge was closed for repairs. Not long after he passed the Parmenter farm, he slowed to a complete stop as his gaze took in the full view. Above the old Sterling place where Annabelle lived, lay the perfect spot for a house. It was the highest point around, which wasn't saying a whole lot. There weren't very many real hills around this area. Glancing in the rear-view mirror, he made certain no one was coming. He wanted to fully examine the possibilities.

A few trees stood on the site, mostly saplings. The old wagon road that led to Sutter's Landing edged the property, dividing it from Annabelle's yard. As far as Tom knew, the land was owned by the Wades. Easy enough to find out. He pressed the gas pedal and drove the few hundred feet to Annabelle's driveway. He noticed Alton's truck parked there and hoped for the opportunity to speak with him. When he got out of his truck, he caught sight of the ladies sitting on the front porch. He removed his hat and lifted his hand in greeting. "Good day, Miss Annabelle, Miss Connie."

Annabelle stood and moved toward the steps. "Good afternoon, Tom. You making another delivery out this way?"

As he approached the front of the house, he scanned the area for Alton. "I'm just out visiting. Thought I'd see how you fared through the weather."

"A whole lot better than you did. Riley told us about your house. I'm so sorry to hear it. Such a beautiful old place."

The light in her eyes reminded him of the former days of their youth. For a moment, he stood there, gazing into her face. He rubbed his chin. "It was indeed. I appreciate your sentiments. But, I suppose it's time for me to make a change."

While his attention had been held by Annabelle's sparkling eyes, Miss Connie had risen and entered the house. Perhaps Alton was inside? He sent a glance over his shoulder toward the driveway. "I thought maybe Alton was here."

"Come on up and have a seat, Tom." Annabelle indicated the rocker Connie had vacated. "We were out here enjoying this fine weather." Once he was seated, she turned her gaze on him. "Alton left his truck here. He's been crossing the floodwaters in a fishing boat for the last couple of days. But I imagine the water has receded enough, he won't have to do that much longer."

"I reckon not, but the bridge is still out. They're working on it, but I expect it'll take some time."

Connie stepped back out, carrying two glasses of iced tea.

As she set them down on the small side table, Tom thanked her. She gave him a warm smile and turned back to the door. "I'll be inside for a bit, Momma. I hear Joseph waking up."

For several minutes, they rocked and sipped their tea, enjoying a companionable silence. Tom didn't want to interrupt the mood. He breathed it in, savored it like the flavor of the sweet tea in his glass. Is this how it would be between them? He sent a furtive glance toward Annabelle's face and found her watching him. Warmth crept up his neck, headed straight for his cheeks.

"By any chance, do you know who owns that property up there above the house?" He crooked his thumb in that direction.

She glanced where he'd pointed, then back at Tom. "I do know. It belongs to me."

Annabelle scrutinized Tom's face. Riley had told her Tom was going to build a new house, but she'd assumed he meant in town, close to his work. Could he really be looking to settle out here? Of course, it was only a fifteen-minute drive from the town square, but still … that was fifteen minutes he'd have to travel twice a day, six days a week. She waited patiently for him to tell her why he was interested. He sure was a quiet man, at times. He always had been. He'd lived in Riley's shadow most of their growing up years. At one time, she thought he had a crush on her. But he never said a word about it.

Finally, he set his glass down, sat forward, elbows on his knees, and clasped his hands together. "I'm hunting for a piece of land to build a house on. I figured this was the best time to look, while the water's high."

She nodded. "That's real smart, Tom. Wise. But out here—isn't it a little far from your work?"

His gaze met hers, held for a moment. "It's not that far. I prefer country living, Miss Annabelle. I'd much rather have birdsong than the constant noise of traffic. That's why I stayed in my parents' old house. It was quiet out there on the Forked Deer. Good fishing, too, most of the time." He sat back and rocked a bit. "I don't guess you'd be interested in selling me a parcel."

Now that would be a fine thing. How much could she make off that land? She could almost feel the comfort of a nest egg sitting in her savings account. But reality crept in. She fingered the collar of her shirtwaist dress. What would Jensen think of her selling off a piece of what he considered his family's rightful property? Though the land had long ago been deeded to her grandfather, Jensen still viewed it as belonging to the Sutter grant. She drew a long, slow breath and eased it out as quietly as possible. The land belonged to her. She should be able to do whatever she wanted with it. After all, Jensen had been most eager to take it off her hands after her mother died.

"I'll sure give it some thought, Tom."

He pressed his hands against his thighs as if to dry sweat from his palms. Had he been worried about her answer?

The kitchen door opened, and Connie stepped outside, carrying Joseph in her arms.

"Here, Miss Connie." Tom rose and offered his chair. "I'm just about to leave anyway."

Annabelle stood. "Don't rush off, Tom. We'll have supper in an hour or so. Why don't you join us?"

"I appreciate the invitation, but I need to get on back. Thelma's expecting me." He turned his hat in his hands and looked from Annabelle to Connie, then back to Annabelle. "Perhaps another time."

Annabelle followed him down the porch steps. "Will we see you in church tomorrow, Tom?"

He froze. "Um … uh …"

Annabelle could see the red creeping up his neck from several feet away. She wanted to laugh out loud. Of course, he wasn't going. But she needed to ask him. If she made a practice of asking each time they met, he'd know exactly how she felt about it, wouldn't he? And if he didn't like it, he'd quit coming around. It was as simple as that. And maybe now, he wouldn't want to buy that parcel of land.

Tom took a backward step, inching toward his truck. As he donned his hat, he gave her a rather sheepish grin. "I reckon you already know the answer to that, Miss Annabelle."

"I do, Tom. But it doesn't hurt to ask, does it? I just wanted to extend the invitation, and let you know you'd be most welcome."

He continued to back toward his truck, probably eager to be away from her church talk. "I appreciate it, Miss Annabelle—that I'd be most welcome, I mean. You think about what I asked you. I'll check back with you in a few days." With a final nod, he hurried to his truck and climbed in.

Annabelle watched until he'd passed from view. One thing was certain, she sure knew how to run a man off.

Chapter Seven

Connie drew a deep breath and tried to concentrate. The worst thing about sitting in the second row at church, especially a small-town church like theirs, was the feeling—no, the knowing—that dozens of eyes were focused on you. All because of Alton's presence by her side. Again. It's not like it was the first time. She pressed her lips into a firm line.

Alton had driven that roundabout route to get to their house so his mother could come. Miss Lillian hadn't wanted to ride in the rowboat. Connie couldn't blame her. But they'd arrived at church too late for Sunday School. Only a few folks were in the sanctuary when Connie, Momma, and Miss Lillian walked in. But that number grew steadily. Apparently, a lot of people were running behind this morning. Alton entered and sat down beside Connie. That's when it started—those gazes boring into the back of her head. She may have imagined the stares, but she didn't imagine the titters.

After only a few minutes, Joseph soiled his diaper. Connie sent Alton an apologetic look and excused herself. On her way back to the sanctuary with a clean baby boy, she paused at the door of the nursery. Classes were letting out, so she held back until the hall cleared of people. In the room next door, a conversation between two women caught Connie's attention. She meant to ignore them, until her name was mentioned.

She recognized Maggie Arnold's voice right away. Maggie's family ran the largest grocery in downtown Trenton. Maggie had always been very friendly, but lately, Connie had detected a slight chill.

"It hasn't even been a year," Maggie hissed.

Connie held her breath. Were they talking about what she thought they were talking about?

Maggie continued, "She probably never really loved him. Otherwise, how could she even think of another man so soon?"

"I thought you liked Connie."

Though familiar, Connie didn't recognize the other woman's voice, but she must be one of the young ladies in her Sunday School class.

"That was before she threw herself at the most eligible bachelor in Trenton. She ought to have more respect for the memory of Joe Cross."

There it was—the reason for Maggie's hurtful words—she was jealous. But knowing that didn't make the conversation any easier for Connie to take. Her blood boiled. She was sorely tempted to step through the doorway and surprise them both. Tears burned her eyes. She turned away to gaze out the window.

"I feel sorry for Alton." Maggie's voice again. "Maybe she doesn't love him, either. She just needs someone to take care of her, and be a father for the baby."

Connie bit down on her lower lip to keep from gasping and giving herself away. What nerve—in church, of all places—where folks are supposed to show God's love. Her stomach in knots, she returned to her seat, ignoring the stares of probably everyone seated in the pews.

What an awful thing for anyone to think, let alone say aloud. How could Maggie believe something so vile of her? Alton's gaze penetrated her soul, but she couldn't meet his eyes. For some strange reason, guilt pressed in on her. She kept her head down, pretending to give all her attention to little Joseph.

But her thoughts stayed on those accusations. Had she brought this on herself by moving too fast?

At all the right moments during the service, she stood, bowed her head, sang words to songs, but didn't really hear them.

When they finally sat again, Momma touched her arm. "Are you all right? Do you need me to hold the baby for a bit?"

Connie shook her head. Without Joseph to hide her distraction, she'd never make it through the service. Even now, she was half tempted to leave. When Pastor Nathan announced his scriptures, Alton held his Bible so she could read along.

Her heart calmed as the Word of God flowed in.

Ye have heard that it hath been said, thou shalt love thy neighbour, and hate thine enemy. But I say unto you, love your enemies, bless them that curse you, do good to them that hate you, and pray for them which despitefully use you, and persecute you...

Was Pastor Nathan aware of the talk going on behind her back? Or was this just a coincidence? She drew in a deep breath, and exhaled. Of course, it wasn't anything to do with her. The whole world did not revolve around Connie Cross. She forced her attention to remain on the words being spoken, but it was all she could do to keep her attention on the page. She wanted to turn and scan the congregation, find Maggie, and glare at her. Like a second-grader. She knew better. By the time the pastor began his benediction, her struggle had come full circle.

The congregation stood and began their exodus toward the door.

Momma asked to hold Joseph, so Connie gave him up. Of course, Momma wanted to show him off to her friends. Comments like, "Oh, look how he's grown," soon filled the air.

When someone touched her arm, Connie turned her head and gazed into the face of Maggie Arnold.

"We missed you in Sunday School this morning,"

Maggie's voice exuded warmth.

Connie produced a matching smile that almost seemed real. "Thank you, Maggie. It's nice to know I was missed. How is your family? I hope you were not inconvenienced by the flood?"

"Not at all, thank goodness. I'm so glad our house sits on a knoll." As she spoke, she glanced around Connie, toward the place where Alton stood in quiet conversation with one of the deacons. "I hope Alton's land will recover in time to plant. Daddy said they were under water over there. In fact, I'm surprised they made it here this morning, with the bridge out."

"They came around the back way. It's longer, of course." She waited until Maggie's gaze returned to her. "That's why we were late."

Maggie barely hid a wry smile. "Of course, I forgot you ride with them." After a polite nod to Miss Lillian, she continued. "I'm amazed at how much your baby has grown in the few days since we've seen him. My goodness, he must be such a comfort to you since the loss of his daddy. I know you must miss your late husband terribly."

At that moment, Alton raised his eyes to Connie's face. Had he heard Maggie's comment? Connie's breath caught; her knees went weak. Did anyone else notice the subtle change in his countenance? The warmth of his gaze? With some degree of difficulty, she brought her attention back to Maggie, who was still chatting away.

After a deep, cleansing breath, Connie willed her

expression to relax. "You're so kind, thank you." She was about to excuse herself when Maggie's piercing gaze faltered. Her eyelids lowered as she took a backward step.

Alton touched Connie's shoulder. "I'm sorry to interrupt such a pleasant conversation, but we need to head home, Miss Connie."

Connie fought to maintain her countenance, to keep the prideful glow from her face. She smiled at the woman in front of her. "Enjoy your Sunday, Maggie."

Maggie gave no answer, but Connie read the truth in her eyes. Maggie Arnold had feelings for Alton.

Annabelle emptied the slop jar into the chicken pen and watched as the young birds gobbled up the leavings of the dinner. She gave the jar a quick rinse at the pump before heading toward the side yard where Connie was pinning diapers on the line. The girl had been uncharacteristically quiet all morning. In fact, since they'd come home from church yesterday.

The baby kicked and gurgled in his basket as Connie shook out a cotton square and draped it over the line.

Annabelle set the jar on the porch, and wiped her hands on her apron. She picked up a diaper and shook out the wrinkles.

"Is there something troubling you, Pumpkin?"

Connie's hands paused. She fastened a pin and bent for another cloth. "Nothing I can talk about. Not yet." She sucked in a breath and let her hands drop to her sides. "Am I a terrible person, Momma?"

Annabelle's jaw dropped. She closed her mouth and propped a fist on one hip. "Of course, not. What's this all about?"

Connie's lip trembled. She covered it with the back of her hand.

Annabelle moved quickly to wrap an arm about the girl's waist. "Oh, dear. Has something happened between you and Alton?"

"No. Nothing like that. It's just … do you think I've moved too quickly?"

"Are you having doubts?" *Please say no.* Alton would be crushed.

Connie pulled in her lower lip, but shook her head. "No. Not really. It's just …"

"Folks are talking. Aren't they?"

The girl lowered her head.

Annabelle stepped around in front of her. "Look at me."

Connie raised her eyes.

"Do you love him?"

A smile tugged at the corners of Connie's lips.

"I know you do. You've been so happy these last few months. Both of you have been."

"But maybe they're right, Momma. Maybe we should

wait. Some are saying I didn't love Joe."

Annabelle blew out a breath, and threw down the clothespin she'd held onto. "They've got no right. Of course, you loved Joseph."

Connie swiped at tears. "I did love him. But what I feel for Alton—" she cast a glance at Annabelle. "It just seems different."

"That's because it is different. You're different. You're more mature. And Alton's a man." She bobbed her head to help make the point. "Joseph was so young, full of life and …"

"Yes." Connie gave a short laugh and swiped at her eyes again. "In so many ways, he was like a boy, playing at life."

Unbidden moisture filled Annabelle's eyes. She lifted a corner of her apron and dabbed it away. "A beautiful boy."

A soft sigh from the basket brought their attention to the newest Joseph, another beautiful boy.

Connie crouched to check on him. "Did you think we were talking about you, sweetie? Well, maybe we were. Maybe you'll be like your daddy. Instead of quiet and brooding, like your mother."

"You don't brood. You *are* sometimes quiet. You're a deep thinker, that's all. Smart. If he takes that after you, he'll be a blessed little man indeed."

Connie rose and returned to the clothesline. "A good mix of both would be nice." She hung up a diaper.

"That's a good thought. Most likely, he'll pick up traits from Alton, too. Just think how nice that will be." When they'd finished their chore, Annabelle took the clothes basket and headed toward the porch. "Bring the little one around front. I'll meet you there with a glass of tea. That'll lift your spirits."

In the kitchen, Annabelle added a plate of freshly baked teacakes to the tray. The afternoon was a warm one, for early spring. If the weather held, the floodwaters would be dried up in no time.

Seated in the rocker, munching on a cookie, Annabelle could almost forget the troubles of the past. The day was a perfect one. A mockingbird sang in the oak tree, cattle lowed in the pasture across the way. Joseph snoozed in his basket.

She sipped her tea. Setting the glass on the table, she sneaked a peek at Connie, who had rested her head against the back of the chair. Annabelle didn't think she was sleeping, though. Was she still thinking about those selfish gossips?

Connie's eyelids fluttered open. "Why is it different?"

"What, Pumpkin?"

"Remember when we received Emily's letter before Christmas, saying she was getting married? You were upset that she'd moved on to another man so quickly." She turned her full gaze on Annabelle. "You haven't seemed upset with me—about Alton."

Annabelle beamed as she gave her chair a little push.

The gentle clack and squeak of the rocker had a calming effect. "Emily's such a scatterbrain. I worried that she'd latched onto someone else too quickly. And I still mourned so deeply. I couldn't understand it. How could she be ready to love again—so soon?" She reached to touch Connie's hand. "But you're level-headed and wise. You think before you make a move. I know that. Alton's our kinsman redeemer, just like in the Book of Ruth. God's choice for you. I knew it right away, when I saw how he looked at you—as though he adored you."

Connie smoothed her braid twisting the loose ends between her fingers. "We are a bit like those women in the Bible. That's encouraging, Momma. God provided for them just like He did for us. Then why do I still feel a twinge of guilt every time I think of marrying Alton?"

"That's how it is, girl. Sorrow exacted a heavy toll on us. But what it took, our Heavenly Father promised to return, and much, much more. Whenever you feel that guilt, just send it packing. You've got no reason for shame. You and Joseph were a loving couple, but that part of your life has ended. You and that baby boy need a chance at happiness. And if that's not enough to decide you, think of Alton. He's waited all this time, and he loves you."

Connie gave a soft sigh. "I know he does."

Doves cooed from someplace overhead. A gentle breeze caressed Annabelle's cheek. She breathed a contented sigh. What a beautiful, peaceful afternoon. But when her gaze drifted to the dry grass in the field beside the house, a memory disturbed her content. "Fiddlesticks."

Connie turned a glare on her. "What is it?"

"I forgot all about talking to Alton about that land." Why had she thought of it so suddenly? Smack in the middle of their peace and quiet. Did she really want Tom living right next door? The money sure would be nice. She wouldn't have to depend on anyone for her livelihood. Depending on how much he was willing to pay for it, of course. She blew out a breath.

And supposing Jensen Wade would allow such a thing to proceed. That man had far too much power. He had a way of making things happen, or not. Now Annabelle experienced a twinge of guilt. She shouldn't be thinking such unloving thoughts about Jensen. After all, he was her first cousin. She should be praying for him. Nothing was impossible with God. And if it was meant for her to sell the land, God could do that too.

Chapter Eight

Following Judith's graduation, Annabelle stood next to Cousin Thelma in the Franklin's side yard, ladling fruit punch into paper cups. She was trying hard to ignore Thelma's latest implication.

"There's nothing wrong with you entertaining the man. Maybe all he needs is a good woman to guide him."

Annabelle snorted. "I've been that route before, and you know it. I'd rather be alone for the rest of my life than be unequally yoked to another." She turned a warm smile on a line of thirsty guests. "You know I loved Ray with my whole heart. I was so young and silly when we married. I thought I could change him. He was a good man, but he had no need of church."

"I remember. His church was anywhere on the water with a fishing pole in his hand. My Riley's of the same mind, only he expands his sanctuary to include the woods and a rifle. We were both young and silly, Annabelle.

Green as corn in June."

"That was one of your Grandma Puckett's favorite sayings." Annabelle giggled as she wiped up a few drops of bright red punch before it stained the plastic tablecloth. When she glanced up, Tom stood in her line of vision. He nodded and smiled. The temperature in the shade of the old oak tree seemed to skyrocket. She turned away and shook out the rag before hanging it over the edge of the table. A long, slow intake of breath seemed to help.

Memories dropped into her mind of a much younger Tom Franklin, red-faced and nervous, asking her to dance with him. "Dance with you?" she'd said. "I would, but you know I'm not allowed. Dancing is frowned upon by the Baptists."

Of course, most of her church friends ignored that rule. But she had no intention of leading poor Tom on. He wasn't bad to look at, a little too skinny perhaps, but she had other plans. She was headed out of Trenton. She didn't know exactly where or how, but hoped to get as far away as possible from the snooty Wade family. Mr. Charles Wade, Sr., in particular, who had turned her mother out of his house after his son died. She had grown up in their shadow, having their name, but never accepted as one of them.

So, she'd married a man who knew nothing about any of that. A good-looking man in a uniform, whose home was far away from West Tennessee.

"Miss Annabelle?"

Annabelle focused on Tom, now standing right in front of the punch bowl. She darted a quick look toward Thelma, who was deep in conversation with Lizzie Carter. Had Tom asked a question she'd been too distracted to hear? With a slight shake of her head, she offered up a smile and a cup of punch.

He accepted the cup and the smile. "Our Judith did well, didn't she?"

Annabelle nodded. This line of conversation seemed safe enough. "Yes, she did. I'm so glad that new principal allowed both girls to speak."

"It was the right thing to do, since they scored the same all the way through." He continued to gaze at her as he sipped the punch.

A tremor ran through Annabelle's fingers as she handed a cup to another neighbor. She usually had no problem with small talk, but when accompanied by a piercing stare from a man who most likely held an affection for her ... that was another situation altogether.

"Alton tells me he's having a work day over at the Sutter place."

Annabelle nodded. "He wants to plant a garden where the old slave cabins were. Have you seen it since they cleaned it all out?"

"Did they tear it all down? I hated to see Miz Liza's old cabin go. A lot of memories around that place."

"It went of its own accord, I believe, a year ago, this past winter. Connie suggested they plant a flower garden—

kind of like a memory garden—keep the chimneys and foundations in place. Alton liked the idea." She topped off Tom's cup. "Are you planning to help out?"

He nodded. "Once I close up for the day, I'll probably come on over. I don't like to turn down Regina's fried chicken."

Annabelle had to laugh. Nobody she knew would turn down Regina's fried chicken.

Connie snapped a couple of pictures of Miss Lillian sitting on the slider swing, Joseph in her lap. Moving through the garden patches, she took more photos to document the day. What a wonderful memory this would make. She'd fill an album, maybe finish it with the photos of their wedding. She hadn't discussed it with Alton yet, but this wonderful garden would make the perfect backdrop for their nuptials. A funny little fluttering sensation greeted that thought. She'd heard of butterflies in the tummy, but did one get them in the heart?

She glanced at Alton, his shirt drenched with sweat. He removed his hat and used his sleeve to wipe his brow. The man seemed tireless. He worked all the time. Once he began a task, he finished it. Did he have any faults? Certainly, he must, and perhaps she should seek them out. Better to know the worst now, before they married. She almost laughed out loud at the thought of Alton leaving dirty socks on the floor.

Alton shot a glance at her. "What are you smiling at— do I look ridiculous?" He replaced his hat. "I hope you're not taking unkind photos."

"Not I. No, I'd never do that."

Regina rang the dinner bell, ending their conversation and causing a frenzy of excitement among the neighbors.

Willie and his boys had set tables around the side yard, under the shade of some maple trees.

Neighbors who had worked side-by-side now segregated themselves at the tables. Connie watched with interest. White families sat near the food table, colored families sat farther away. Her heart ached a little at the scene, though they probably never gave it a thought.

Miss Lillian walked over with a hungry baby, so Connie excused herself to go inside for a few minutes. By the time she returned, everyone had their food.

Momma filled Connie's plate and sat next to her.

A moment later, Regina appeared with a frosty glass of iced tea.

"Regina, you read my mind."

The men were talking baseball—Mickey Mantle's three consecutive home-runs. What a game that was. Unlike California where the Dodgers were next to food and drink in importance, Tennessee didn't have a team. So, they followed after the heroes of the game. Connie enjoyed watching Alton's animated expressions as he carried on with his neighbors.

While the ladies cleared away the food and washed the dishes, the men sat in the shade, whittled, talked, and napped. When cleanup had ended, most of the women joined the children, who were playing games in the field. The white children played near the house, the colored children down near the creek.

Connie gave an absentminded shake of her head. Once again, they'd segregated themselves.

By mid-afternoon, most everyone had gone home to chores of their own. Joseph was fast asleep in his cradle on the side porch. Connie relaxed in the slider swing nearby.

Alton reached for her hand. "Come take a look at the garden. We made pretty good headway, I think."

They walked along the newly-laid brick paths, where the ladies had planted settings of thrift. Old-fashioned climbing roses were in place, one or two at the base of each of the old chimneys. Alton told her they'd be pale pink, with a sweet aroma. Rows of ancient daffodils had already bloomed, but their bright green leaves bordered the foundations. They'd planted petunias and zinnias, cleome, and cosmos, leaving empty seed packets on little stakes to mark them. This would be a very pretty place in late summer.

After that short stroll, Alton went to help Willie gather up the tools. Connie headed down to the creek, now running low, but still quite pretty.

"Watch out for snakes!" Alton called out.

Connie waved to let him know she'd heard. She could see Samson up ahead, so figured the dog would protect her from reptiles. Drawn by the clear, rushing water, she kicked off her shoes, removed her socks, and rolled up her pants.

Samson had already dashed in. He splashed around, pausing from time to time to sniff the air.

It was dark and cool here, and smelled earthy and clean. She gazed up at patches of clear blue between the brand new leaves of the trees. Sycamore-scented air filled her lungs. Her ears thrilled to the expert mimics of a mockingbird. She stepped into the water, so cool to her tired feet, and waded upstream, keeping a sharp eye out for snakes, as Alton had warned. Mayflies scudded by, weightless on the water's surface. Minnows swam beneath them, tickling her ankles, but nothing larger appeared.

In a few short days, all the water would be gone. The creek would be dry again. Just a rugged, rocky bed. She'd miss the relaxing sound of running water.

Up ahead, Samson whined.

She looked to the place where he stood, his back to her, tail erect. A sudden chill crept up her neck. Was it a warning whine? Did he see a snake?

He stood near an overhang, where the floodwaters had cut deep into the steep embankment. She watched as he crept further into the hollow. Moments ticked past until there came a clipped bark, followed by a whine that sounded almost mournful.

What on earth?

She swallowed her fear of snakes and crept nearer. Sun sparkled on the water, temporarily blinding her. When her vision cleared, she could see Samson standing just inside the newly carved-out space, his ears and tail drooping. He turned his head and gazed at her with another mournful whine, but didn't move.

Her heart in her throat, she waded nearer. "What is it, boy? Did you find something?" Still, she couldn't see anything. "What?" She was near enough now to touch the dog. She smoothed his head and neck, reassuring him.

Her breath caught as her eyes lit on what he'd found. The unmistakable shape of a human skull, partially unearthed by the floodwaters.

The evening sun illuminated the front porch at Sutter's, where Connie sat with Alton, Momma, and Miss Lillian. Judith reclined on the porch floor, playing with Joseph.

After taking a quick look at Samson's find, Alton had called Sheriff Jordan. "Most likely, it's old bones buried along that creek," Alton told the women. "Got washed out by the flood waters. It's not unusual. Sheriff said he'd come out and take a look tomorrow after church."

"They should at least be removed to a safer spot." Miss

Lillian's words echoed Connie's thoughts.

Alton nodded. "I agree. If Sheriff Jordan gives the OK, Willie and I will move what's left to the old cemetery."

"Could be a slave," Judith said. "Or someone that died in the war. Or maybe murdered and …"

"That's enough of that," Miss Lillian interrupted. "You've been watching too much television, young lady."

Judith giggled. "I don't watch much at all. But I do read, Miss Lillian. I love murder mysteries."

"There you go. Puts all kinds of ideas in your head."

Regina spoke from inside the screen door. "I've got food on the table in here, if anyone is interested."

"I hope everyone is," Miss Lillian pushed up from the chair. "We could almost feed half the county with the leftovers from dinner."

Regina hung back as everyone filed inside.

Connie touched her arm. "You've had such a long day. You must be tired."

"It ain't that, Miss Connie. I don't like you finding that grave. It troubles me some."

"Samson found it, not me. So, there's nothing to worry about." She smiled and hoped her light tone would reassure Regina.

"I suppose, but I have a bad feeling, Miss Connie."

Alton barely had time to change his shoes after church before Sheriff Jordan arrived.

"I hope you don't mind me stopping in before I go to dinner," he told Alton. "The wife made plans for us to eat with her parents over at Windy City."

"Not a problem at all," Alton assured him. "But you're going to need to wade in the creek. Do you need a pair of boots?"

The sheriff rounded his car and opened the trunk. "I carry a pair of waders." He lifted them out and grinned at Alton. "Just in case I need to throw in a line somewhere."

Alton chuckled. "Always good to be prepared."

After donning the waders, the sheriff picked up a long-handled flashlight and a small shovel before lowering the trunk.

Alton led the way to the creek, relating the story of how Samson had located the body as they walked.

"Dogs'll whine like that, real mournful-like, when they find someone dead."

They stepped into the water and waded forward to the overhang.

The sheriff didn't hesitate, just waded on in, aiming the flashlight at the skull. "Looks to me like it's been here sometime." He cast the light overhead. "You may need to fill this in, or else collapse it. You wouldn't want someone to fall through and hurt themselves."

"We've already roped it off. Willie and I plan to move the remains to the family cemetery. Afterward, we'll fill in the hole and smooth this out."

"Good idea. I don't know though. Lookie here—" he tugged at a ragged piece of cloth. "Looks like a bandana or a scarf, maybe. I'm wondering if we ought to have the county doc come out and take a look at this. Just in case, you know."

"Whatever you think. You want us to leave it as-is, I guess?"

"Let me talk to the man. I'll call you, probably in the morning."

Deep in thought, Alton watched the sheriff pull away. This was turning into more of a chore than he'd expected. His mind was already cluttered with things to do. He had a trip to Nashville planned for sometime early next week. And the cotton was nearly ready for chopping. With all that rain, weeds had popped up all over.

Samson thumped his tail as Alton approached the back porch steps. He crouched to rub the dog's head, but his mind was far away. How long would it take to receive an answer back from someone living in the territory of Hawaii?

Chapter Nine

"Was it your idea to send Tom Franklin my way?"

Alton took in Jensen's florid complexion as his brother mopped his face with an already damp handkerchief. "I don't know what you're talking about."

Jensen carefully folded the cloth and returned it to his pants pocket. "Right. I'm sure you had nothing to do with it. Trying to piece-parcel our land now, huh? First you give it back to that woman over there—" he made a wild gesture toward the old Sterling house. "And then you send Tom Franklin in to see about that hilltop."

Alton suppressed a chuckle. One of these days, Jensen was going to worry himself into a heart attack over land that didn't even belong to him. "I'm telling you, I haven't spoken to Tom, and I don't know what you're talking about."

"Ever since you took up with that foreign woman, your brains went out the window." Jensen spat at the ground and slapped his hat against his knee.

As his brother's words sank in, Alton clamped his teeth together. He would not allow the man to rile him. He concentrated on the few hairs on the top of his brother's head. But not reacting to a barb only urged Jensen on.

Samson rose from his resting place and shook himself. Always sensitive to his master's moods, the dog stood— wary and alert—watching Jensen.

"You do realize what you're doing? She and her lot will end up owning everything. It makes me sick to my stomach, knowing that half-breed boy of hers will stand to inherit part of what should rightfully go to mine."

Alton's patience met a quick end, as though he'd been sucker-punched. "Did you think I would never marry? Never have any children of my own?"

Jensen huffed. "Truthfully? No. I'd a bet the big house on it. You've had plenty of chances. Some of the best little fillies in the state waved their caps at you over the years. But you were too much of a momma's boy, I reckon."

Jensen's eyes narrowed to slits in that way Alton hated. He was egging Alton on. Prodding, pushing, hoping to rile him up. But why?

Samson whined, and took off toward the creek.

Alton watched him for a moment. Probably after a more interesting varmint than the one standing here.

Jensen leaned closer, his voice low and gravelly. "I was beginning to think you were rooting for the other team, till that half-breed came along. You prefer dark meat." He let out a wicked laugh.

Something deep inside Alton broke free. Before he could catch himself, his fist had connected with Jensen's jaw. Hard.

Jensen's expression showed actual surprise as he stumbled backwards. He reached up to rub his jaw, then opened his mouth wide till it popped.

His heart beating wildly, Alton swung around and strode toward the barn, hoping to put as much distance as possible between himself and his brother. Otherwise, he was going to do something he'd really regret.

Connie greeted Miss Lucy and her family, armed with well sharpened hoes, on their way to Alton's field.

"How's that baby, Miss Connie?" Miss Lucy asked. "I been missing him since the work took up."

"He's doing well. Fat and sassy."

Miss Lucy cackled. "Well, you give him a kiss for me."

Judith had walked part of the way with Connie and now continued on with the workers. A twinge of guilt passed through Connie as she watched them go. Surely, she should be working too, instead of nosing around Sutter's Landing, but she was curious. She wanted to know what the sheriff had said about the body they'd found.

Her steps faltered just below the house as she watched Alton punch his brother in the face. Had that actually happened? A moment later, Alton swung away and stomped off toward the barn.

Samson, who had rushed to greet her near the crossing, took off after Alton.

"Your man has a temper!" Jensen called out.

Connie gazed at him, but didn't respond. She took a step nearer.

He mopped his face with a handkerchief, settled his hat on his head, and glowered at her. "If I was you, I'd give careful thought to your future. You have a child to think of." He nodded toward the barn. "Is that the kind of father you want for your son?" While he was speaking, he carefully folded the handkerchief before stuffing it in his pocket.

Revulsion churned in Connie's chest. She'd never known Alton to lose his temper or show any negative emotion, for that matter. No doubt she was looking at the reason for it.

Jensen sucked his teeth. His ample lips settled into a smug smile. "I'll bid you good day, Miz Cross. I reckon you have a lot to think about." Moving faster than she'd thought him capable, Jensen jumped in his car and backed out of the drive.

The screen door swung open. Regina stepped onto the porch. "You come on inside, Miss Connie. I got you a glass of iced tea ready."

Something in Regina's tone urged Connie forward. With a last look toward the barn, she stepped inside.

Heat and the spicy aroma of Regina's delicious cooking enveloped Connie as she took the chair offered by the cook and housekeeper.

"Don't you pay no mind to Mr. Jensen, Miss Connie. He's a troubled man, looking to push his trouble off on whoever happens to be near." She shook her head and set a plate of molasses cookies in front of Connie. "Thank the good Lord Miz Wade ain't to home. It would worry her to no end."

"I'm glad of that, too." Connie bit into a cookie and savored the taste. "These are wonderful, as usual, Regina. Have you any idea what the argument was about?"

Regina turned away, took up a long-handled spoon and began to stir one of the pots on the stove.

Connie sipped the iced tea while she waited. There was no rushing Regina. If she wanted to talk, she would.

After another ten minutes or so, Regina pulled out a chair and sat. She held a pint-size Mason jar filled with cold water. "I hope you don't mind me settin' a spell, Miss Connie. It's been a long morning." She drank most of the water, then patted her lips with the corner of her apron.

Connie smiled. "Not at all, Regina."

"Miz Wade laid out those things for you upstairs. She hopes you'll like one of those patterns for the paper. She shore is set on getting that room done. I tried to tell her you might want to have more say." She took up a fan and waved it in front of her face. "Land sakes, it's hot for so early in the year."

Connie thought about asking Regina what the sheriff said, but remembered the woman's reaction to finding that grave. She might not want to talk about that either. After a moment's consideration, she took the safe road. "Thank you for the cookies and the tea. If you're not going to tell me what those two were arguing about, I guess I might as well go upstairs."

Regina laughed. "Miss Connie, since you gone be living here soon, I'll tell you. I don't ever talk behind Mr. Alton's back. But I will say, he's always a gentleman. Always. So, you know if anything went bad out there 'tween those two, it wasn't his fault."

Connie chuckled as she patted the woman's arm. "Thank you, Regina. That makes me feel a little better."

On the way up the stairs, she paused on the landing to peer outside. Still no sign of Alton. She wasn't even sure he'd seen her approach, so why would he hurry home? She climbed the remaining steps and crept to the front of the house. The main bedroom took up the full width of the upper story on the front side. Three tall windows overlooking the ample front yard let in plenty of light. According to Miss Lillian, this was the room her parents had shared. It had not been used since her mother died.

The wallpaper was dove gray with a large floral pattern throughout. It seemed a bit dark, even with all the light in the room. Several framed portraits had been removed, leaving darker ovals where they'd been. A large fireplace adorned the side wall. Connie ran her hand along the ornate mantel. It was clear this house had once been quite a showpiece.

She crossed to the table in front of the windows and touched the wallpaper samples lying there. How could it be that she was choosing the colors for the room she'd share with Alton? She pressed shaky fingers against her lips. It all seemed unreal. Yet Miss Lillian insisted she take part. What if she made the wrong choice—chose a color Alton would hate?

Glancing behind her, she lowered herself into a straight-backed chair and drew a deep breath. She'd seen the room he slept in. It was quite ordinary, with plank walls, painted white. No frills there. It might as well have been a servant's room. Perhaps it had been at one time. Or a closet. She smiled at the thought. He was such a humble man, he wouldn't object. And he probably wouldn't mind what pattern she chose for their room either.

She tugged at the edge of one of the samples and set it aside. The background was the color of cream with a hint of vanilla. Tiny sprays of dark pink flowers intertwined in a soft lattice effect. She closed her eyes and imagined creamy lace sheers at the windows, billowing in an early morning breeze. Her imagination stretched forward to include Alton sharing this room; this moment. But Connie couldn't allow it. She shook herself alert and wrote the information needed for the wallpaper choice on the notepad

Miss Lillian had provided.

Downstairs, the clock began to chime. It must be noon. Surely Alton would head home for dinner. She rose to go, hoping to slip out the side door and meet him in the yard. She didn't know why, but she didn't feel quite comfortable in this part of his house. She hurried toward the stairs just as Alton stepped out of his room, directly into her path.

His eyes widened as he reached out to catch her before she crashed into him.

"Alton. I'm sorry, I didn't even hear you come in."

He gazed down at her, but said nothing.

Chills danced up and down her spine. For a long moment, she thought he might be going to kiss her. What was the holdup, anyway? In just three days, they'd celebrate the 4th of July—and three days later, the one-year anniversary of Joseph's death—the end of her other life. She gazed into Alton's eyes, doing her best to invite him. What would it feel like to be kissed by him? Should she make the first move? Joseph had loved it when she did.

She dropped her gaze as another thought penetrated her soul. Alton was not Joseph.

A moment later, Alton drew her into his arms and held her against his chest. She closed her eyes and allowed herself to relax against him, feel the beat of his heart. When she dared to raise her face again, he kissed her. It was short, but certainly not chaste. She knew in that moment, there was a fire burning deep inside Alton, but he kept a very tight rein on his emotions. Regina's words returned to her,

"He's always a gentleman."

She smiled into his eyes.

"I love you," he whispered.

"I love you," she answered.

"Do you?"

Did he really doubt her feelings? She reached up to touch his cheek, allowed her fingertips to linger there. "Yes, Alton. I do."

His grip on her relaxed. A smile tugged at the corners of his lips. But the heat in his eyes remained. "Let's go downstairs." He turned quickly, as though he needed to escape.

Joy swirled in her heart. They had turned a corner. She'd caught a glimpse of the future—of what it would be like to spend her life with this man.

With a backward glance, he extended his hand. "Are you coming with me?"

She settled her hand in his and nodded. Oh, yes.

Under Regina's watchful eyes, Alton passed a steaming bowl of creamed potatoes to Connie. If they were alone, he might be able to relax and enjoy the meal. But Regina had warned him Connie had witnessed the argument. It weighed heavily on his conscience, along with the liberty he had taken upstairs. He barely suppressed a smile at the memory of her lips pressed against his. She hadn't exactly objected.

He cleared his throat. "Regina told me you … overheard my conversation with Jensen."

She shook her head. "I didn't really overhear. I did see what happened at the end."

"I guess you're probably wondering why I hit my brother."

"I am acquainted with your brother."

Alton chuckled. He loved her sense of humor. "Still, I feel I owe you an apology for my outburst."

"I forgive you, Alton. But if you were defending my honor, as I suspect you were, no apology is necessary."

"We'll just leave it at that?"

"Sounds good to me."

Regina shook her head as she returned to the kitchen.

Alton gathered a forkful of green beans. "Have you heard anything about Tom Franklin wanting to buy some property out this way?"

Connie nodded. "He asked Momma about the land next to the house, on the other side of the old wagon road. He didn't realize the land was hers."

"Did she make any kind of agreement with him?"

"Oh, no. She told him he'd have to clear it with you. Or Jensen."

He chewed a bite of chicken and washed it down with a swig of tea. "It's not really our land, it's hers. If he doesn't mind having deed restrictions, I don't see a problem with it."

"You might not see a problem, but I imagine your brother would." She sat back, her gaze searching his face. "Oh."

"What?"

"That's why Jensen was here, wasn't it? You weren't defending my honor."

Those eyes. He set his fork down. "Well, yes, I was. The conversation started with the land, and ended ... badly."

"I see."

Tiny frown lines creased her lovely brow. The brow he longed to kiss. He swallowed. What did she see?

"He really doesn't like me, does he?"

Alton reached for her hand. "I don't care how my brother feels about you. That's his problem. I'm in love with you, and I plan to marry you as soon as possible."

Her eyes flashed as the color rose in her cheeks. "I like the sound of that."

Chapter Ten

Alton glanced up as his mother stepped out onto the porch, waving an envelope.

"Who's writing you from M—how do you pronounce that—Ma-oo-ee?" Mother raised questioning eyes to Alton.

Alton took the envelope. Was this it? The letter he'd been waiting for? "Mother you know better than that. It's Maui, one of the Hawaiian Islands."

"Mow-wee? So, that's how they spell it. How was I to know? Who are you writing over there?"

The high arc of her brow told him she already knew the answer. He sent her a sideways glance and a knowing grin. "I'm pretty sure you read the envelope."

She shrugged. "I don't know anyone by the name of Pruitt."

"Connie's father. I wrote to formally ask his permission to marry his daughter."

Mother lowered herself into a porch rocker. "I thought as much. You're such a gentleman. Stirs a mother's pride."

"I also invited him to the wedding." He sat on the top step and carefully tore open the envelope.

Inside the kitchen, Regina sang. Mother's rocker creaked in accompaniment.

Alton leaned against the porch railing. It was a good thing he was seated. He might have fallen over.

Mother sat forward. "What's the matter? Did he refuse his blessing?"

His eyes still fastened to the letter, Alton shook his head. "No, he's given his blessing …"

"Well, what's the trouble? Is he asking for a bride price?" She chuckled and slapped her knee.

Alton looked at her. "It's surprising, that's all. He's impressed that I would take the time to write. He appreciates the invitation and offer to pay his transportation. But he can't make the trip."

"Land sakes, Alton. Is he sick? Too frail to travel?"

"No, he says he's a wanted man in Kansas."

Mother's jaw went slack. "What?"

Alton waved the letter. "He says it's a possibility. That's the reason he never returned to the States. It was years ago, and he thinks someone may have died as a result of something he did."

"*May* have? So, he doesn't know for sure?" She sat back in her chair and continued rocking. "Sounds sketchy. I remember Connie saying he didn't have any family left, so never saw the need to return. Maybe she doesn't know the real reason?"

Alton shrugged. "Maybe. I'm going to do some snooping around."

"I figured as much. Don't be disappointed if you can't make it right. You're not Superman."

He folded the letter and returned it to the envelope. "What makes you so sure?"

She cackled. "You haven't been able to resolve the case in your own backyard, for one thing. Have you heard any more about it?"

"No, and we do need to get that reconciled. I'd hate for someone to get hurt over there. Willie said the washout goes nearly eight feet back. That's going to be a good chunk of land we've got to fill in."

"I guess it's rather low on the medical examiner's to-do list."

"Understandably so, if we lived in the big city. Crime is low out here. Don't know what the holdup is. I'll check with Jordan while I'm in town."

"Good idea."

Samson hopped up when an ancient pickup pulled into the drive.

Alton stood. "There's Walter. I'll bet he's got your wallpaper. Are you ready for this?"

Mother joined Alton at the base of the steps. Shielding her eyes with her hand, she watched Walter's approach. "I sure am. I loved Connie's choice. I can't wait to see how it looks."

His meeting with Sheriff Jordan over, Alton crossed the street and entered the newspaper office. Bentley Crockett, the paper's owner and editor, was on the phone. He waved Alton to a seat in front of his desk. As he hung up the receiver, he grinned ear-to-ear. "Good to see you, Alton. Are you ready to publicly announce your nuptials?"

Alton shook his head. "That's not why I'm here."

Bentley sighed. "That's disappointing. So, what's going on?"

"If you needed to research something that happened in another state back in … say … the late twenties, how would you go about it?"

Bentley sat back. "Is this about that body y'all found in the creek?" He sat forward again and took up his pen. "Does the sheriff suspect foul play?"

Alton shook his head. "No, sir. It's not about that. I need information is all, about a friend of a friend. Jordan's checking to see if there are any outstanding warrants, but he suggested you might be able to find information that might have been in the local newspaper." Alton cleared his throat. "It was in Topeka, Kansas."

Bentley propped his chin on his palm. "And you don't know the exact date?"

110

"Yes, but I'm asking if it's possible to do. To find out, I mean."

"It's possible, depending on the alleged crime."

"Could've been wrongful death or accidental death."

Bentley scratched his head and concentrated. "I can try, but I'd sure need to know more facts."

"Well," Alton leaned forward. "I need you to keep this on the quiet, Bentley."

"Understood." He passed a scratch pad and pen to Alton.

Alton jotted down the information.

Bentley read what he'd written and nodded. "All right. I'll check into it, and give you a call if I find anything." He sat back in his chair again. "Now, about those nuptials. Don't try to tell me you aren't thinking on it."

Alton chuckled. "You'll get your story, Bentley."

"I'd better. It'll be the social event of the season."

Alton doubted that, since Connie had already hinted that she didn't want to make a big to-do. He hadn't objected, in fact he'd been relieved. He was not the pageant type. Which was exactly why he had always avoided Maggie Arnold. Besides the fact she was a good ten years his junior, her uppity attitude had always repelled him.

After leaving the newspaper office, Alton headed to the drug store where he hoped to catch a moment of Tom's time, and maybe grab a sandwich and a soda pop.

Tom was with a customer when he entered, so he slid onto an empty stool at the soda fountain.

"What can I get you," Freddie asked.

"Ham and cheese and a cola."

"Coming right up."

Finished with the customer, Tom jotted something on a pad, then nodded toward Alton. "Good to see you." He pushed through the half-door and headed over.

"I hoped you'd have a minute, Tom," Alton glanced around. "When we could talk."

"Well sir, it's been a right busy day." He sat next to Alton. "Freddie, fix me one of those ham sandwiches."

"You wanna cola too, sir, or your usual?"

Tom glanced at Alton and grinned. "The usual."

"You still drinking black cows?" Alton chuckled. "I thought you'd grow out of that."

"Why change a good thing?" Tom leaned on his elbow. "I reckon your brother talked to you."

Alton nodded. "He did."

Freddie served the sandwiches and drinks.

Alton had to admit, Tom's drink looked scrumptious, all frosty and frothy. He bit into the ham sandwich. In between bites, they discussed the problems with the property. "So, if you aren't opposed to deed restrictions, you and Annabelle could probably come to some agreement."

"I'll mull it over." Tom chewed thoughtfully.

Alton watched his face. What was he thinking?

Tom sipped his black cow and fiddled with a ketchup bottle. "Do you think I'd have problems other than the deed restrictions, Alton?"

"You mean from a certain lawyer? Who knows. It depends entirely on his mood these days. But you're practically family, Tom." He wadded his napkin and tossed it on his empty plate. He lowered his voice. "Of course, if you became family, you'd have no problem at all." He raised his eyebrows and smiled.

Tom's face nearly matched the ketchup in that bottle. He shook his head. "Don't look like that's gonna happen anytime soon."

"I know you're a patient man, Tom. I've seen you fish." He paid for his food and drink, slid off the stool, and turned to go.

Tom rose and walked with Alton to the door. "Thank you for stopping by. Like I said, I'll give it some thought. I'll let you know, either way."

Alton gripped Tom's hand in a firm handshake. "I'll see you around."

"I reckon you will."

Alton and Willie each aimed a high-beam flashlight into the washout while Dr. Otis examined the remains. In Alton's mind, the echo of voices from the cotton patch lent an air of surrealism to the scene.

Dr. Otis said little, beyond muttering from time to

time. Finally, he held up his hand. "You can turn those off now."

Alton nodded to Willie. They clicked off the flashlights and moved aside for Dr. Otis.

He rinsed his hands in the stream. Standing, he barely topped five feet. "Well, sir, that appears to be male, fully grown."

"Could you tell how he died?"

"No visible signs of violence. Could be sickness, or natural—or he could've drowned."

Alton removed his hat and mopped his brow. "Can you tell when?"

Dr. Otis shook his head. "Not without testing in a lab. Since there's no sign of foul play, I don't think you really want to go to all that trouble. Most likely, it was someone buried in this century. Could've been the flu epidemic the winter of 'eighteen. Judging by the bandana around his neck, I don't think it would've been as far back as the war." He headed for the creek's edge. "Of course, it's possible he drowned and got trapped up under there. Last bad flood was some time ago, I believe."

Alton led the way up the incline to the driveway. "Can I offer you a glass of iced tea, doctor? You're welcome to stay to dinner, of course."

"I wouldn't turn down a glass of tea. I have to get on home for dinner, though. Mrs. Otis is preparing my favorite today—liver and onions."

Willie gave Alton a nod before moving off toward the

garage.

Alton stopped by the kitchen window to ask Regina to bring tea to the front porch.

Mother joined them there, sitting beside Alton on the porch swing. Dr. Otis relaxed in a chair, fanning himself with his hat. "Shore enough hot for so early in the year."

"Yes, it is," Mother said. "So, you couldn't really identify the remains?"

"No ma'am. Sheriff might want to check into missing persons. The more I think on it, it was probably someone washed downstream in the last flood." He took a long drink of iced tea, then resumed fanning.

Her face drained of color, Mother glanced from Alton, back at the doctor. "How long ago?"

"Hard to say. I'd guess that last bad flood. When was that?"

"There was a bad one in 1920." Her voice trembled.

Alton watched her. "What are you thinking, Mother?"

"Uncle Pen got washed away in that flood. They never did find his body."

Dr. Otis set his glass down. "Well, it could be him. Was he a tall man?"

"No, as I remember, he was slight of build and not as tall as my daddy."

"Well, it would fit." He set his hat on his head and sat forward. "Alton, you might want to have those tests done to prove his identity. Up to you."

"Just a minute." Mother stood and went in the house.

She returned a few moments later, holding a photograph. "Here's a picture of him, taken shortly before he disappeared."

Alton took the photo and held it so he and Dr. Otis could see the man dressed in work clothes, leaning against the barn fence. He wore a dark-colored hat. A kerchief adorned his neck.

"He's wearing a bandana all right."

Mother gave a soft sigh. "He always wore one."

"I believe you've found your man." Dr. Otis stood. "You can give him a proper burial now." He started down the steps. "I better be on my way. I'll file my report with the sheriff's office."

As his car left the drive, Mother walked to the other side of the porch. "I want it done right, Alton. Let's call the funeral home."

He looked at the picture again. "I was just thinking the same thing."

Chapter Eleven
July 4, 1955

The sky blushed pink with the dawn as Annabelle stepped outside. She eased the screen door shut, hoping not to wake Connie and Judith. Sometimes she couldn't get a good breath of air inside. She didn't mind sharing her room with Judith, the girl was quiet as a mouse. But every once in a while, Annabelle just needed some time to herself. This was definitely one of those moments.

The Fourth of July. One year ago, over the Fourth of July holiday, a simple three-day fishing trip turned tragic. Her life had changed forever. The tears started before she could make it off the porch. She needed to put some distance between herself and the house, so she trotted toward the garden patch.

The chickens were beginning to stir, already clucking contentedly inside the hen house when Annabelle lowered herself to the ground. She didn't care that dew soaked her dress. Great sobs tore from her breast as she allowed herself to mourn. All the emotion she kept hidden inside came out in a wild rush. The handkerchief she'd tucked in her pocket was next to useless against such a torrent. She hugged herself and rocked slowly, focused on catching a breath.

How long before the constant ache in her chest dulled? Folks liked to say time heals all wounds. They remarked on her great strength. If they could see what teemed inside her, they wouldn't think that way.

The worst over, she gazed at the azure sky. "Praise God from whom all blessings flow…" she quoted the doxology. It always set her heart at ease. "Praise Him all creatures here below." Her words drifted into song. "Praise Him above ye heavenly host. Praise Father, Son, and Holy Ghost. Amen."

How did folks survive without faith in God? She surely would've shriveled up and died this past year, if not for her belief that God would rescue them. And He had done it. Warmth flooded through her as she remembered all He had done. Alton. The house. The land. Little Joseph. She sat still and quiet, wondering at the presence of God.

She was just beginning to consider getting up when an odd noise drew her attention. She turned to see their silly young rooster, eying her. Fumbling in her pocket, she drew out a handful of dried corn deposited there for just such an occasion. He pecked at the palm of her hand, gobbling up the kernels. Of course, this attracted the attention of the rest of the flock.

Time to get moving, Annabelle. Feed the chickens,

gather the eggs, start the breakfast. It was how she got through the days. Staying busy. Filling up her life with moments in close fellowship with God and family.

She wouldn't think about what loomed ahead. Days on her own, after everyone had gone their separate ways. She'd just open her heart and enjoy the summertime. Relish each moment of every day with her loved ones. She hoped it would be enough to get her through. It would have to be enough.

Annabelle continued to hum while scattering kernels of dried corn for the chickens. With a last look toward the sky, she gave thanks to God. Apron pockets weighed down with fresh eggs, she headed toward the house.

The Fourth of July was just another holiday. Connie tried to convince herself, but all she had to do was look at her mother-in-law's face to know the truth. The strain in the woman's eyes told a story only Connie knew. Momma carried deep pain. She tried hard to cover it, but it was there. This would never be "just another day" for her.

Though their lives had completely changed in the last twelve months, all the years before those remained. Years filled with memories of love and lives cut short. Too short. Joseph squealed and giggled in his playpen, sending a painful twinge deep into Connie's heart. How would she feel if she lost her child? The baby she'd carried and labored into this world—how would she survive if his life ended before he'd had the chance to really live?

"What a sweet sound to wake up to," Judith said as she entered the room. She bent over the side of the playpen. "Good morning, sweet boy." He laughed as he reached for her. She lifted him into her arms and began to dance around the room, which drew more gurgling laughter from the child.

Connie looked up to find Momma standing in the doorway, her face aglow. She reached for Connie's hand and squeezed it. "There's nothing like baby laughter to lift a person's spirits. Will you come and set the table, love? Breakfast is almost ready."

Judith paused by the window. "Looks like it might rain today. I hope it doesn't delay the fireworks. I love watching fireworks." She followed Connie and Momma into the kitchen. "Do you think Joseph will be scared? Stevie always screamed. Ma had to hold her hands over his ears and sing to him."

Connie smiled at the picture Judith painted. She could well imagine Stevie screaming in fear of the noise. Would Momma feel up to attending the celebration?

Momma stirred the eggs, humming. It's what she did when she was trying not to think, so she wouldn't cry. Connie had seen the behavior often enough to know.

After they'd eaten, Connie washed the dishes and Momma dried, all the while, planning what they'd fix to take to the picnic. She seemed not to notice Connie's hesitance, until she dried the last dish and put it away.

"You are planning to go to the picnic, aren't you, Pumpkin? I know Alton's looking forward to it."

Connie swiped out the sink and hung the washrag over the drying rack. "I haven't thought much about it."

Momma sniffed and touched Connie's hand. "Shall we sit home and nurse our sorrows, while everyone else enjoys the day? Don't you think we've been through enough?" She pressed a kiss against Connie's cheek and smiled.

She was right. Connie knew it, but she couldn't seem to push past the guilt. Yes, it was guilt. Weighing heavy on her shoulders, like a thick, wool coat. How she wished it would move on. If she could go back and change things, she would. Why had God allowed such a tragedy? Why had He topped it off with a good man like Alton? Was it fair to him that she suffered guilt with every loving thought?

Momma nudged her arm and handed over a bowl of potatoes to peel. "You know what I thought about this morning?" She didn't wait for a reply, just raced ahead. "How God has blessed us in so many ways since we came here." She pressed her fists against her chest. "Doesn't it just bless you to bits?"

Connie could only nod and keep peeling the potatoes. Of course, Momma was right to count their blessings, but it still didn't explain the valley they had to travel to get there.

"Thunderstorms pass. Remember that." She set her

fingertip against the center of Connie's brow. "Let that go before it becomes permanent."

Connie angled a gaze at her mother-in-law.

"Your forehead is much too pretty and much too young to be so creased with worry. Let it go."

The night sky lit with millions of man-made stars as another skyrocket burst. The beauty of the evening, the fireworks, and the sweetness of Alton's presence closed in on Connie like a warm embrace. Joseph slept through it all. She wasn't sure how, with all the noise, but she was thankful.

A triple explosion preceded showers of dramatic color.

"That's called a willow," Tom told Momma.

Poor Momma didn't know how to handle Tom's attentions. Connie suspected she enjoyed it just a little, but always managed to keep her distance. They sat surrounded by all the Franklins, including Tom. Alton and Miss Lillian seemed perfectly comfortable with the lot. Miss Lillian came to life in the midst of a big family. The sight was as entertaining for Connie as watching the fireworks.

After a final bright burst, everyone began to pack up their blankets and chairs. Connie reached for Joseph, who immediately snuggled against her and sighed.

Judith leaned close. "Maggie at ten o'clock. I'll cut her

off."

Funny, the things that spur memories after the loss of a loved one. Joe used to say that when he was pointing something out to Connie. It had taken her a moment to catch on. She thought at first, he was telling her the time, till he'd explained he meant a direction.

"Here we go." Alton encircled her and the baby with his strong arm and steered her toward the car. "Let's take advantage of the distraction." He nodded toward Judith who had waylaid Maggie Arnold. As soon as they were away from the bright lights of the fairground, Connie relaxed a little.

"Thank you, Alton." She sat in the front seat with him. Momma, Miss Lillian, and Judith sat in the back. Connie prayed Judith wouldn't feel compelled to tell all of them about Maggie.

Miss Lillian sighed. "What a wonderful celebration. It seems like the fireworks get bigger and better every year."

After Alton steered the car onto the highway, he found Connie's hand and held it.

She was glad of the darkness. The warmth of his touch comforted her. The conversation in the backseat soon faded as anticipation filled her mind. The year of mourning officially ended in a couple of days. When would he want to announce their engagement?

Joseph picked up his head, stretched, and yawned. She pulled her hand from Alton's grip to calm the baby. An ache throbbed at her temple as she bent to kiss his sweet head. She closed her eyes. Her lungs emptied of air. Would it always be this way?

Her memory returned to that day upstairs at Sutter's, when Alton had kissed her. She hadn't given Joe a thought. Maybe there was hope.

"Don't you think so, Pumpkin?" Momma's voice, punctuated by a jab to Connie's shoulder, brought her back to the present.

Again, she was glad of the dark. "I'm sorry, Momma, I guess I drifted off. What was your question?"

"Judith wants to go shopping in Jackson one day next week. She thought we'd like to go along."

Connie opened her mouth to say no, but Miss Lillian spoke first.

"I think it's a fine idea. We'll all go. I'll treat you to lunch at my favorite restaurant."

"That never happens," Alton whispered.

"Alton, keep a civil tongue in your head," Miss Lillian answered.

This was closely followed by a snort from Judith and a giggle from Momma.

Connie took advantage of the light from approaching headlights to glance at Alton and found a smile on his face. How could she say no?

Alton kept close to home the next day. The funeral director sent a special crew out to remove the remains of Penuel Sutter, a crew that normally dug graves. They took all day and made sure they got everything. Toward sundown, the lead man approached the house, carrying what looked to be a small bag. Alton met him halfway.

"What do you have there?"

The man handed him the bundle. Turned out, it was the bandana. "Found a few personal items in the man's pockets. Thought y'all might want to have them."

"That's thoughtful of you, thanks."

"We wrapped it in that kerchief. It was mostly rotted, so you ought to take care with it. If you had any doubt of the man's identity, you have positive proof now."

Alton took the bundle into the house. Mother should be the one to have it. He found her in the back parlor, reading.

She sat forward when he entered. "Did they find something?"

"They did." He laid it carefully on the hassock near her chair.

When she looked up at him, a deep crease furrowed her brow. "This is the neckerchief he wore?"

He nodded. With great care, he revealed what was inside—several old coins, and a leather packet. Alton lifted the folded leather and opened it. He gazed at his mother's face. "It's Penuel, all right. This here's a card showing he was a U.S. Army veteran of World War I."

Mother took a breath and slowly exhaled. "Yes, that'd be right. I remember when he came home. He never was the same."

Alton gathered the items. "Where do you want these?"

"Lay them on the chest over there. I'll find a place for them. Reckon we ought to ask for a military funeral?"

"The director will take care of it. I'll make the call as soon as I get cleaned up."

After freshening up, Alton stepped into his room to change his shirt before supper. On the way out of the room, he stopped to open the top drawer. It was the smallest of all the drawers, where he kept his cuff links and dress watch, and a small velvet box. He picked it up and flipped the top open to reveal the sparkling ring he'd bought in Nashville. Sometime later this week, he hoped to see it on Connie's finger. He carefully closed the lid and placed the box in the drawer. She'd never had an engagement ring. That's why he wanted to give her one. It was something he could do that would be different from the first time. He meant to make new memories for her—not to outdo anything Joseph had done, not to better the man who'd come before—but to create something. Construct a new layer upon the strong foundation of love in Connie's life.

Chapter Twelve

Connie had mixed feelings about the shopping trip. A long, drawn-out discussion ensued, in order to choose a day to go to Jackson. The carpenter was due at Sutter's Landing on Monday. Miss Lillian wanted to be there to oversee the changes being made. The solemn assembly and interment of Penuel Sutter's remains was set for Thursday morning—they were all expected to attend. Wednesday was out, because many businesses closed at noon on that day. Of course, Friday was much too busy a day in town. So, that left Tuesday.

Alton gave Judith a day off from the field. He suggested she drive his mother's car, since it was roomier than Judith's.

Connie hadn't seen Jackson since the day she and Momma passed through the Greyhound depot. It seemed a nice town, not overly big. Like Trenton, it was a county seat.

"Pull in here at the Esso," Miss Lillian told Judith. "Might as well gas up."

A friendly young man appeared at the window.

"Fill her up," Miss Lillian ordered from her seat in the back.

An older man sidled over and began to wash the windshield. The gas tank full, the young man raised the hood and checked the oil before pausing at Judith's window to collect the money. He gave Judith a sideways smile that made a dimple pop out.

Connie barely suppressed a giggle as Judith's cheeks flushed bright pink.

"Isn't he a cutie." Miss Lillian jabbed at Judith's shoulder.

Judith sank down in her seat, as though she wanted to slide beneath it.

Momma laughed outright, and Joseph sent up a gleeful squeal.

"Do you think we're laughing at you?" Momma asked him.

Miss Lillian patted the baby's hand. "Of course, he does." She glanced up. "Here we are."

Judith, still red-faced, eased into a parking spot, shifted into park, and turned off the key.

A few minutes later, pride shone from Momma's eyes as she pushed the stroller through the door at *Carriage's Department Store*.

Connie bit her lip and peered around the shiny store. It

smelled heavenly, like really expensive perfumes made up of florals and rich spices, but the looks on the clerks' faces nearly sent her out again.

Miss Lillian insisted this should be their first stop, so Connie pressed forward. Judith quipped that her pocketbook was more *Sears and Roebuck*. Connie tried to smile in response, but her nerves got the better of her.

Customers were looking at them, too. Well-dressed, neatly coiffed women who definitely belonged in such an establishment. Connie fought the urge to smooth the front of her best dress. It wasn't completely out of style yet, but the clothes worn by the nearby mannequins made her feel downright shabby.

Miss Lillian greeted one of the salesladies, a middle-aged woman with dark, curly hair and very red lips. "Good morning, Barbara."

The woman gazed over Miss Lillian's shoulder, directly into Connie's face before turning aside. "Perhaps your girl would rather wait outside, Miss Lillian?"

Miss Lillian looked around. "My girl?" Her gaze lit on Connie. "Oh, you mean Connie?"

To Connie's horror, Miss Lillian waved her over. "Barbara, I'd like to introduce you to Alton's fiancée, Mrs. Connie Cross. She's a widow."

"Oh." The clerk's red lips pursed. Uncertainty flashed in her eyes as she gazed at Connie. "She's … young to be a widow."

"Yes, she is. But quite lovely, don't you think? My son

has good taste." Miss Lillian laid her hand on Connie's arm and gave her a reassuring smile before turning back to Barbara. "Your assumption that she is a woman of color is false, my dear. She's Hawaiian by birth on her mother's side. Even so, if I was to bring my long-time housekeeper and good friend Regina with me—perhaps to buy her a new dress—or a hat, say. You'd turn her away? You'd have her wait outside while I made the purchase?"

The woman lifted her chin as her gaze slid between Miss Lillian and Connie. "We must be respectful of our other customers, my dear Miss Lillian. Surely you can understand that."

"Oh, I most certainly do."

Connie wanted to crawl beneath the nearest row of dresses, but supposed that would only increase the humiliation.

Behind them, Joseph let out a wail.

Momma, followed by Judith, pushed the stroller down the aisle toward the entrance.

Hopefully, Miss Lillian would not feel compelled to tell her friend whose baby Joseph was. She needn't have worried. In a matter of moments, Miss Lillian linked arms with Connie and turned toward the door. "I regret that we must take our shopping elsewhere."

"I'm very sorry you feel that way," the woman said. "Perhaps another time …"

"You have all those other customers to think of, dear. You don't need me. There won't be another time."

As they exited the store, Miss Lillian shook her head. "I've known Barbara since she was a girl working her way through college."

"I'm so sorry." She really was. But her sorrow was mixed with relief. She would not return to *Carriage's*. Ever.

Together, they walked down the street. Connie kept her eyes ahead of them, on Momma with Judith, who pushed the stroller.

"There are a couple more stores we can check," Miss Lillian tapped her finger against her pursed lips. "There's *Kisber's* and *Holland's*, but I prefer *Rosenbloom's*."

Connie slowed her steps. "Maybe we should just go home."

Lillian stopped to look at her. "My dear, I've always thought you so strong. So brave. You left the safety of your life in Southern California. Surely, you can face a bit of bigotry in West Tennessee." Her face brightened. "You leave it to me. I know what to do."

In front of *Rosenbloom's*, they found a bench in the shade.

"You wait out here with Annabelle and the baby," Miss Lillian told Connie. "Judith, you go with me."

Judith sent Connie a woeful stare. Connie suppressed the urge to laugh out loud. The mischief in Miss Lillian's eyes warmed her heart. She settled on the bench beside Momma.

"What's that all about?" Momma asked.

Connie gave her the short version of what had occurred in *Carriage's*.

Momma giggled behind her fan. "Oh, I would love to know what's going on in there."

They didn't have long to wait. A smiling Judith opened the door and waved them in.

Joseph was sound asleep, so Momma decided to wait on the bench.

Inside the store, Connie drew a deep breath and blew it out. She leaned close to Judith. "How do I look?"

"Wonderful, as always." Judith's eyes twinkled.

Miss Lillian's voice sounded from somewhere nearby. "I'm hoping we can find her a suitable wedding outfit—for a second marriage, of course." She turned at Connie's approach. "Here she is. Isn't she lovely?"

The blonde clerk looked to be in her late forties. Her smile and greeting set Connie at ease. "I'm pleased to make your acquaintance, Mrs. Cross." She looked Connie up and down, then addressed Miss Lillian. "You're quite right. She is lovely." Turning back to Connie, she gestured toward the aisle. "If you'll come with me, I'm certain we can find something that will appeal to you."

Judith leaned close to Miss Lillian. "Maybe I should go on over to the *Sears*, while y'all are doing that."

Miss Lillian waved her on. "That's a good idea. We'll be here, or maybe over at *Kisber's*."

"All right."

Connie watched as Judith walked out. The girl looked

a little too happy to be going. Her cotton-chopping salary wouldn't go far in a place like this. Did they even have price tags? She'd read that some stores didn't. Surely Miss Lillian realized Connie and Momma didn't have this kind of money.

Momma crept in as Connie was modeling the third outfit, a mint green suit with a white lace under blouse.

"I hope you realize what a blessing this is. Miss Lillian is set on buying your wedding outfit."

"What? Momma, no. It wouldn't be right."

"Why not?" Momma shook her head. "She's going to be your family. You'll need to look smart when you're married to the Wades. It'll be expected."

"I don't like it. I should be working to make the money for myself." Or maybe she should swallow her pride and write to Dad. Maybe he'd have mercy on her.

Miss Lillian swept by, modeling a new hat—royal blue with white roses.

"If you don't find what you like here, we can go elsewhere. Jackson has a good variety of shops," she removed the hat, and straightened her hair. "I'm glad. If I had to drive to Memphis, I'd order from the Sears catalog."

The fourth outfit won Connie's heart, though she tried not to show it. The lovely, pale yellow dress cost more than she'd ever paid—or ever planned to, for that matter—even if she was marrying a Wade.

The shopping expedition ended with a delicious meal at the *Fox Restaurant*. The southern penchant for smoked meats brought back childhood memories for Connie, but if she ate like that very often, she'd definitely need a new wardrobe.

The staff took great care of them. There was no repeat of the episode at *Carriage's*. It was almost as though they'd been warned ahead.

Miss Lillian told Connie and Momma what she'd done in *Rosenbloom's*. "I walked right up to that woman and told her how I wanted to help my son's fiancée find a dress. I told her the story of how you two came to be widows, and how you'd traveled all the way back home to your family."

"She nearly had the woman in tears." Judith giggled. "We had an audience surrounding us. They all stood around listening. Several of them were wiping their eyes."

Momma clapped her hands. "No!"

Miss Lillian nodded. "Oh yes, it's true. That clerk looked at Judith and said, 'Let's see what we can find for you.' I told her, 'Oh, this isn't Mrs. Cross. This is my sweet friend, Judith.'"

"I sent Judith out to get you, and while she was gone, I told the woman you were a native Hawaiian, pretty as a picture, and you had a little baby boy." She chuckled into her napkin. "It was so much fun."

Peace settled over the ladies on the drive home. Judith nudged Connie and pointed in the rear-view mirror. Both Momma and Miss Lillian had dozed off.

Thankfully, so had Joseph, but his little body snuggled into Connie's arm put out a lot of heat. She tested his forehead with the inside of her wrist. It wasn't overly hot, so it must be the weather, not a fever. What she wouldn't give for a cool glass of tea right now—or a breath of fresh air. Most of the roads they traveled were dusty gravel, so they didn't dare keep the windows down.

She noticed Judith swiping at dampness, too. Judith glanced her way. "I bet it's hot enough to fry an egg on the hood."

"Is this normal for July?"

"No, but we've had an abnormal weather year. All that rain, now all this heat. At least we didn't have any tornadoes this spring. I hate those."

Connie had heard all the horror stories about tornado damage. There was a storm shelter up the road, but she had no desire to enter that thing. Talk about creepy crawlies. At least Sutter's had a cellar. One that Willie kept very clean. Regina made sure of it.

The white house at Sutter's Landing appeared on the horizon. What a welcome sight.

"Y'all come on to the front porch and set a spell," Miss Lillian still sounded a bit drowsy. "I'll get us some iced tea. When Alton comes in, he'll run you home. It's too hot to walk."

Connie wanted to object. She would have, except for the baby. It was awfully hot, so she sat down on the front porch swing. It was somewhat cooler there.

Judith joined her. "It won't be long, this'll be your home," she whispered. "Are you looking forward to it?"

"I ... uh ... mostly." Should she confess her innermost fears to Judith?

"Nervous, huh? I would be, too. Especially after today."

At that moment, Miss Lucy rounded the corner of the house and called out, "Lookie who it is. Heaven done shone down a blessin' on me."

Judith waved. "Hello, Miss Lucy."

Not content with a spoken greeting, Connie hopped up and descended the steps to give Miss Lucy a hug. "It's so good to see you."

"How's our boy?"

"Fat and sassy," Momma held Joseph up for Miss Lucy to see.

"Oh my, look at the size of that boy. What yo' momma been feedin' you?"

Momma brought Joseph to Miss Lucy, who took him in her arms.

He chuckled when Miss Lucy tickled his neck. She laughed out loud. "You done made my day for sure. I was longing to get a look at him. We been so busy these last few days, working the cotton. Hoo! It's shore enough been hot. And the weeds is thick as can be."

"Come and set a spell, Miss Lucy." Miss Lillian opened the screen door and held it for Regina, who carried the tray filled with glasses of iced tea.

"Don't reckon I better," Miss Lucy said. "I got to git on home and start the supper. Got more mouths to feed than I can count. Don't never know who's gonna show up at my table."

Miss Lillian brushed her hands together. "You need anything? We have aplenty coming in. Green beans, early corn."

"I don't reckon I do right now, Miss Lillian, but I'm mighty obliged to you. Soon as the cotton's chopped, I'll come round, help y'all put that up."

"That'll be fine, and you can take some home with you to help feed that brood."

Miss Lucy planted a final kiss on Joseph's cheek before handing him back to Momma. With a wave to everyone, she strode off down the drive toward the road.

"She certainly is a ray of sunshine," Momma said.

"Good hearing, too!" Miss Lucy called out. "Jesus is my sunshine. I got that all the time." Her voice faded as she kept walking.

Miss Lillian nodded. "No greater love. I've just been telling Regina what happened to us in town. She got a chuckle out of it."

Regina cackled as she passed the tea glasses around.

Momma sighed. "We did have a good time, didn't we?"

"Don't look as if y'all bought anything," Regina said.

"Just me." Miss Lillian folded her hands in her lap and smiled at Regina. "I bought a hat."

Momma looked at Connie and grinned. "Where is that hat?"

Miss Lillian drew back. "I reckon we left it in the trunk. It's so hot, I don't even want to go get it."

Connie held her glass to her cheek and sighed. "It's so hot, that hat may be melted by now."

Laughter rang out—the contagious kind. They all laughed till they cried. Connie wiped her eyes and sat back, barely able to draw a breath. "Why was that so funny?"

"Because we're all hot and tired, that's why," Momma said.

Miss Lillian rocked contentedly. "Oh my, but it feels good. This has been such a wonderful day. Thank you, dear friends."

Her gratitude eased Connie's injured pride. Making Miss Lillian's day was worth any amount of discomfort.

"What's all this noise?" Alton stood looking through the screen door. "Sounds like a fox got in the hen house again."

Chapter Thirteen

Connie carried Joseph as she, Momma, and Judith crossed the dry creek bed on their way to Sutter's Landing for a day of canning beans. Miss Lillian had gone to sit with her sister for the week. Before leaving, she'd asked for their help with the beans.

Alton dropped a kiss on Connie's cheek when she entered the kitchen. "Good morning, sunshine."

He smelled of *Palmolive* soap. Connie smiled into his eyes. "We've come to help Regina put up beans."

"Glad to hear it. But would you mind coming upstairs first? Walter finished installing the wallpaper yesterday."

"Wonderful." She handed Joseph to Momma.

"We'll be in the old kitchen," she told Connie. "One of Miss Lucy's granddaughters is watching the young'uns."

"All right, Momma." Connie accompanied Alton up the back staircase. The smell of fresh paint and wallpaper glue drifted down the second-floor hallway. So much had happened since that day she'd chosen the pattern, she had only a vague memory of what it looked like.

Alton opened the bedroom door and stood aside.

Her hands flew to her mouth. "Oh, my goodness."

He stepped inside the room. "Is it … what you expected?"

Was he unhappy with it? Something in his tone made her think so. She took a moment to examine his expression before answering, "I love it. I hope it's all right with you."

He nodded. "Good, I'm glad you like it. It was so different—so much lighter than the old—I was afraid you might not care for it."

She touched the paper and smiled. "I love it, really. It's beautiful." Still, there was something in his demeanor.

He stood with his hands in his pockets.

Was it because this would one day be their bedroom? A thrill of excitement ran through her. She pivoted to look at the windows, tried to concentrate on the finished decor.

Through the glass, she noticed a small figure on the lawn. She moved nearer to see better.

Alton spoke from across the room. "What are you looking at?"

"A little boy."

"A little boy?"

"Yes, with blond hair." She glanced back at Alton. "He's just standing there, looking up at the house."

Alton moved closer.

She touched his arm. "I've never seen him before. Do you know him?"

He frowned and rubbed his chin. "I believe I do. That's Chase."

"Chase?"

"Chase Wade. My nephew."

"Jensen's boy? He looks too tall to be Jensen's boy."

He grinned. "You're thinking of Landers. This is Chase, the older one."

"How did I not know there were two?"

"He's been away at military school."

"Good gracious, he's so young. Do people really do that?" She turned to look at Alton who raised his brows. She took that as a yes. "What's he doing here?"

Alton bent to gaze into her eyes. "I'm going to go find out." He reached for her hand. "Want to go with me?"

"Of course, I do."

Alton searched the boy's somber face as he walked slowly toward him. "Hello, Chase."

"Good afternoon, sir."

"You don't have to be so formal. You used to call me Uncle Alton."

"Yes, sir, Uncle Alton."

"What're you doing out here?"

"Is Grandmother here?"

Alton looked over his shoulder at Connie, who waited on the back porch. Regina stood beside her. He turned back to the boy. "She's not here right now."

Chase clamped his jaws tight.

Connie spoke from the porch. "Are you hungry, Chase? Regina baked some cookies this morning. And we have fresh lemonade."

The boy licked his lips.

Alton straightened. "Come on in. We'll talk while we sample some of those cookies."

They sat at the kitchen table where a plate of cookies waited.

As Regina poured lemonade into glasses, Connie set them on the table. Alton noticed several meaningful glances between the two women.

Chase wolfed down a half dozen cookies. The boy was hungry. But not very talkative.

"We'll fill his belly, see if it loosens his tongue," Alton winked at Connie.

Chase peered at them. "Are there any more cookies?"

Regina set a ham sandwich in front of him. "You've had enough sweets, Mr. Chase."

He finished off the sandwich in record time.

"Why are you here, Chase?" Alton asked.

"I want to talk to Grandmother."

"She's visiting her sister in Bells. Your Great-Aunt Susan. I can take you there, if you like."

Chase nodded.

Alton stood and slid his chair beneath the table. "I'll take him to see Mother."

Connie followed him to the back porch. "What about his parents? Shouldn't we let them know where he is?"

He met her gaze. "Do you want to call them?"

She twisted the ends of her braid. "No."

Alton stood still and bowed his head. Of course, he should call Jensen. It wouldn't be right not to, but he sure dreaded the confrontation. "I'll be right back." He sent up a silent prayer as the phone call went through. A woman's voice greeted him, one he didn't recognize. "Wade residence."

"This is Alton Wade. I need to speak to my brother."

"One moment, please."

Several moments passed before Jensen's exasperated voice came on with, "What do you want?"

Since Alton had never apologized for nearly decking Jensen, he figured the man had a right to be angry.

At first, he didn't believe Alton. "What do you mean, you have Chase? He's away at summer camp."

"Do you mean to tell me they haven't reported him missing? What kind of camp is it?"

Jensen blew out a breath. "Never mind that. What's he

doing at your place?"

"Right now, he's having a bite to eat."

"Well, I'm coming to get him. He's due for a bruising."

"Why don't you let him stay here for the night? I'll bring him to town in the morning."

"Tomorrow's a work day," he grumbled.

"All the more reason to stay put. I'll bring him home in the morning after I've done my chores."

"If I didn't have a big to-do this afternoon, I'd come out there and give that boy a piece of my mind. I'd send him right back to camp. He's a worse momma's boy than you ever were. Which is why he's spending the summer at a camp that'll toughen him up. I had to pull some pretty tight strings to get him accepted." After a bout of unintelligible muttering, he gave a heavy sigh. "You go on and keep him tonight, but you better not have that woman in there."

Alton held the phone away from his ear, rolled his eyes toward heaven, and prayed for strength. "I hope you don't mean Regina. I'd hate to have to send her home. I'm pretty worthless as a cook."

"You know who I'm talking about."

Marla's voice sounded in the background. "Get off the phone, Jensen, we have to go."

Jensen covered the phone with his hand, which only muffled his retort to Marla. He was still muttering under his breath when he returned to the call. "You just bring him home in the morning." Click.

Alton stared at the receiver. His brother had just hung up on him.

Chase was so quiet all the way to Bells, Alton kept glancing at him. Any attempt at conversation drew a clipped answer of, "yes, sir," and "no, sir." So, Alton gave up and drove in silence.

Samson lay curled up between them, snoring softly. Alton thought the boy had also fallen asleep. Well, this day had certainly not turned out as planned. He'd been about to give Connie her ring when she caught sight of Chase on the front lawn. He glanced at the boy, looking so forlorn. What had happened to make him do something so desperate?

Mother nearly lost her balance when Chase jumped out of the truck.

"Is that Chase?" She glanced at Alton. "What on earth has happened?"

Chase strode right up to his grandmother and announced, "I've run away from summer camp, Grandmother. I'm requesting refuge."

Mother looked at Alton over Chase's blond head.

Alton chuckled. "It's true, Mother. He's left his old life behind, and he knows what it means—he can never return home. So, he's thrown himself on our mercy."

She enveloped Chase in a brief hug. "It's good to see you, whatever the circumstances. You come up here and take a seat so we can talk this out."

"Yes, ma'am."

Alton thought the boy might salute, he was so formal. Instead, he followed Mother to a double-wide rocking chair and sat down. Alton perched on the corner of the porch.

Samson curled up at his feet.

Mother spoke to Alton. "Have you at least fed him?"

Alton nodded. "Regina made sure he had plenty to eat."

"Of course, she would." She turned to Chase. "All right, tell me what happened."

"My attempts at fitting in were thwarted, Grandmother."

Alton watched his mother try to sustain a serious expression at the boy's very proper speech.

She patted Chase's hand. "What do you mean? What did you do?"

"I tried to be friendly, like Mother told me. They laughed at me. They called me names. I tried to ignore them." His eyes filled, but he sat up straight and clamped down on his lower lip.

Flames kindled in Alton's chest. "What kind of names?"

Mother frowned at him.

Chase sucked in a deep breath and slowly exhaled. "It doesn't matter. Daddy said I have to toughen up. I tried.

I'm not a momma's boy—"

Mother sat forward. "Of course, you're not. You attend military school."

Chase sniffed and wiped his nose on his sleeve. He nodded. "Yes, ma'am."

"Is there anything else you need to tell us?" Alton crouched in front of him so he could look him in the eye. "Did they harm you in any way?" The boy shook his head, but Alton didn't believe him. It was no telling what they'd done to him.

Mother laid her hand on the boy's arm. "I've got to stay a few more days with your Great-Aunt Susan. After that, I'll be home. If it's all right with your parents, you're welcome to stay at Sutter's Landing awhile. Your uncle Alton will take good care of you."

Chase kept his head down. "They won't let me stay. They'll make me go back. And if they do, I'll not stay there. I'll hop a freight train and head out West."

Mother grimaced. "Oh, my goodness. You mustn't do that."

Alton smoothed the boy's hair. "If they force you to go back, and you can't take it, you call me. I'll come get you. Don't you go hopping a freight train. Is that understood?"

Chase nodded. "Yes, sir."

Alton glanced up when Chase entered the kitchen bright and early.

"May I help with your chores, Uncle Alton?"

Could the boy be serious, or had he inherited his father's cunning? After a close examination of Chase's expression, Alton decided to trust him. It's possible he'd been hurt by those folks at the camp. In that case, he'd need sympathy. Keeping him busy wouldn't hurt.

"I'd be obliged."

"After he's had his breakfast." Regina placed a heaping plate of food in front of the boy.

Chase sat down and went right to work cleaning his plate.

Other than an initial wariness of the animals, the boy did well at chores. Later, Alton found him admiring the fishing rod collection. "Do you fish?"

Chase shook his head. "No, sir."

"Seems like something they ought to be teaching at summer camp." He opened his tackle box and showed the boy the lures he'd collected over the years. Meanwhile, his mind worked, full steam ahead. Besides the hundred or so questions he had about what went on at that camp, he had a few ideas beginning to percolate. The "what if" kind of ideas. Maybe he ought to stop by and have a quick word with Connie on the way into town.

While Alton got ready to go, Chase tossed a stick to Samson. It hurt Alton's heart to see the change that had already begun, especially when laughter rang out. He peered through the window to see Chase and Samson in a tug-of-war with a length of old rope. A ten-year-old boy should be doing this kind of thing on a daily basis.

Alton saw Connie and Annabelle working in the garden when he pulled into the drive. He cut his eyes toward Chase. "You don't have to get out if you don't want to. But Samson will want to." He followed the comment with a quick wink and a grin.

As predicted, Samson hit the ground running.

Alton shook his head and chuckled. At least they'd know company was coming.

The boy opened the door and jumped down. "Are these people my kin?" He fell into step beside Alton.

"Yes, they are. Miss Annabelle is mine and your daddy's cousin."

"Why does your girlfriend live with your cousin?"

This boy was smart as a whip. "She was once married to Miss Annabelle's oldest son."

The boy stopped. "The one that died?"

"Yes."

"So, she's a widow."

Alton kept walking toward the garden. "Yes. And she has a little boy of her own."

Chase caught up to him. "Are you going to marry her?"

Though he fought it, Alton could not stop the grin from breaking out. "I plan on it."

Connie approached, removing her work gloves. "Good

morning, you two. Can I offer you something to drink?"

Alton shook his head. "We can't stay."

Annabelle picked up Joseph and joined them. "My goodness, is that Chase Wade?"

Chase nodded.

"You're practically grown."

"I'm ten," he told her.

"And nearly as tall as I am. You must take after the Sutters."

His gaze on Connie, Alton lost track of the conversation between Annabelle and Chase. "I stopped by to ask your opinion on something." He kept his voice low, hoping the others would not overhear. Annabelle seemed to take the hint. She moved away, pointing out some of the plants in the garden.

Connie smiled into Alton's eyes. "What's up?"

How could she always look so beautiful? Even when she was working. Oh, how he wanted to kiss her again. He cleared his throat. "I uh … I've been thinking what to do about Chase." He looked to where Annabelle and Chase stood.

"You're taking him home?"

"Yes, but I'm thinking about asking if he can stay with me the rest of the summer."

She took a backward step. "Really?"

He angled a glance at her. Did she think it was a bad idea? "If I can get Jensen to agree, I thought the boy could work for me. Chores and such. And I could teach him to fish and hunt."

"They don't teach those things at summer camp?"

"He said not. I don't know what they do. He clams up every time I ask."

Baby laughter pierced the air. Alton and Connie paused to look.

Joseph laughed at Chase, and Chase was smiling.

Alton and Connie exchanged glances. He turned back to her. "What do you think?"

"I think that's a great big 'if' you're dealing with. *If* your brother agrees. That's your first hurdle. Are you wanting my approval, or encouragement? You have it. If it's something you want to do, I have no doubt you can."

Now he really wanted to kiss her. She sure would've made a good teacher. And maybe she would yet. He ran his fingers down her arm, gathered her hand into his. "Thank you. I guess I just needed to know you'd approve."

Should he tell her the rest? "Um, it's not exactly out of the blue. It's something I've thought about before."

Her eyebrows arched. "What do you mean?"

"Before you came along, I thought of hosting a summer camp at Sutter's Landing. Teach some of the town boys at our church to fish and hunt, and maybe other things like taking care of animals. A few of those boys lost their daddies in the war."

The look she gave him sent shivers into his neck and scalp.

"You're a good man, Alton Wade."

"Uncle Alton," Chase called out. "Samson chased a rabbit out of Miss Annabelle's garden."

"He loves doing that." He let go of Connie's hand and gestured toward Chase. "Let's get on the road so the ladies can get their work done before it gets too hot."

"I wish we could stay here a while," Chase mumbled as he passed.

Alton winked at Connie. "So, do I, boy. So, do I."

Chapter Fourteen

Dread cast its shadow over Alton as he pulled into the drive at his brother's house. He forced a smile, hoping to calm Chase, but it looked to be a losing battle. Marla stood in the doorway. As he approached, Alton examined her expression. A mixture of joy and relief preceded the usual stone face she reserved for her brother-in-law. He gave her a wry grin. "Marla."

"Alton." She drew a breath and faced her son. "Chase, you are in so much trouble."

Chase stood with his head bowed. "Yes, ma'am."

"You'd better go up to your room."

The boy sent a pleading glance toward Alton.

"I was hoping to speak with you … and Jensen about the boy, Marla."

Marla rounded on Alton. "Jensen's at work."

"I'm aware of that."

Marla eyed him for several moments before turning

her back to him. "I'll have Edris prepare us something. Coffee or tea?"

"Tea is fine." He followed her inside. So many changes had been made to the front parlor, he hardly recognized the room. He sat in a high, wing-backed chair facing the Italian marble fireplace. The chair was almost comfortable.

Marla returned and sat on the sofa across from him. "What is it you want to say to me, Alton?"

With Marla around, a person wouldn't have to worry about the heat. He was convinced she was made of pure ice.

Edris entered and set a tray on the table between them. She caught Alton's eye and smiled before whisking away again.

Alton accepted the glass from Marla and took a sip. The cool, sweet liquid tickled his tongue. Oh, how he'd missed Edris. "I don't think you should send Chase back to that camp."

Sparks flashing in her eyes, Marla sat forward. "What business is it of yours?"

Alton sipped his tea and set it down. "He's a good boy. I suspect he's been through something … difficult."

The storm calmed. Haughtiness relaxed into curiosity. "What did he tell you?"

"He wouldn't talk about it. But I think something happened to him there. A boy like Chase doesn't run."

"I'll speak to him." Her fingers trembled as she lifted

the glass of tea. "It won't make any difference, you know. Jensen will send him back on principle."

"You don't have any say?"

"I don't interfere."

Alton waited, watching her. She sat very still, kind of like a statue, kind of like she was dismissing him.

Her high-and-mighty attitude set Alton's teeth on edge. But he couldn't argue, it would do no good. Before he lost her attention, he spoke. "I have a suggestion to make."

She turned her gaze on him.

"He can spend the rest of the summer with me—at Sutter's."

"What?"

"He'd have to work—do chores, earn his keep—but he'd also learn to hunt and fish."

Marla drew a breath, like someone bursting up through water. "I don't think ..."

Sensing a crack in the ice, he rushed forward. "Those are manly pursuits."

"It doesn't matter. There's such an enmity between you and your brother. I can't see Jensen agreeing to such a thing."

Alton made eye contact with her. "He would if you urged him to."

She offered him a humorless smile. "Now, why would I do that? I've never liked you, Alton. You're too ... uptight. Holier than thou. You might try to change my son into a religious nut, like yourself."

So, that's what she thought of him. He'd always wondered, now he knew. He had to smile, it was too good. "I'm glad you feel that way. It tells me I'm doing something right. I won't be easy on the boy. He'll have to work hard." He drained his glass before setting it down.

Something indefinable flashed in her eyes. "I don't doubt that. There has to be something of your father in you. I'll talk to Jensen. I doubt it'll do any good, but I will talk to him." She stared into the empty fireplace.

Dismissed, Alton stood. "Guess I'll head out."

"Alton."

He met her gaze.

"Will he be allowed to be a boy?"

"Absolutely."

She turned her back again. "I'll let you know, whatever is decided."

"I thank you for that, Marla."

Chase was standing in his open bedroom window when Alton got to his truck. He waved, but the boy didn't return the gesture. The look on his face broke Alton's heart.

With Judith's help, Connie finished all the laundry and they hung it out to dry. It was a perfect day for it, hot and only slightly humid. Afterward, they emptied the wash water and wiped out the inside of the washing machine.

Judith blew out a breath and wiped her brow. "If only there was water in the creek still. We could go wading. It was always so cool."

"There is a pond over there, but Alton said you have to be careful of moccasins this time of year.

Judith sat on the edge of the porch and fanned herself with her apron. "You mean the lake? Here in the south, that's what we call those." She sent Connie a teasing smile. "Snakes are everywhere out here. Just easier to see in the creek, so it's safer. I just miss it, that's all."

"Are you back to chopping cotton tomorrow?"

"Yes. Alton's transporting all of us over to his other field, near the highway. So, I'll need to take something to eat. I reckon we'll be there all day."

"You've already worked over there, haven't you?"

"It's ready for the second round, but just weeds this time, no thinning out. So, it'll go faster."

Connie had watched some of the workers thinning out cotton. They'd leave about ten to twelve inches between plants, so the cotton would have room to branch out and produce better.

Momma opened the kitchen door. "Are y'all about ready for a sandwich?"

Judith hopped up. "Yes, ma'am, I worked up an appetite."

As Connie rounded the porch on the way to the front steps, her gaze swept the fields, coming to rest on the big, white house at Sutter's. What was happening there? Had Alton taken Chase home?

She tugged on the screen door and let herself in.

Judith was already seated at the table. "It's tuna salad sandwiches."

Her exuberance made Connie smile. The girl loved tuna salad.

Momma stood in the window, Joseph tugging at the loose ends of her hair and cooing. After washing her hands, Connie took her place at the table. "I can hold him if you need me to, Momma."

"You go on and eat. He's fine right here." She lowered herself into a chair.

They bowed their heads as Judith spoke the blessing over the food.

Momma broke the silence first. "I was just thinking and wondering about that little boy."

Judith glanced up. "You mean Chase?"

Momma nodded. "I'm worried that Jensen will be his usual stiff neck and send the boy back to that mean camp."

"It's his decision. He is Chase's father." Connie bit into her sandwich and savored the taste. Momma had a way with tuna.

"I know he is. But he's too stubborn for his own good. He'll ruin that boy." She sighed and planted a kiss on Joseph's fat cheek. "But I suppose that's his mistake to make."

"Where's your faith, Momma?" Connie asked. "We

prayed, didn't we?"

Alton mashed the gas pedal and sped down the Milan Highway toward home. On the way out of town, he'd stopped at the newspaper office. He finally had some information for Mr. Pruitt. He'd write the letter tonight, and get that in the mail first thing tomorrow. But before doing that, he meant to get a moment alone with Connie.

Her ring was burning a hole in his pocket.

He found her sitting on the porch with Miss Annabelle, shelling crowder peas.

"Have a seat, Alton. Tell us what happened with Chase." Miss Annabelle kept her eyes on the peas as she spoke. "Connie told me about your plans." She glanced at Connie, then back at Alton. "I hope it's all right—that she told me, I mean."

"Of course." He winked at Connie. "I talked to Marla. Told her what I wanted to do, then left it up to her. She said she'd talk to Jensen, but she didn't hold out much hope."

Annabelle gave an exaggerated sigh. "Oh well, at least you tried."

"If it's God's will, it'll work out." Connie's gaze caught in his.

Alton swallowed and rubbed his hands together. "Would you like to go for a drive tonight?" He asked loud enough for Miss Annabelle to hear it. She was always his best ally. She didn't disappoint.

"What a wonderful idea. I'll be happy to look after Joseph."

Connie glanced at Annabelle before answering Alton. "I'd like that."

"I'll be by after chores and supper. We'll stop at the Dairy Whiz, if you want."

"You know the way to a woman's heart," Miss Annabelle's eyes held humor. "Ice cream."

Connie gathered up another handful of peas to shell. "I'll be ready."

When he stopped back by later, she wore that pale blue dress he loved. Her hair looked freshly braided, and she smelled real pretty, like summer flowers. His heart thudded as he led her to the truck. Maybe he should have driven Mother's car.

She didn't seem to care.

For a while, they just chatted, revisited their earlier conversation about his summer camp dreams. "I guess it's because Daddy never had much time for us. Mr. Franklin—Riley's father—used to take me fishing once in a while. And an uncle taught me to shoot and hunt. It meant a lot to me."

"What about Jensen? Did he go, too?"

"No, Jensen never had any interest. He mostly ran around with his friends. They were all too good for such lowly pursuits." He tried to soften his words with a smile, but the memories still rankled him a little. He pulled into the parking area beside the Dairy Whiz. "What'll it be?"

"Vanilla swirled with chocolate."

They sat at a well-worn picnic table while they ate their ice cream. The weather was perfect. All around them, folks carried on conversations, children laughed and played. If not for the constant pressure of the ring in his breast pocket, Alton would've been completely at ease.

When they'd finished eating, he helped her back into the truck. Right on time. The sun was going down. He drove toward home, but turned off the road onto a narrow lane. Connie glanced at him, but didn't say anything. The lane dwindled down to a cow path. He slowed, but kept driving.

"I hope you know where you're headed." He didn't miss the note of laughter in her voice.

"I do." On the crest of a low hill, he backed the truck into position. He hopped out and trotted around to open the door for Connie. This was a part of his property she'd only heard him talk about—the route he'd driven after the flood. From this location, they could see the entire lake.

"I know it's not much, but I like it here."

She stood aside while he let down the truck's tailgate. He drew out a rolled blanket and spread it out before helping her climb up. They sat side-by-side, with their legs dangling.

"It's beautiful here. There's even a symphony."

He laughed out loud. "You're right, there is. A frog symphony—nothing better." He removed his hat and laid it behind him. When she leaned against him, he put his arm around her for support. Could she feel his heart beating like a drum? He opened his mouth to declare his love, but she spoke first.

"So, did you bring me out here to make out?" She twisted to gaze up at him.

Was she teasing him? The humor in her eyes settled his guilty, racing heart. He chuckled. "No, I brought you out here …" He fumbled in his pocket for the ring. "… to give you this."

She gave a little gasp and straightened.

"If you'll let me, I'll put it on for you. That is, if you're still of a mind to marry me."

She grinned. "Oh, Alton, you're such a romantic."

Was she disappointed? Maybe he should have knelt on one knee. But no, she was laughing, until she wasn't anymore. She leaned forward and kissed him. Really, really kissed him. Left him aching for air. But he wasn't quitting until she did.

When she backed away, he noticed her hand in front of his face. Barely able to put two thoughts together, he took hold of it and slid the ring onto her finger. It was a perfect fit. Thank you, Miss Annabelle. He'd only had to ask her—she'd been more than happy to find out the right size. She'd traced Connie's wedding band and given him the slip of paper to take with him to the jeweler's.

"Oh, Alton, it's beautiful. I've never had a diamond before."

"It's only a half-carat, but I hope to add to it over time."

"I'm perfectly happy with it." She leaned against him.

He encircled her in his arms and breathed in, as his heart filled and overflowed. Heat lightning lit the night sky. A battalion of lightning bugs twinkled all around. "I guess we need to decide on a date." If it was left up to him, he'd marry her this minute, or at least as quick as they could get someone to speak the words over them. But he didn't reckon she'd want that.

She gave a soft sigh. "I've been thinking about it. I figured you'd need to wait until the cotton is in."

"If you want to take a … a wedding trip, we'll have to wait till late fall, at least." He couldn't bring himself to say the word honeymoon. It seemed too intimate.

"You mean a honeymoon?" She laughed into his eyes. "You're such a prude, Alton Wade."

Marla's less than kind words came back to him. "Is that a bad thing?"

"Not at all. I like that about you. It's kind of sweet … and funny."

He grinned. "Ah, and you do like to tease me."

"I do. So, about the date, I was thinking about mid-

November. How does that sound?"

It seemed like an eternity at the moment. "I guess that'll give us enough time to make our plans."

"It's plenty of time, but we won't be able to have the reception in the new garden like I'd hoped. It's liable to be cold."

"We can do something out there in the springtime. Get the family together, maybe make it an annual event."

"That sounds perfect."

Perfect described everything about this night. These were surely the most pleasant moments of his life so far, but the rising moon reminded him it was time to go. He didn't want it to end. He jumped down to help her. After one more mind-numbing kiss, he drove her home.

Chapter Fifteen

Connie watched as just after dawn, Alton stopped by to pick up Judith. The truck's bed overflowed with workers, mostly Miss Lucy's family, large and small.

Samson yipped in excitement as the truck pulled away. Connie pictured the dog settling down on Judith's lap in the front seat.

An hour later, that same truck rolled up Sutter's drive across the fields. Connie stood in readiness, waiting for his uplifted hand. He didn't disappoint. He always knew she'd be watching, waiting for their morning greeting, though divided by twenty-odd acres.

Before she turned away, a light blue Cadillac convertible pulled into the drive behind Alton's truck. A woman was driving. Connie nearly lost her footing. She made a quick grab for the porch support. "Well, if it isn't Marla Wade," she spoke under her breath. "I hope that means—" At that moment, Chase's blond head appeared on the other side of the vehicle. He carried a suitcase. Connie nearly jumped up and down. She pressed her hands together. "Praise the Lord."

"Amen." Momma's voice sounded through the open window. "What're we praising God for now? Did you blind yourself in the reflection off that rock on your finger?"

Connie opened the screen door and stepped inside Momma's room. "Ha ha. You're really funny. It's so much better than that. Marla's brought Chase to Alton's."

Momma's eyes widened. "Really? Well, praise the Lord. You were right. I shouldn't have spoken against it."

Together, they made their way to the front room, where Joseph kicked at the air, his little eyes intent on the ceiling.

He giggled when Connie's face appeared above him. He gazed up at her, adoring expectation in his eyes.

Connie gathered him in her arms. "I can't even imagine leaving my child anywhere. But I am happy Marla and Jensen made this choice. I just hope Alton's up to it."

Momma folded Joseph's blanket and laid it in the now empty playpen. "He will be. But will you?"

"What do you mean?"

"I don't know if you've thought about it. This could keep him too busy to spend time with you." She propped the front door open to catch the morning breeze. "It could delay the wedding, if you'd thought to marry anytime soon."

Connie settled into the chair and prepared to feed

Joseph. "We plan to wait till after the cotton is picked, anyway. Alton can't leave while the crop's at stake."

"That's right, I reckon. I didn't mean to cast a shadow on Chase getting to come stay with Alton. That's a miracle, however you look at it. I suppose the two of you will have to talk it through, but don't be surprised if you see less of Alton for a while."

Connie hadn't thought about that, not really. She'd assumed things would go along as usual. She agreed with Momma, though. Alton would be busy with his charge. He was the kind of man to take his duty very seriously. If that meant less time with her and little Joseph, that's the way it had to be. It was only for a couple of months, after all. She glanced at the wall calendar and mentally ticked off the weeks until the second week of September, when school usually started.

Joy flooded Annabelle's soul, followed closely by a sharp twinge of guilt. Connie and Joseph would be here till after cotton-picking season ended. That probably meant sometime in November before they'd have a wedding. Wonder if she could talk them into waiting until after the holidays? Would that be too much to ask? The thought of spending Christmas on her own did not appeal at all.

She scrubbed the last pot and set it upside down on the

drainer to dry. Why did the thought of living alone terrify her so?

It wasn't that she was afraid of being by herself. She wasn't. Her trust in God would see her through. The fact remained and hung constantly over her: she had never lived alone.

Another thought popped into her head—just as scary and real. Alton had already mentioned the fact that as soon as the land was ready for replanting cotton, she might want to consider renting the house to someone who would farm it. Receiving an income from the cotton sales appealed to her all right. But where would she live?

"Maybe I could find someone to work the land for me." With the present limits on growing cotton, Alton couldn't do it, so she'd have to find someone else willing to take it on. "I'd have to pay them a portion of the profits, though." She chewed the inside of her jaw. When had she become such a worry-wart? It would be at least another season before they could grow cotton on the land. She gazed out the kitchen side window to the spot Tom had spoken to her about. Was he still interested? She'd be mighty tempted, though having him in such close proximity … good gracious, the thought set her heart to racing. How could she even consider it?

"I'm headed out to the garden, Pumpkin." She kept her voice low so she wouldn't wake Joseph.

Connie waved her on.

That girl needed rest, too.

Annabelle took a moment to dead-head the zinnias growing at the base of the front porch before moving on. She hadn't gone far when she heard a vehicle on the road, followed by the unmistakable crunch of gravel on the drive. She sincerely hoped it was Alton coming by for a visit. But as she rounded the side of the house, her hopes sank. It was Tom, wearing a smile that rivaled the sun in brightness. What was on his mind?

He didn't waste any time. "I want to talk about that land, Miss Annabelle. See if we can come to some sort of agreement."

Annabelle opened her mouth, but nothing came out. Her mind had gone completely blank. She stood there like a post, blinking at the man.

He wore a white cotton shirt, open at the collar, with the sleeves rolled up. His hair was windblown. He must've driven with the windows open. Of course, he would, in this heat. She fanned herself with her hand, feeling a bit too much warmth herself.

"Miss Annabelle? Are you all right? I reckon I must have caught you by surprise. Maybe we should go sit on the front porch?"

Annabelle managed a nod and started walking.

"Uh … Miss Annabelle?"

She turned her head to look at him.

He nodded toward the house. "I believe the front porch is this way."

What must he think of her? "Of course, it is. It must be

the heat. I'll go through the house and pour us a glass of iced tea. I'll meet you on the porch."

Land sakes alive, Annabelle. She chided herself as she entered the back door and crept through to the kitchen. A peek into the parlor told her Connie had fallen asleep. Annabelle worked quickly, but as quietly as possible, filling glasses with ice and sweet tea.

Tom sat in one of the rockers, looking quite content. He accepted the glass, but kept his eyes on her. "I hope you're all right, Miss Annabelle. You seemed a bit ... confused back there."

"I'm fine, Tom. Nothing to worry about. It's been so hot, is all."

"Yes, it has been. Worse in town, I think. Must be all that pavement. Anyway, about that land. I've looked around a good bit. Didn't find anything I liked better. So, I was thinking we might be able to make a deal."

Annabelle swallowed some tea. "I still don't know, Tom. I talked to Alton. There'd be some problems with it."

"He came by the store. He explained about the deed restrictions, the mineral rights, and all. And of course, he didn't know what his brother would have to say about it. Since Jensen's in a legal position to block a building permit, I thought I should talk to him first. I think we've come to a ... an agreement of equal ... er ... benefit."

Tom's hesitance troubled Annabelle. She watched his expression, but that only worried her more, in a different way. He'd grown into such a handsome man. The gray at his temples made him look so distinguished, and those laugh lines on either side of his mouth made her wonder … why had he never remarried? Had he been so deeply in love with that woman?

What was she thinking? Wake up, Annabelle. She cleared her throat. "What kind of agreement?"

"I will lease the land from you. I can build my house—that would be considered improvements. I'd own the building, of course, but not the land it sits on. Businesses do it all the time."

"I don't know, Tom, is that wise? What if something happened? How would that work?"

"I suppose you mean, what if something happened to me?" He grinned and shook his head. "That's the beauty of it, Miss Annabelle. It'd be yours, if I was to die."

She sat back. "Mine? How so, Tom?"

"I'd leave it to you legally. It'd be yours."

"That doesn't seem right." She shook her head slowly, ruminating his words. "It'd be your investment. You should leave it to your family."

He was quiet a moment, staring into his tea, as if he contemplated something, like whether or not he ought to speak. She considered stopping him now, before he said something she'd regret.

When he spoke, his voice was so quiet, she barely understood. "I consider you my family, Miss Annabelle."

She opened and shut her mouth several times before she found something to say. "No. No, Tom, I'm not."

He set his glass on the table and faced her. "You know how I feel about you—how I've always felt."

Her hand trembled. Annabelle set her glass aside also. This could not be happening. She didn't want it to happen. Why did he have to have feelings for her?

"I'm sorry," he waved his hand in the air, as if to shoo away those last words. But they couldn't be brushed aside. They were out there, and Annabelle would never forget them.

A fist to his mouth, he cleared his throat. "I know it's still too soon. I just want you to know how I feel. I won't ever speak of it again. Not until the day you're ready to hear it."

"Oh, Tom, I—" she took a deep breath and slowly released it. The very thought of him—his nearness, his manliness—sent shivers down her spine. She didn't like it. Not one bit. She bowed her head and prayed silently. Prayed for wisdom, and strength.

"I've loved you a long time. It's why I want to do this. I want to take care of you. If I'm close by, I can do that. I can make sure you're safe. And if anything happens to me, you'll have a nice place to live out your days. You can tenant out this house, let someone raise your cotton for you."

He had it all figured out, didn't he? He must have been thinking about it for a while. Sure, she'd known he was sweet on her, but loved her this much? What was she supposed to do about that?

She shook her head. "I can't, Tom."

"You can't lease me the land?"

Oh, the look in his eyes. She was hurting him, disappointing him for sure. "Oh. I can lease you the land, but … I can't be what you want. I promised myself, I'd never—"

"You'd never love anyone again? Are you afraid of losing someone else, Miss Annabelle? Because that's perfectly normal. And in time …"

"No, Tom, it's not even that."

After a quick intake of breath, he nodded. "It's because I won't go to church with you, isn't it?"

"I promised myself, I'd never be unequally yoked again. You grew up in church, Tom. You know what that means."

He shrugged. Poor man, he looked so forlorn. "I do."

"I did that. My Ray, I loved him, but he wasn't a church-goer. If I ever marry again, Tom, I want a man who believes what I believe. Who shares my faith, and will go to church with me."

"I am a believer, Miss Annabelle."

She looked him in the eyes. "I believe you are, Tom. And I do respect you. You're a good man—a good friend."

"I see what you're saying, Miss Annabelle." He gripped the chair arms.

She watched the muscles of his jaw tighten and loosen as if he chewed on her words.

His fingers relaxed with the air leaving his lungs.

"That's all right. You can think of me as a friend. I hope you'll love me as a friend. And if I never find my way back to the church, I hope you'll forgive me."

Annabelle fought the need to touch him. Reassure him. She laced her fingers together in her lap and concentrated on breathing slow and easy. "I'd rather believe that you will, Tom. I'd much rather believe that you will."

Wake up, Annabelle. It was the voice of reason. Listen to it. Don't give in to a handsome face. A pleasing smile that envelopes your heart and takes it captive. You're just missing Ray. You're just lonesome.

Annabelle sat up in bed, her heart thumping wildly. She could barely get her breath. And it was hot. So hot. She slid out of bed and padded into the kitchen for a drink of water. Afterward, she found her way to the sofa and sat down. There'd be no more sleep tonight, she just knew it. Her long conversation with Tom ended with a promise to think about everything he'd told her. She hadn't been able to not think about it.

Supper was a blur, and all the way up to bedtime, she'd been so distracted. She couldn't even be entertained by little Joseph, or her favorite gospel singing on Judith's radio.

Connie had been worried, so Annabelle claimed to

have a headache. It wasn't really a lie. Her head was aching. Spinning with all this information. With feelings and emotions she didn't understand. And guilt. Oh, the guilt and pain, knowing she'd disappointed such a good man. A man who loved her.

And what if her hard stance—her stubbornness—made him even more determined not to go back to church? Could she live with that?

She closed her eyes and let her head rest on the back of the sofa. "Dear Lord, only You know the answer. You've led me this far. I know You'd never lead me away from You. Touch that man's heart, Lord. Bring him back—fully back—and strong."

She could love him. In fact, she might already. That thought scared her more than anything. How could she do that? How could she love another man so soon, only a year after the love of her life had died? The fact that both Emily and Connie had already fallen in love with others didn't matter. They were young. Their marriages to her sons had been short, compared to the lifetime Annabelle had spent with Ray. Fresh tears poured from her eyes as misery filled her soul.

"Momma?"

Annabelle opened her eyes. Morning light streamed in the window. She tried to blink away the confusion. Had she slept?

Connie stood over her, a worried frown on her face. "Are you all right, Momma? Is your head feeling better?"

"I'm fine, Pumpkin. Don't you worry about me. I got a little rest." She pushed up from the couch. "I'll get started on breakfast."

"No, you won't. You stay right there. Judith and I will get breakfast."

As soon as she sat up, Annabelle's head pounded, and her stomach roiled. Guilt consumed her anew. She had brought it on herself by lying about having a headache. She had some serious repenting to do.

Chapter Sixteen

"For serious cane pole fishing in a pond or a lake," Alton told Chase, "there's no better bait than a fat earthworm. We have plenty around here. Willie knows all the best places."

Chase frowned in concentration as he impaled the pink worm with the hook.

Alton never took his eyes off the boy's progress. "And remember what I said about fish hooks. They go in a whole lot easier than they come out. You don't want to find out, believe me."

It was a perfect morning for fishing. A little on the cloudy side. Alton hoped the time spent together would loosen the boy's tongue. This was the third day since Chase arrived, and he still had not said a word about that camp, except when Alton asked how he'd gotten here from there.

"I took the bus to just outside Trenton. I walked the rest of the way. I didn't want anyone to see me and tell my daddy. Except for not having anything to eat, it was fun." He managed a wan smile. "An adventure."

Alton shook his head, silently thanking God that no harm had come to the boy during his adventure.

The first part of the week, they'd been busy as cows in a patch of new spring grass. So far, the boy had learned to groom and feed the horses, muck out the stalls, and clean the blades on the cultivator.

They'd ridden the fields, checked on the cotton, and talked to the workers. After they'd discerned the amount of work yet to be done, they hiked up to the dam to check for clogs in the runoff. It was while they were at the dam, Alton decided to take a break and teach the boy how to fish.

Plop! Alton glanced up to see the ripples from a fish jumping. "Did you see that? They're coming up to feed. Just sit still, and do like I showed you. Make 'em think that worm fell into the water. They'll go for it."

Chase nodded, never breaking his concentration. Within minutes, the line tightened. The boy jumped and nearly jerked the line.

Alton caught it just in time. "Easy there, you'll jerk it right out of the fish's mouth." He crouched beside Chase, who was standing now, a look of pure joy on his face. Together, they hauled the bluegill out of the water.

"It's not much, is it?" Chase frowned at the fish flopping on the ground.

"It's a good size for a bluegill. If we catch several, Regina can fry 'em up for supper. They're right tasty."

Two hours later, a beaming Chase carried his load of bluegill back down the trail to the house.

"Oh my, will you look at that," Regina exclaimed. "Looks like enough for your supper and mine, too."

"We'll get these cleaned up for you," Alton told her. He meant to do the work himself, and show Chase how it was done, but the boy insisted on trying. Didn't help Alton's nerves any, watching the boy wield a fillet knife. But he needed to show the boy he trusted him, so he sat quietly by, only interrupting once.

After delivering the cleaned fish to Regina, Chase turned to him. "What now?"

Alton mussed his hair and grinned. "Free time for you, young man."

With a shrug, Chase headed for the door.

"Listen for the dinner bell," Regina said.

He'd a pretty good idea what Chase would do, so Alton didn't worry about the boy. He did check on him a time or two, and found him tossing a stick for Samson to catch. That dog was gonna miss Chase when school started. Thinking about missing and loneliness, Alton's gaze traced a path across the fields to the old Sterling place. His heart ached for time alone with his beloved.

His beloved. Such an intimate, cherishing phrase. He almost groaned aloud for missing her so. But he'd made a promise and he'd hold to it. He'd head over there for a few minutes this afternoon, have a talk with her. She'd understand, because she knew how important it was to make a lasting imprint on Chase.

His mind had only wandered a moment. He looked down and couldn't see the boy or the dog.

Samson's bark drew Connie's attention. She and Momma worked, clearing a section of the garden, to make room for a few late plantings. She swiped a drop of sweat headed for her eyes, and gazed toward the sound. Samson wasn't visible, but Chase was. He was dashing across rows of cotton, headed first one way, then another.

"Look, Momma. Samson must be on the trail of a rabbit, and Chase is hot on his heels."

Momma stood and stretched her back. "That's a sight, ain't it? That boy being allowed to run free. Does my heart good."

The smile on Momma's face did Connie's heart good. Those had been in short supply ever since Tom's visit. She would love to know what they'd talked about, but Momma had not confided in her, so Connie had not pried.

Within moments, Samson burst through the final row of cotton and shot across the drainage ditch into the open, Chase right behind him.

Farther afield, Alton hollered, "Chase!"

Connie propped her hoe on the fence and set off toward Chase. "I'll be right back, Momma."

Samson made a beeline for Connie, nearly falling over at her feet. He panted hard to catch his breath.

Connie crouched and rubbed behind his ears, watching Chase's approach. "Hello there, Chase."

"Did you see that, Miss Connie? Samson almost caught that rabbit." His face was beet red, his hair sweat-soaked.

"I did see. You both look as if you could do with a rest in the shade, and a cool drink of water."

Chase licked his lips. "Yes ma'am, I sure could."

Connie lifted her hand to gain Alton's attention before she set off for the garden and the shade of a nearby tree.

Momma was already there, checking on Joseph, who slept in his playpen. She looked up at their approach. "Well, Chase, how are you faring these days? Are you enjoying your stay with Uncle Alton?"

Chase nodded. "Yes, ma'am. Lots. Today, we caught a whole mess o' bluegill up at the lake."

"You don't say?"

"Yes, ma'am. My first time ever, and I caught five. Uncle Alton said he'd never seen a first-timer with such good luck."

While they were talking, Connie poured water into a cup and handed it to Chase. He downed it in one gulp. She soaked her kerchief and wiped his face.

He gazed up at her. "Thank you, Miss Connie. I was mighty hot."

"Yes, you were, and so is your uncle, I think."

Alton arrived, removed his hat, and wiped his forehead with his sleeve. "Chase, you shouldn't run off without telling me."

The boy's face went blank, like when they'd first seen him in the front yard at Sutter's.

Connie wanted to comfort him, but held back. She filled the cup with water and passed it to Alton.

"I'm sorry, Uncle Alton." His expression pierced Connie's heart. He kicked at a clump of dirt. "I wanted to see what Samson was after."

Alton took the cup of water Connie offered, and sat down in the shade. "No harm done. Rest a spell."

Chase sat next to Samson.

"He was telling us about his good luck fishing this morning," Connie told Alton.

"I've never seen the like." He finished off the water, then handed her the cup. "Chase here is a natural at everything. He takes it right up like he was born to it."

Chase beamed.

Connie's heart swelled at the look on his face. He basked in the glow of encouragement—was starving for it. Well, he had come to a good place.

Momma talked of the garden, her plans for the fall crops. Late peas and cabbage. Connie listened to the even breathing of the two little boys. Joseph in his playpen, and Chase, lying with his head propped on Samson's side. He'd fallen right to sleep.

Momma got up. "I'm going on in to start our dinner."

"Okay, Momma."

After she'd gone, Alton slid next to Connie. "I was meaning to come by later this afternoon." He glanced at Chase. "I'm sorry I haven't been sooner."

Connie searched his face. "That's all right. You've been busy."

"I have." He took her hand and squeezed it. "I sure have missed you."

"I've missed you, too."

"It'll have to be this way, most days. That's a stipulation of him being able to stay."

"I can't say I'm surprised. Will he go home weekends?"

Alton shook his head slowly. "No. He'll go with me to church, but he'll sit with his daddy. After church, he'll return home with me."

"My goodness, Alton. That's rather demanding, isn't it?"

"It is, but I believe in the greater good. It's only for a short season." His gaze slid from her lips to her eyes. "I'm intending to have a lifetime with you."

At that moment, Joseph stirred and gave a little sigh.

Samson's head jerked up.

Catching sight of the dog, the baby laughed and rolled over.

"Well, I'll be." Alton released her hand. "I didn't know he could do that."

Chase sat up, bleary-eyed. "I guess I fell asleep."

"You sure did," Connie told him.

"Come on, boy. Reckon we better get on back. Regina should be ringing that dinner bell any minute. We don't dare be late."

Chase and Samson jumped up and started across the field. "Last one home's a rotten egg."

Alton dropped a kiss on Connie's lips. "Guess I'll be a rotten egg."

"I'll see you at church on Sunday."

A spark of mischief in his eyes, he smirked. "Oh, you'll see me before Sunday."

A letter awaited Alton at the house, from Thomas J. Fowler, Topeka, Kansas. Someone had answered his inquiry. His gut twisted as he tore it open.

Dear Mr. Wade,

I was notified of your interest in my case by Charles Dodge at our local newspaper. He's a personal friend of mine, and a man I worked with for over thirty years. I have to tell you, I was quite shocked by the contents of your letter. I had assumed Mac Pruitt died at Pearl Harbor. Your inquiry opened an old wound, but his only transgression was running out on a lifelong friendship. There was an accident in which I was badly injured. I did recover, but it took a number of years. Mac was not responsible, though he may believe he was. He'd had quite a lot to drink, so his memory may have been impaired. We were broadsided by another young driver who'd also drunk too much alcohol. And all this happened during a time when alcohol was prohibited.

My only regret is, Mac didn't stay by my side. I would never have left him, even if it meant I went to jail for what we carried in the trunk of the car we drove. Thank the Lord for a good-hearted deputy who destroyed the evidence. He was an old friend of the family who didn't want our name sullied. So, there you have it, Mr. Wade—the whole ugly history—a chain of events which resulted in me not having to go to war. I was given a full scholarship at the University of Kansas, married a beautiful wife who still loves me, and recently retired from an excellent position as a journalist.

I would dearly love to know how to contact Mac. If you prefer, send him my address and ask him to write me. It's time the past was laid to rest.

Yours truly,
Tom Fowler

Alton blew out a breath, releasing the tension in his throat. He folded the letter and returned it to the envelope. His fingers itched to write the reply. But dinner was on the table. It would have to wait.

"I like Miss Connie," Chase announced after the blessing.

Alton lifted his eyes to the boy's face. "You do, huh?"

"Yes, sir, Uncle Alton, I do. She's not what Daddy said."

Alton arched his brows, but held off any response. He wasn't completely sure he wanted to know what Jensen had said about Connie.

Regina set a bowl on the table with a bit more fervor than necessary.

"What did … um … your daddy say about Miss Connie?" He set his fork down a moment, and tilted his head forward. "You don't have to answer that."

"It's all right, I can answer." He chewed a bite of food and swallowed. "Daddy says she's colored, but not the typical kind. He said she's part South Pacific colored, but that's still colored. I don't think he's right. She seems very white to me. And kind. She's very kind."

Alton glanced at Regina, standing in the middle of the kitchen, staring at him. Her smooth, dark complexion had paled somewhat, her eyes round as saucers. He'd better come up with something to say and quickly. "Folks can be kind, Chase, no matter what color their skin. Regina, for instance—and Edris—she practically raised me. Miss Connie is kind because she was sort of raised by Miss Annabelle, who is one of the kindest of God's creatures. Well, when she's not on a tangent." He grinned at Chase. "Don't tell her I told you that. But she does have a stubborn streak."

Chapter Seventeen

Her eyes wide, Connie stared at the excited women of her Sunday school class. They pulled her into their circle as soon as she entered.

Matilda Grace grabbed her hand. "All right, show us that ring."

Giggles filled the small room with the exception of one dark corner, where Maggie sat. Connie had only a moment to glance at her before being swallowed up by the others.

"Oh, look how it sparkles."

"You're so blessed, Connie."

"Alton must love you a lot."

Julie Reynolds closed her eyes and hugged herself. "Isn't it romantic? I thought he'd never marry."

Their elderly teacher, Bertha Tuley, cleared her throat. "Ladies, let's get started on our lesson."

As Connie took the seat Matilda had saved for her, Matilda whispered, "Not everyone is happy about it."

"I see that."

Matilda shrugged it off, but Connie couldn't let it lie. She needed to find a way to make peace with Maggie Arnold.

As soon as class had ended, several of the girls made plans to meet during the week.

Matilda touched Connie's shoulder. "They're putting together a shower."

"I hope it's not supposed to be a surprise."

Matilda cackled. "No, silly. I'll see you later. It's my turn in the nursery."

Connie's mind was already racing ahead. What could she do to soften Maggie's hard heart?

Entering the sanctuary, she noticed Chase sitting with his father. That meant Alton was already here, but he wasn't in their usual seat. She crossed the distance and sat next to Momma.

Momma leaned close, "The church is abuzz this morning."

"Talking about our engagement?"

Momma nodded. "I don't know how word gets out so fast. That's not all, though. They're also talking about Chase. No one can believe it."

"What, that he's staying with Alton?"

"You have to admit, it is unexpected."

Alton slid into place next to Connie. He shot her a heart-stopping smile that sent a quiver up her spine. He smelled so good, she even had trouble focusing on the hymn-singing. How was she going to get through the next few months?

"It's too sad," Momma said to Connie as they walked to Judith's car.

"What's too sad?"

"I'm gonna miss our Sunday afternoons with Alton and Miss Lillian."

Judith opened the door so Momma could climb in. "Well, you have something almost as good. Ma invited us all to dinner."

Connie opened her mouth to speak, but thought better of it. She'd almost said how she missed Thelma's mouth-watering biscuits, but held her tongue. Someone might find that insulting.

That someone slid into the backseat of the car with no comment.

Judith held the door for Connie and Joseph. "Y'all are mighty quiet this morning. I hope it's all right I told her we would come. Ma couldn't abide a Sunday dinner without me at the table." She closed the door and trotted around to the driver's side and got in. "I told her it was just until Chase goes back to school. And it'll be worth it. That's what you keep telling me, Aunt Annabelle. It's a season, is all. Just like the summer. When summer ends, things will go back to the way they were."

"Aren't you a sharp one." Momma gazed out the window. "You're going to do all right over there at the university."

"I know I will."

Connie couldn't decipher Momma's mood. Was she upset over something that happened at church? Or maybe she was still troubled by Tom's visit. Joseph bounced and giggled at the sight of a dog running alongside their car. After calming him down, Connie brought her attention back to Judith. "Are you looking forward to college?"

"Yes, I am. I intend to get as much as I can out of the experience."

"Well, I know your parents are proud of you," Momma still sounded preoccupied.

Judith signaled a left turn and waited for an oncoming car to pass before proceeding. "Daddy thinks the only good reason for a girl to go to college, is to meet and marry an educated man."

Momma cackled. "That sounds like Riley."

"I knew some girls at Southern Cal who held the same opinion."

Judith glanced at her. "Did they find what they were looking for?"

Connie nodded. "I know a couple of them did. They dropped out after their sophomore year to marry. I thought it was sad they didn't stick with it, get their degree."

"You did, but I guess you were already married."

"Yes, I was, but my husband was still overseas."

When Judith pulled into the drive, Joseph squealed as the youngest Franklin children ran out to greet them.

As soon as Connie opened the door, Judith's little sister Raydeen reached for the baby. "Can I hold him, Miss Connie—please?"

Connie handed him over. "Just be careful. He's picked up some weight since you saw him last."

"I'll be careful." Raydeen scooped him up and held him close. He reared back to look at her face, but she managed to keep him steady.

Stevie helped Momma out of the car. "Daddy and Uncle Tom went fishing over at the Tennessee River."

Momma's face brightened to such an extent, Connie came to a full stop. What on earth was going on?

"Well, I hope they catch a passel of fish." She reached for Connie's arm.

As they walked up the steps into the house, Connie couldn't help thinking Tom and Momma had had a falling out of some sort. What other explanation could there be?

Tom cast his line into the placid blue water of the Tennessee River. "Looks like you got a nibble, there."

Drowsy, Riley reclined against the edge of the fishing boat. "It's probably the same one that's been eating my bait all morning. Never will take a good bite on the hook. Kinda like a certain cousin of mine."

Tom frowned into the bright sunshine. "You talking about me?"

Riley gave a soft chuckle. "You recognize yourself?"

"I've done all I know to do." He slowly reeled in his line for a recast.

"So, she knows exactly how you feel about her?"

"Pretty much." He had no intention of relating the entire conversation. It was just too intimate, even to share with his best friend. He released a sigh.

"Sounds like you got it bad." Riley pushed up from his position and reeled in to check his hook. Sure enough, the bait had been taken. "Guess we need to move again. Shade's done gone. Fish got lazy."

Tom agreed. He was having a hard time concentrating. All he could think about was his conversation with Annabelle. He'd been blindsided. Had he completely misjudged her? Had he only fooled himself when he thought he detected a light in her eyes—a softening of her countenance when she talked to him?

Riley found a well-shaded cove and pulled into it. After they cast, he took out their baloney sandwiches. He handed Tom a mason jar of iced tea and a sandwich. Settling back, he tasted the tea, and smacked his lips. "I sure never thought to see you broke down over a woman."

"I'm not. We're friends, just like we always were. She's not ready anyway. She was married a long time to a good man she loved. Can't expect her to bounce right back from that."

Riley slugged down a long drink of tea, which he managed to spill. He used his shirt sleeve as a napkin. "I guess I never could see you married. I thought you'd always be a bachelor."

"I was married."

Riley glared at him. "That was so long ago, I don't even remember it. I'm not even sure it really happened."

Tom chuckled. "You don't remember it because you weren't there. You and I were both in the service. I was in Virginia, and you were in Memphis."

"I sort of remember. How'd she die? I done forgot."

Tom adjusted his line. "She had stomach cancer, they said. I never saw her again after that furlough when we got married."

"That ain't like a real marriage. You never spent any time with her. You got to live with a woman for several years, just to get to know her. Even then, you don't really know her. You think you do, but you don't." He slapped his knee and laughed out loud. "Till you buy her some doodad and she thinks you're crazy for thinking she'd like it."

Tom grunted.

"You know I'm right. You and Annabelle, you're just getting to know one another again. She'll come around."

"I don't know. It's complicated."

Riley baited his hook with a bite of baloney. He cast it

in toward the shore. "Naw, it ain't. I know what the problem is. You tell me if I'm wrong. But I know I'm right. She won't go with you unless you go to church with her." He sat forward to make eye contact. "Am I right?"

Something tugged Tom's line. Perfect timing. He gave all his attention to the fish, and soon hauled in a big cat.

"Look at that." Riley caught it in the net. "That's a four-pounder for sure. Your luck's about to change, old boy."

After a couple more hours of fishing, they returned the boat to the rental dock and began the two-hour drive home. Tom was content to drive in peace. He was hoping Riley would nod off. But no, the man was on the scent of something, and he would not let it be.

"The way I see it, you got two choices. You've loved this woman since we were in grade school. You lost her once, 'cause you wouldn't speak up. Now you're about to lose her again. You got to decide, is it worth it? Get up and go to church with her, sit in the pew for an hour a week. See what comes of it."

"That's what you did. You made Thelma think you were a church-goer and as soon as she said, 'I do,' you quit going." Tom caught Riley's eye and nodded. "Didn't you?"

Riley slapped his knee. "It worked, didn't it? I still go with her once and again."

"Once in a blue moon. Christmas and Easter, and when one of your kids get baptized."

"Hey, it works for me. And I can be here with you of

a Sunday, hauling in fish. Good times."

Tom shook his head. "Well, I can't lie to Miss Annabelle. She's a good Christian woman who deserves my honesty."

"Oh, yeah, you always did have a soft way about you. So, you've made your decision? You're just gonna let her go again?"

"I haven't made up my mind what I'm going to do." He intended to give her some slack, let her swim for a while, maybe wear her down. Maybe.

Riley stretched his arms over his head and yawned. "Well, wake me when we get there. I done my bit. I said my say."

Too much say, in Tom's mind. Nosing around in another man's business. But Tom would never let on to Riley. Because Riley cared for him like a brother, and he'd always been there for him. Like this spring, when he'd offered hospitality till Tom could make other arrangements. Yes, Tom helped out, paid rent to defray the cost of feeding him. But even if he couldn't pay, it wouldn't matter. And if Riley had a need, Tom was there. They'd always been the best of friends.

So why was it so difficult for Tom to take his advice now? He knew Riley was right. He was about to lose Annabelle. Again. And all because he was too proud to walk back in that church building. He'd made peace long ago with Jensen and everything that had happened. Tom always believed Jensen was half right about that mansion house. It belonged in the Wade family. Uncle Jeb would never have wanted it. If he'd been alive, he would've given it back. That's the kind of man he was.

He gripped the wheel as he drove past the church. He had some serious thinking to do.

Mid-August weather turned searing hot with only an occasional pop-up storm to cool things off. Alton lifted another bale of hay onto the conveyor. Willie and his boy Anthony moved the bales to neat stacks in the barn loft. Chase was much too small for this chore, so Mother had put him to work cleaning the back porch. This time of year, she liked for everything to be moved, cleaned, and swept. She swore it cut down on spiders coming in the house.

When they'd emptied the hay wagon, Alton removed his straw work hat and swiped his brow with his handkerchief. He glanced toward the loft door. "Willie, I'm going to go check on the boy."

Willie responded with a wave. He and Anthony sat in the opening and let their legs dangle.

As Alton approached the house, Chase's laughter rang out, a sound that always warmed his heart. He strode toward the side yard. There was Chase, paddling around in the large, galvanized horse trough they used to catch rainwater.

Mother stood nearby, intermittently spraying Chase with the garden hose. She looked nearly as wet as the boy.

Samson lay on his back, his belly fully exposed to the spray. Alton chuckled. What a ham bone. That silly dog had trailed his master for years. Now he dedicated most of his time to Chase.

"Jump in, Uncle Alton. It's really cool."

The screen door opened and out stepped Connie, carrying a jug of iced lemonade. "You're just in time."

Alton stood still, drinking in the scene. A rush of love and longing rolled over him. This is how his life would look in just a few short weeks. But what about the boy and the promise he'd made to his brother? Of course, it was wrong of Jensen to require such a thing. After all, Connie was going to be part of the family, whether Jensen liked it or not.

Connie drew near, carrying a glass of the lemonade, which she offered him. He accepted it, took a long drink, and grinned down at her. "Thank you, darling."

She smiled into his eyes. "I was about to bring it over to the barn, but I saw you headed this way." She glanced toward Chase. "Your Mother sent Regina's girl over to the house this morning. They thought I'd like to help put up the pear preserves."

Alton nodded. He understood all too well. Mother wanted Connie here, though his brother was liable to show up at any time. He'd already "dropped by" twice—while he was in the neighborhood, of course. Jensen was hoping to catch them together—exactly like this. Alton tried to ignore the churning in his chest. Downright irksome, that was Jensen.

His gaze remained riveted to Connie as she glided back across the lawn to the porch. He could watch her all day. Just as she disappeared into the house, a horn blasted from the road. One that sounded an awful lot like Jensen's.

Chapter Eighteen

Alton shrugged his shoulders to loosen the kinked muscles in his neck as Jensen got out of the car. The splashing noise behind him quieted as Chase stood up, dripping wet.

"Ain't this a homey scene," Jensen spoke around the cigarette clamped in his teeth. "I expected to find you laboring in the field, boy."

Before Chase could answer, Alton stepped forward. "He's been working all day. Mother thought it would do him good to cool off."

Jensen scratched his cheek and grinned. "That would be nice, wouldn't it? Looks like you could use a dip, too. It's sure enough hot." Pulling a folded kerchief from his pocket, he removed his hat and mopped his forehead.

Alton indicated the glass in his hand. "This is how I prefer to cool down. Can I offer you a glass?"

"Lemonade?" He glanced toward the back porch. "I

would love some, thanks."

Alton followed his gaze to the place where Mother stood, just inside the door. She lifted a glass to let him know she'd heard. As long as Jensen didn't enter the house, they'd be all right.

Jensen dropped his cigarette butt, and ground it into the dirt. He leaned against the car, arms crossed over his chest.

Mother brought the ice cold lemonade. "Good afternoon, Jensen. I hope you're faring well."

"Mother." He gave her a curt nod and accepted the glass. "I'm as well as can be expected in this infernal heat."

She sent a small smile toward Alton. "Chase, if you're about finished, I believe the porch floor is dry. We can move the furniture back in place."

"Yes, ma'am." Chase stepped over the side of the trough, grabbed a nearby towel, and draped it over his shoulders.

As he walked past Samson, the dog thumped his tail, then turned his head to gaze at Jensen.

Alton could almost read the dog's thoughts. If Jensen made even one move toward the boy, he was in danger of attack. Alton clamped his jaw tight, though he wanted to chuckle.

"What brings you out this way, Jensen?"

"Driving back in from Jackson, thought I'd take a gander at the crops." He tipped his glass toward the field. "Cotton's looking good, but the corn's not doing well, is it? This heat's wreaking havoc."

"That it is."

"What of the Sterling acres? Will they be ready to plant come spring?"

"Probably soy for a couple of years, before going back to cotton. That soil is depleted. It needs a blast of nitrogen, so I think soy's the ticket."

"Well, I reckon you're the expert on that." He drained his glass and handed it to Alton. "I better let you get back to work. I noticed the bales above the dam. Looks like a good haul there, anyway.

"Oh, by the way, Tom and I worked up a lease agreement I think Miss Annabelle will profit from. Tom can build his house, but he won't own the property outright." He brushed at a spot of dust on his pants leg. "The way I see it, the land will still be in the family."

The prideful look in his brother's eyes disgusted Alton. He turned aside to set the glasses on the back porch, taking that moment to gain control of his emotions. When he turned back, Jensen had opened the car door.

"Chase, I'll see you on Sunday. Your mother wants you to come have dinner with us."

Chase straightened, looking almost as if he meant to salute. "Yes, sir."

Jensen fiddled with a pack of cigarettes in his breast pocket. He pulled one out and held it between his fingertips. "Good day to you, Mother, Alton. I'll see y'all on Sunday." He gave a low chuckle. "If not before."

Hands on his hips, Alton watched as his brother backed out of the drive.

Mother descended the two porch steps and reached for the glasses.

He knew she wouldn't speak in Chase's hearing, but she didn't have to. Her thoughts rang through loud and clear. "I'm headed back to the barn," he told her. "We've got a couple more wagon loads to bring in before dark." He turned to Chase. "When you've finished the porch, you can take advantage of that water in the trough. I'd hate for you to waste it. Just be ready to do the evening chores."

Chase grinned. "Thank you, Uncle Alton."

Connie didn't know the exact agreement between Jensen and Alton, but she suspected she was at the heart of it. After being warned by Miss Lillian, she twisted her braid into a coil and donned a straw hat, keeping her hair tucked under it. While Jensen was talking to Alton, she carried lemonade across the back lot to the barn. Even if he could see her, she doubted Jensen would recognize her, dressed in one of Regina's loose-fitting work shirts.

Willie and Anthony were happy for the refreshing drink. Afterward, she took water to the workhorses who were tethered in the shade.

"That's mighty kind of you, Miz Cross," Willie called

from his high perch in the barn. "We were jes' about to do that."

Connie smiled up at him. "I'm happy to. It gives me something to do while I wait."

Willie chuckled. "I know what you mean. I regularly keep my distance from Mr. Jensen."

"There's a new batch of kittens in the stables." Anthony jerked his thumb toward the back of the barn. "The mama cat is friendly. She won't mind you paying a visit."

"Thank you, Anthony, I believe I will."

Connie was admiring the adorable new babies when Alton strode into the barn.

"I wondered what happened to you." His voice echoed in the breezeway.

"Just keeping out of sight." She pushed up from a crouch.

Alton took a step nearer, his gaze locked on hers. "Don't get too attached. Most of those will go to good homes. Always somebody needing a good mouser." His lips curved into a smile. "I like the disguise, by the way."

She removed the hat and let her braid fall down her back. "Would you have recognized me at a distance?"

"I might not, unless I saw you walking." Before she could respond, he bent to drop a light kiss on her lips. "I'd do more than that, but I'm afraid I reek of sweat."

She tilted her head to the side. "I'll take a rain check." She glanced past him. "Looks like the guys have the team ready. I guess you're going after another load?"

"Two more, I hope." He turned toward the front of the barn.

She followed, carrying the hat. "I'll probably head home pretty soon."

He paused and looked at her. "Connie, I'm sorry about all this."

She reached for his hand and held it in hers. "We'll deal with it."

"You're too good for me."

She drew in a deep breath, slowly releasing it. "Well, if we had time, we could argue that one back and forth." She let go of his hand.

"I'm sure you'd let me win." He tugged the brim of his straw hat and smiled big enough so she could just make out the dimple in his cheek. As soon as he climbed onto the wagon, Willie slapped the reins and clucked to the horses.

Connie watched their departure, her thoughts in a tangle. Did she really understand? Or should she be disappointed that Alton would allow anyone to come between them? Especially his selfish, bigoted brother.

She reached for the two mason jars Willie and Anthony had emptied, then set off down the path toward the house.

Would he make similar decisions later, after they'd married?

Chase's laughter rang out, followed closely by Samson's high-pitched bark. Connie peered through the tree branches to see the boy playing in the trough, splashing water toward the excited dog. Her steps faltered. As she watched the scene, a slow smile loosened the tight muscles of her jaw.

"Worth the sacrifice." She'd said it before. In the long term, there was no knowing whether the boy would even remember these few weeks. It would be years before they'd know the outcome. And, if Alton's plans came to fruition, there could be more sacrifices ahead.

She let go of a pent-up breath. Life was filled with decisions and sacrifices. A mother knew all about giving until it hurt. Moving toward the house, she allowed a smile to dominate her expression. This boy had seen enough trouble. She would not add to it. But she did intend to have a serious conversation with his uncle.

Several days passed before Connie had the opportunity to speak with Alton. When they finally had a moment in private, she hesitated. They had so little time together. Should she bring up something that might cause friction?

"You're very quiet tonight. What's on your mind?" Alton asked. They were sitting in the truck outside the Dairy Whiz.

She had just polished off a hot fudge sundae. "I can't believe I ate that whole thing."

He laughed, but she could tell he wasn't buying it.

"I said I wouldn't ask, but it's bothering me."

His brow crinkled. "Ask about what?"

Keeping her eyes on his face, she twisted the end of her braid around one finger. "The agreement between you and Jensen."

"I see. Well, it was a simple one. He didn't want the boy exposed to … whatever might happen between a man and his intended." He grinned. "Of course, Jensen didn't put it so politely."

She eyed him a moment. Was he serious? This whole thing was about discretion? She was not a floozy. She could be discreet.

He held up his hand. "Now, calm down."

"I didn't say anything."

"No, but I could feel your pressure rising. I figured you were about to blow."

"Does he think I'm the kind of girl to hang all over you, show public displays of affection in front of a ten-year-old?"

His mouth twisted in a crooked grin. "I wouldn't mind the occasional display of affection."

She shook her head. "That's not all there is to it. He doesn't want me around his son. And he wants to keep us apart."

He drew his fingertip across her jawline to her chin. "He's not going to keep us apart. And it doesn't matter what his reasons were. They were wrong, and I was wrong to make the agreement. I just wanted Chase. And I'm glad I've had these weeks with him. The boy's changed. I'm sure you've noticed that."

"I have. I just … it irked me so, that Jensen has such a hold on you."

He drew back, as though he'd been slapped. "He has no hold on me." His voice had changed. His words were clipped.

Connie looked down at her hands. She'd said too much. Now he was angry with her. "I'm sorry, I—"

He blew out a breath. "No, it's my fault. I can see why you'd think that way. I don't always know the right thing to say, especially to women." His lips quirked into a smile. "You may have noticed that."

He massaged the back of his neck. "Connie, I let my brother come between us. I won't do it again. You mean too much to me."

She gazed at him in silence. Outside the truck, voices echoed, as folks talked among themselves while they enjoyed their treats. "Maybe we better head out."

"Are you mad at me?"

She shook her head. "No. I just don't want to be guilty of showing public displays of affection."

He started the engine and shifted gears. "Let's get out of here."

Alton marked another day off the calendar. Just ten more to go before Chase went back to military school. Ten more days before Alton could spend all his free time with Connie. He dropped the pencil on the desk. After a moment's thought, he reached up to rub his neck. He wasn't so sure more time with her was a good thing. She was mighty tempting.

Outside his room, he paused. The door to the front bedroom stood open. Would he ever get used to the room's lighter coloring? He had to admit, it was right pretty. Kind of feminine, like Connie. He walked inside, drew a deep breath. It still smelled new.

He remembered the day they'd all stood around the bed as Grandma lay dying. He'd been fifteen years old. Jensen was nearly twenty. Daddy sat in the chair by the window. Alton couldn't remember who else was there— probably Aunt Susan, and maybe Aunt Bertha. Grandma held Mother's hand as she passed from life into the sweetness of Heaven. He'd wanted to close his ears to the rasping, laboring breaths. But after she'd passed, her expression relaxed into one of ease.

He gripped the carved post of the four-poster bed. It was a lovely piece of furniture, but Grandma had died in that bed. Of course, the mattress and all the linens were new. But would he still think of her, as he lay in bed beside his beautiful new wife? Another thought occurred to him.

Would Connie think of Joseph when she lay in bed with Alton?

The thought jolted him. He knew she still thought of her first husband. It had only been a little more than a year since her loss. Had Alton rushed her into marriage?

He wasn't sure how long he'd been standing there, staring at the bed, when the phone rang downstairs.

Mother answered.

"Alton," she called. "Alton!"

"I'm on my way."

Downstairs, he picked up the receiver. "Alton Wade." The line crackled. "Hello?"

"Mr. Wade, it's Mackenzie Pruitt."

"Oh, I'm sorry to keep you waiting."

"It's all right, I'm not in Hawaii. I'm in Memphis."

Chapter Nineteen

Annabelle had never been a graveside visitor. She'd never really contemplated or desired to talk to those who had passed on. She figured they were either asleep, or maybe celebrating. Who knew, really? But sometimes, of late, she longed to visit Ray's grave, and those of her sons. The thought came to her a couple of weeks after talking to Tom. She'd pretty much left things hanging with him. Although she'd signed the lease agreement for the property, he'd kept his distance.

Out walking of an early morning, she found her feet headed in the general direction of the old Sutter family cemetery. Towering black oaks kept the place deeply shaded and quiet, except for the singing of a million insects. She let herself in at the gate in the three-foot-high wrought iron fence and wandered among the ancient markers. Many of the names were familiar. She remembered standing here as a child, when someone of the older generation passed.

Outside the fence, there was another plot, bordered by smooth stones, neatly kept by someone. This is where the Sutter family servants were buried. Miss Lucy's mother was the last of that lot. On the other side, and less neatly kept, were the graves of the Sterling family. Granny and Grandad lay there, but Annabelle's mother had been buried in the cemetery behind the First Southern Baptist Church.

The raucous cry of a jay bird pierced the air and sent shivers down Annabelle's spine. Why was she even here? She turned and started back, but stopped near the granite stone marker that belonged to Miss Lillian's mother. A woman who had always been kind to Annabelle, especially after she and her mother had been turned out of the Wade home. Annabelle laid her hand on top of the stone.

"I wish you were still here, Miss Lutie. You always had a good word for me. You could turn most any bad circumstance into something good." Annabelle blew out a puff of air as she lowered herself to the ground beside the grave. "I've been pining away these last few weeks, and I don't know why. I went through most of the entire first year, keeping my head up, not letting myself be overcome by the heavy weight of sorrow—" Her voice broke. She took a moment to get control.

The crack of a branch sent chills scrambling up her neck. Annabelle pivoted, following the sound. A small, dark figure stood outside the wrought iron fence.

Was it an apparition?

"Beggin' yer pardon, Miss Annabelle, didn't mean to intrude."

Miss Lucy. Annabelle released the breath she'd held. "You're not intruding. I can't even tell you why I'm here."

"I overheard that last part, and I have an opinion, if you care to hear it."

Annabelle pushed up from her position on the ground and brushed off the back of her skirt. "I'd love to hear it, Miss Lucy. You're one of the wisest women I know."

The woman stepped nearer and rested her gnarled hands on the fence. "I don't know about that. But I will say, it was full-speed ahead all them months, with you making a new life for yourself, Miss Connie, and the baby. You gave yourself no time to properly mourn the passing of your loved ones. I know that all too well, having done it myself. Now, Miss Connie is fixing to marry Mr. Alton, and you're left looking in life's mirror. What you've pressed down deep inside for so long, is needing to come out, and it will. One way, or the other."

Miss Lucy's warm tone calmed Annabelle's frayed nerves. "I know you're right. I knew all along I was · pushing it aside, but I hoped that if it would just get left long enough, I'd forget."

"Some thangs we don't forget. We can't forget. Like that one little grave there in the middle." She pointed to the servants' section. "I don't know if you remember my boy."

While Miss Lucy spoke, Annabelle stepped carefully among the graves to join her. "I remember." Miss Lucy's second son had been run over when he was only ten. It was such a tragedy, folks all around gathered for the funeral.

Miss Lucy pressed a balled fist against her chest. "I'll carry that ache to my grave."

Annabelle stood beside her, gazing at the small marker on the boy's grave. Standing there, sharing in the woman's deep sorrow filled a need in her, like water to a parched soul.

"We's like clay pots, sista. They needs to be baked in a real hot oven till they's set and they true color rises to the surface."

Annabelle opened her mouth, but closed it again as Lucy's wisdom pierced her heart. "We have certainly been through the fire."

"We shore enough have, Miss Annabelle. You and me, we sisters in loss. I'll be praying for you to heal up inside, so you can go on. Set one foot in front of the other, that's how you start. I know you can, 'cause you strong."

Annabelle draped an arm around Miss Lucy's shoulder. "So are you."

Miss Lucy curled her lips into a smile, revealing only a couple of teeth. "Well, I reckon I best get on back. I put up a mess of my summer soup early this morning. I'll bring y'all some."

Annabelle stood beneath the shade of the black oaks, long after Miss Lucy's footsteps faded into the distance. For a little while longer, she remained there, recounting Miss Lucy's words. *Tried in the fire.* She pressed her hand to her cheek as tears welled in her eyes. "I'm about done. I don't know how to go on. Just show me where to go from here."

Miss Lucy had said to put one foot in front the other. "That's how you start," Annabelle forced her feet forward and began to walk toward the old wagon road. Back toward home.

Connie and Momma were just finishing the dishes when someone knocked at the front door. Judith was entertaining Joseph, so Connie dried her hands.

Without turning around, Momma said, "It's probably Alton, anyway."

Connie stepped through the door into the parlor and came to a complete halt. The man standing outside the screen door looked just like—but it couldn't be. "Dad?"

He removed his hat. "You going to open the door, or am I not welcome?"

He'd lost most of his hair, had a few more wrinkles in his ruddy face, but the eyes—the voice—definitely Dad's. All the way from Maui. Here. On their front porch. She pushed open the screen door. "Dad, it really is you—but how?" No vehicle sat in the drive.

Dad chuckled as he stepped inside. "The usual way, daughter. I used my feet."

"All the way from … where?"

He laughed again. "I wish I'd brought Lila's Brownie. I know she'd want a picture of your face right now." He grabbed her in his arms and gave her a squeeze. "And I suppose that woman is your mother-in-law?"

Connie stepped back, both hands covering her mouth.

"I'm Annabelle Cross." Momma thrust her hand toward Dad. "It's a pleasure to meet you, Mr. Pruitt."

He shook her hand. "You might as well call me Mac. Most do."

"Come on in, Mac." She waved a hand toward Judith and the baby. "That young lady in the corner is my cousin Judith. And I reckon you can guess whose baby she's holding."

His gaze rested on Connie's face. "Is this my grandson?"

Connie couldn't seem to find her tongue. Tears stung her eyes as she nodded. It was too much to expect a person to recover so quickly from such a shock.

Judith answered for her. "This is Joseph."

"He's a good-sized boy. Looks like his daddy, from what I remember." He set his hands on his hips and faced his daughter. "I'll have a couple more grandbabies before the year's out."

Finally, Connie sucked in enough air to push out a word or two. "I heard."

"Have a seat, Mac." Momma patted the back of the best chair. "Can I get you a glass of iced tea?"

He settled in. "Iced tea sounds real good, Mrs. Cross. That old wagon road was a longer walk than I intended. Alton said I should wait for him to finish chores, but I needed to stretch my legs after that long bus ride."

"You came by bus?" Connie sat across from him. Confusion clouded her brain. She still had trouble believing he was here.

"By air, rail, and bus. Oh, and Ford truck, this last little bit." He grinned.

Connie searched her mind for a word, a hint, dropped by Alton, but came up empty. If he meant to surprise her, it worked.

Dad leaned forward. "I know we didn't part on such good terms."

How well she remembered his last words. "That boy'll leave you high and dry. And when he does, don't expect me to pay your way home." Well, Joseph had left her, but in good hands. His mother's. Connie had never desired to go back home to Maui, even after Joseph died. But there was something different about her Dad. He was almost nice, even smiling, like he was glad to see her.

"That's in the past, Dad."

Momma returned with a glass of tea.

Dad accepted it, but set it on the side table. He clasped his hands together, and looked at Connie. "Still, I need to acknowledge that I made a mistake. It was wrong of me to say what I said to you. I'm sorry."

"Thank you for that, Dad. I'm sorry for the way I

acted, too."

He touched her knee. "So, we're square, now?"

She nodded.

He relaxed against the back of the chair. "Your young man wrote to me."

"Alton?"

"You got another young man?"

Connie smiled into his eyes. Teasing. That was new. "No, just Alton."

Momma sat beside Connie, and patted her hand.

"Nice ring on your finger." He picked up his glass and sipped the tea. "Seems like he intends to take real good care of you and the boy."

"Did he … pay your way here?"

"No, but he did invite me to the wedding. He wrote that letter to ask for my blessing. I told him you were on your own now, you didn't need my blessing. But I was happy to give it, since he seemed such a nice, polite young man. Educated too, judging by his way with the written word." He sipped his tea. "I met his mother, today. She's good people."

Judith made herself comfortable on the floor with Joseph propped against her.

The baby's head bobbled a bit as he raised big eyes to gaze at Dad. The sight brought a smile to Connie's lips.

When Dad cleared his throat, she examined his face and noticed for the first time how tired he was.

"I don't know if your sisters told you, I sold the farm

to one of those big corporations. Made a decent amount of cash in the deal, so I paid for my own trip. I had a stop to make on the way in. You remember my family came from Topeka? I grew up there."

"I thought your family had all died." Had he lied about that? She still couldn't quite make out the change in him.

"I don't have family there anymore, but an old friend wrote, asked me to stop in. He's a retired journalist. I invited him to visit me on Maui." He looked at Connie as though he expected a response.

"Do you think he will?"

"I hope so, especially since Hawaii's going to be a state soon. He could do an article, call it a work expense."

Momma spoke up. "A state? Surely not. It's so far away."

"It is, but it's good, valuable property. It's already a big moneymaker among vacationers. And a whole lot of that money goes into American pockets. You know, they've pretty much taken over."

He finished his tea and set the glass down. "I hope I'm not putting you ladies out, taking you away from work or something."

Momma waved it away. "Our day's pretty much done. We're happy for the company. Will you be staying with us?"

Connie pulled in a quick breath. Why hadn't she thought to ask that? He must think her so rude.

"Oh, no, your little house is full. Alton and Mrs. Wade

already offered to let me stay over there. They have me tucked away in a nice corner room with a view of the cotton fields. I'm happy as a lark."

"How long will you be able to stay?" Connie hoped he meant to stay at least a month or more. She'd like to have time to get to know the new man Dad had become. And why—what had changed him? He hadn't yet said.

"I planned on staying two or three weeks. I don't want to wear out my welcome, and I know this is a busy time for a cotton planter."

"Well, the crop was so late going in this year, we'll have a break till it's ready to pick." Momma tapped her fingers on the chair's arm. "Of course, we have other crops that'll be coming in."

The sound of a vehicle drew Connie's attention and sent a shiver down her spine. If only she sat nearer the door, she'd run outside to greet her "young man," as Dad called him. He deserved a big kiss for making this happen.

Alton didn't bother to knock. He opened the screen and stepped inside. His gaze went instinctively to Connie's adoring face. He longed to scoop her up and hold her in his arms.

"There he is," Mac Pruitt said. "I was beginning to think I'd have to make my way back in the dark."

"I'm sorry to be so late getting here. One of the calves had an injured leg. Miss Annabelle, Connie, Judith—how are you?"

Momma stood and took Alton's hand. "You must be plumb worn out, Alton. Why don't you sit down?"

"Well, normally I would, but it's so late, I reckon I better get Mac home. He's had a long day."

Mac stood and took a step forward. "I am feeling a bit tired, though I hate to leave such good company. But tomorrow's another day."

Connie leaned forward to pick up Joseph, before following her dad toward the door.

Alton waited for Connie, while Mac and Momma passed through to the porch. As she drew near, he smiled into her eyes. "I hope you'll all come over in the morning. After I'm finished with chores, we'll have time to visit."

"What about Chase?"

"He'll be fine." He laid his palm against the small of her back as she stepped outside. "I meant what I said the other day. I should never have made that promise."

"But you did. I don't want trouble with you-know-who."

"There won't be." Her sweet smile awakened a fierce hunger in him. He'd settle for a kiss, but even that evaded him as she moved toward her dad to wish him goodnight.

Mac rumpled Joseph's soft mop. He kissed Connie's cheek. "See you tomorrow. I'm looking forward to getting to know my grandson."

Alton climbed into the truck and pulled the door shut. Focused on Mac and Momma, he failed to notice that Connie had slipped around to his door.

"Da-da," Joseph said, with a happy giggle.

Alton turned toward the sound. "Did he just say dada?"

Connie's broad smile lit her eyes. "I believe he did."

Alton reached for Joseph's hand and kissed it. "Goodnight, sweet boy." He leaned forward to kiss Connie's cheek, but she turned at the last moment to catch it full-on. What a woman.

Chapter Twenty

Tom stood still, arrested by the sight of Annabelle walking up the church steps looking mighty chummy with a strange man. Someone he had never seen before. A memory pricked at the back of his mind, but he couldn't bring it forward. He rubbed his chin. What was it Thelma had told him last night at dinner? She talked so much sometimes, he tended to tune her out once in a while.

After Annabelle disappeared from view, Tom turned and unlocked the pharmacy door. One thing he'd never considered—Annabelle finding someone else. Someone who'd go to church with her. Could he live with that?

Usually so comforting, the empty store now seemed dark and lifeless. He'd planned to mix up a brown cow to drink while going over his books, but his stomach had turned. He got out his work but found himself staring at a blank wall. He couldn't concentrate. He even pulled out the plans he'd approved for his new house, but the effect on his nerves drove him to slap an open palm on the desktop. The sound echoed throughout the store.

He never should have gotten his hopes up. Why had he professed his feelings to her? Now, his humiliation was complete. He swiveled in his chair and leaned forward, elbows on his knees. If he was a drinking man, he'd surely want one right now. Something good and strong.

A shaft of sunlight, dappled with the shadows of leaves dancing, caught his attention. Surely, he'd feel better outside in the fresh air. Maybe take the plans and walk through the plot. The surveyors had already staked it out. His gut roiled at the possibility of living beside a woman who would never love him the way he loved her. Unrequited love. That's what they called it. He knew all about that.

On the way out, he grabbed an ice cold soda from the cooler. He uncapped the bottle before heading out the door. Arrived at the property, he checked his watch. With very little traffic on a Sunday morning, he'd made the trip in twelve minutes. He left his car on the side of the road, and climbed the small incline to the gap in the fence. One day this week, Alton would run another fence, closing off the back end of the property Tom had leased. Things were moving forward.

Except those that were moving sideways. Annabelle. He sighed. Had he really been such a dreadful sinner that nothing would ever go his way? He crouched in front of a line stretched taut to indicate the front of the house.

He used to think God had smiled on him. He had his own business—a good and profitable one. He lived in a beautiful setting. Though an old house, he'd owned it free and clear. He had family and friends who loved him. And he was his own man. What else could he ask for? Until Annabelle had moved back home and turned his neat little world upside-down.

Tom pushed up from his crouched position and removed his hat. He glared at the bright mid-morning sky. "Lord, I know it's been a long time since I talked to you. I'm empty. That's the truth, plain and simple. I thought I knew what you had planned, but turns out, I don't really know anything. My expectations led me astray. My hopes are dashed."

He slapped his hat against his thigh. "If I have any right to ask anything of you, it's to take away this powerful love I feel for … Annabelle. I'd rather live the rest of my life alone than go through the kind of pain I feel right now."

Inside the plot-lines of the house, he gazed down at the parched earth. Just over an hour ago, he'd been feeling a thrill right here, imagining the finished home, warm and vibrant. He turned and looked toward the whitewashed Sterling house where Annabelle lived. Longing filled his heart. He'd wanted to give her everything. Actually, he already had. He'd made the changes to his will. What a sap he'd become. His lawyer would think he was a very foolish fellow.

He kicked at a clod of dirt. No use in worrying about

it. He might as well suck it up. Most likely, his prayer went nowhere. What had he ever done to deserve anything from God? Well, quite a few things came to mind. Times he'd given money, food, and goods to those in need, just out of the goodness of his heart. He hadn't done it for recognition, or to gain any standing with the Father in Heaven.

"Let my prayer stand, if it's Your will, Lord. If that other man will make Annabelle happy, and it's Your plan for her life, I can live with that. She deserves happiness, and I reckon she deserves a man who will go to church with her. It's what she wants, so that's what she should have." He set his hat on his head and gazed up again. "I trust it to You, Father, to give her what she needs."

On the way home from church, Dad shared the story of Connie's sister Lana's wedding, and how proud he'd been during a father-daughter dance with her. He turned to Connie. "Will there be dancing at your wedding?"

She caught Alton's glance in the rear-view mirror before answering her dad. "Our church doesn't allow dancing."

"Well, that's good, I guess. I'd hate to miss dancing with my eldest daughter at her wedding."

In Connie's wildest imagination, she'd never considered such a thing. This new person her Dad had become intrigued her more with each passing moment spent in his presence. The past couple of days, she'd watched him work with Alton on the farm, interact with Chase, entertain Joseph, and even pet Samson. He'd never been one to care for pets. They were too much bother, and took food from the children's mouths.

She listened as he carried on an intelligent conversation with Alton in the front seat, regarding the latest farming techniques. Who was this man?

Nearly drawing to a full stop in the middle of the road, Alton pointed out one of his better stands of cotton.

Connie barely suppressed a yawn. At this rate, it would be evening before they reached home. Momma and Miss Lillian were unconcerned. Each looked as though they hung on every word exchanged between the two men.

As they pulled in the drive, Dad spied something in the distance and pointed it out. "Who's that man standing near your house, Miss Annabelle?"

Momma squinted toward the house. "My goodness. I don't even know how you can see so far off."

"I've always had twenty-twenty vision. Could've been a pilot, but I wasn't interested."

After Alton put the car in park, he lowered his head to peer out the window. "Looks like Tom. He's probably checking on the stake-out for the house."

Once again, Connie puzzled over Momma's expression at the mention of Tom. She still hadn't been able to find out what had happened between those two.

Momma always changed the subject or just clammed up.

Dad opened the rear passenger-side door for Miss Lillian. "Tom—have I met him yet?"

Miss Lillian headed for the porch. "He's another Franklin. Cousin to Thelma's husband, Riley."

Alton opened Connie's door and helped her out of the car. Joseph was fast asleep in her arms. Once she was safely standing, he addressed Dad. "You'll find we're all cousins down here. All of us are related some way, somehow."

Dad laughed. "It was the same thing back home in Maui, only worse, probably. They didn't really care how close a family relation they married." As Connie stepped near him, Dad put an arm around her waist. "Did you tell them about your royal blood?"

Connie's jaw went slack. "No, and don't you do it, either."

He chuckled. "Why not? It's always fun to watch people's expressions."

"Dad."

He shrugged. "I'm thinking it might solve some of your problems, if folks knew."

She leveled her gaze at him. What did he know about her problems?

"I was talking to Miss Lillian. I thought if people knew about your bloodline, they might not be so judgmental."

"I doubt it would make any difference, especially if they knew how well populated that royal bloodline is." She gave him a wry grin. Practically everybody she knew growing up, was some degree of royalty. It held little importance to her.

"What's happened to you, Dad?"

"What do you mean?"

Connie narrowed her eyes at him. "You know what I mean. You're different. What has changed?"

He rested his arm at her waist and steered her toward the house. "I'm a new man, daughter. Your young man jump-started that change. He helped lift a tremendous burden. And when that happened, it was like I could see, after being blind most of my life."

He related the story of what had happened in his youth, the event that drove him to run away. When he came to the part Alton had played, his voice broke.

She noticed moisture glistening in his eyes.

He met her gaze. "Last thing I did before leaving Hawaii—I stopped in to visit your sister Leila. Went to church with her. They have an outdoor service, and I sat there, gazing at God's beautiful creation all around me. For the first time in my life, I understood what it all meant. He'd brought me full circle."

He sighed. "I remembered sitting in church with my mother, and her telling me how Jesus had a plan for my life. When your sister's congregation started singing *Amazing Grace*, I knew the Lord had released me from guilt. I was forgiven. My past had been cleansed. By the time I got on the plane to leave Hawaii, I felt like a brand new man."

Connie brushed at tears. "I love you, Dad."

He kissed her forehead. "I love you, too, darling. Let's go in now, and join the others. Dinner's waiting."

Alton enjoyed the lively conversation at Sunday dinner. Mac certainly added a vibrant element to their typically quiet household. Connie had apparently inherited his sense of humor, and mischievous nature. But that was really where the likeness ended. Sure, she favored him in looks some, but tended toward a quieter, more introverted way. Mac was ready to tell all and pretty much had. Alton figured he already knew more about Mac Pruitt than Connie.

"I feel I can talk to you," he'd told Alton. "Say things I haven't even been able to share with my family."

He'd struggled most of his life with alcoholism. Alton didn't wonder why. The man had carried a heavy load of guilt since that tragic car accident. He'd seen untold horrors in the aftermath of the attack on Pearl Harbor. He'd received a Medal of Honor for his service. Mac hadn't said it, but Alton understood he'd saved numerous lives.

"I rounded up as many fishing boats as I could," he told Alton. "We pulled bodies out of the water. We didn't care if they were American or Japanese. We just fished them out. Some were still breathing. We delivered those to the base hospital. It was a mess, let me tell you."

But at the dinner table, Mac kept the subject as far from his personal life as possible. He delighted Mother and Miss Annabelle with vivid tales of the islands.

Alton fingered his napkin and tried not to stare at Connie throughout dinner. He could drown in that gaze of hers. One thing Mac had asked him, Alton was now considering. Why wait till mid-November? Why not move up the wedding, so Mac could attend. Alton meant to discuss this with Connie if ever they had a moment alone. Was it normal to be jealous of everyone—to want every word, every glance sent his way—not shared with others?

"Can I have two minutes of your time?"

Connie's softly spoken question startled Alton out of his mental wanderings. Two minutes. How about a lifetime? Her smile hinted she'd read his mind.

"Dad brought me some hibiscus seeds. We don't know if they'll grow here, but it would be utterly amazing to have them. I'd like your help deciding where to plant them."

Was she really talking about planting? Surely, she didn't mean to plant flowers in the fall. "You mean in the spring?"

Mac spoke up. "I told Connie you might consider planting a few of the seeds a bit deep after the first frost. I've been told the winters aren't so bad here. They might do better if they're already in the soil. Come spring, they'll shoot up faster and you won't have that shock of transplanting seedlings. You can grow some in the hothouse too, just in case it doesn't work."

Alton shrugged. "They're tropical, these … hibiscus? I don't know that they'll survive here, but I guess it won't hurt to try." In spring, she'd be living here. With him. Something like true joy filled him up inside.

Mother signaled from her place at the table. "Why don't you three go on out to the garden? Annabelle and I will clean up."

"If you don't mind," Mac said, "I have a standing appointment with that comfortable chair in the parlor. I'm still not fully acclimated to this time zone."

It seemed everyone had something to do, which suited Alton very well. He led Connie out to the flower gardens in the back yard. Though it was late summer coming on to fall, blooms were everywhere. Bees buzzed and butterflies flitted from flower to flower.

Samson dashed ahead of them, sniffing the path.

Connie patted the dog's head before moving past him. "The hibiscus plant gets tall, so we need to be sure and plant them where they won't block anything. Have you ever seen one?"

"I don't believe I have."

"Well, they're beautiful. Dad brought seeds from red, as well as the native yellow. On the islands, they're evergreen, but I don't know how they'll do here. The blooms are trumpet-shaped and they get about this big." She showed him with her hands slightly rounded to a circumference of seven or eight inches.

"That's a big bloom. And you say the plants get tall? So maybe toward the back. How about near that big chimney over there?" He pointed out the largest of the remaining brick chimneys from the old shanties. They'd planted a climbing rose on it, but a taller plant to the side wouldn't hurt. He walked toward the spot and she followed, still going on about flowers and her plans for spring. They were now far enough away from the house he could talk without fear of being overheard. He looked at her, noticed how the sun glinted on her dark hair. If only she wasn't so achingly beautiful. All he could think of was what it was like to kiss those sweet lips, run his fingers through her silken hair. This line of thought would soon land him in trouble.

She stopped talking and gazed up at him. "What?"

He swallowed. His throat went dry all of a sudden. But the time had come. He had no idea how she'd react. "I was talking to your dad, and it occurred to me, that we might want to … move up the wedding date … just so he could be here for it." He clamped down on his lower lip and watched her face.

She was quiet so long, he thought she might be upset, but she didn't look mad. She wandered along the path a little farther from the house, her eyes on the field behind the garden.

The minutes ticked away. Alton stuck his hands in his pockets and kicked at a clump of grass.

She turned to face him. "I think that's a good idea,

Alton. Even though it means we can't go anywhere … afterward."

The sun broke through the clouds that had shadowed his heart. "Well, we could take a few days, if it's not so late in the year. Maybe mid-September? That way, I'd be back in plenty of time for the full picking." He couldn't keep from smiling like an idiot.

She laid her hand at the base of her throat. "That's just three weeks away."

"It's mighty fast, I know."

Her hand moved from her throat to touch her lips. She looked shy, all of a sudden, like a little girl.

He wanted to kiss her in the worst way. He sucked in a deep breath and took a step nearer. She glided right into his waiting arms. Would he ever get used to this? How she just seemed to fit so perfectly against him? Her lips tasted sweet, like the baked apples they'd enjoyed at dinner. He didn't want to break away, but he knew he must. If all went well, he'd only have to wait three more weeks.

Chapter Twenty-One

After the Sunday night service, Alton brought Chase home for his last week at Sutter's Landing. The boy had made a list of all the things he wanted to do before the week ended, which included an overnight camping trip. He'd chosen the spot above the lake, so they could fish for their supper.

Alton looked at the calendar. "How about Thursday for the camp-out?"

Chase sent two fists into the air. "Yes!"

Alton noted it on the calendar. "Thursday, it is."

During Monday morning's breakfast, Chase set his fork down, and with a serious expression on his face, asked, "Uncle Alton, do you think it would be all right if we ask Mr. Mac to go camping with us? He told me he likes to camp out, and especially loves to fish."

The boy had caught him with his mouth full, so Alton finished chewing. He took a swig of coffee. "If you don't mind him going along, I think it would be nice to invite him."

Chase grinned. "Good. Because I was just thinking, it would be bad to leave him here alone with all these women talking about weddings."

"Ha!" Mother drew back to glare at Alton.

It's a good thing Alton didn't have a full mouth this time. He chuckled. Maybe the boy was spending a little too much time with Mac. That statement sounded just like him. He grinned and shook his head at Mother.

She dabbed at her mouth with her napkin, but didn't make any comment.

Alton passed the plate of biscuits. "Do you want to ask him? I'm sure he'll be down shortly."

Chase nodded as he helped himself to another biscuit.

"Ask me what?" Mac strode into the dining room. "Miss Regina, that coffee sure smells good."

Regina filled Mac's cup. "How you want your eggs this morning, Mr. Mac?"

This time, Alton did have a mouthful of coffee he barely managed to swallow. Usually, Regina made whatever she felt like, and you ate it. But she'd taken to Mac right away. Treated him like royalty. Kind of the way she treated his daughter. How would she behave when Connie lived here all the time? He should be happy the two got along so well. Peace in a man's household was surely a treasured thing.

After greeting Mother, Mac settled into his chair. He

peered at Chase over the rim of his cup.

Chase turned a hopeful gaze on Mac. "I was wondering if you'd like to go camping with us."

Mac set the cup down and picked up his napkin. "That sounds like fun. I'd like that."

They spent the rest of breakfast making plans.

Mother excused herself to go make some calls, but before she could start, the phone rang. Mac and Chase carried on so, he couldn't make out the conversation.

From the next room, she waved for him to come, so Alton excused himself. He sure hoped it wasn't bad news.

"That was Marla," she said as he entered the side parlor. "You won't believe this, but Edris wants to bake your wedding cake. Marla told me it's just fine with her— and Jensen. Said it was the least they could do for all you've done this summer. What do you think of that?"

"I'm not sure what to think." Had the earth stopped turning?

"Well, I think it's wonderful. See, what you did for Chase this summer, it made a real impact. Maybe things are going to change now."

Alton hated to see Mother get her hopes up again, but he didn't want to appear negative, either.

"Prayers do work, we know that. We've seen some real miracles this season." That was certainly true. He hoped he was wrong, but he suspected Jensen of an ulterior motive.

Jensen stopped by just before noon on Wednesday. He timed his visits well, knowing they'd be at the house around noon for dinner.

"Won't you come in and have dinner with us?" Mother called from the doorway.

Alton winced at the hopeful look on her face as his brother uttered a well-practiced refusal.

"No, thank you, Mother. I'm on my way to an appointment. Just in the area, so thought I'd stop by." Jensen's gaze settled on Mac and Chase as they approached from the barn.

Samson ran ahead of them, barking a warning.

Alton kept a watchful eye on his brother. What did he think of his son spending time with Connie's dad?

Jensen frowned, but didn't make his usual complaint about barking dogs. He sniffed. "Chase is fond of Mr. Pruitt."

"They get along very well."

Jensen leaned against the side of his car and picked at his nails. "It's not often a boy gets to spend time with a celebrated veteran of Pearl Harbor." He sucked his teeth and mashed his lips together in a flat line. "I'm thinking we should have him over to the house this Sunday."

Alton had no words. None at all.

"All of y'all should come—Mother, Miss Annabelle,

and your intended—of course."

Alton nodded. "That's nice of you."

Jensen looked down at his feet as though contemplating Alton's remark. "It was Marla's suggestion." He cleared his throat. "We're pleased with how Chase has behaved this summer. He's benefited by his time out here."

"We've enjoyed having him. He's a good boy."

Jensen nodded. "Well, I'd best get going. I'm sure Marla will call Mother and repeat the invitation, so I'll see y'all on Sunday."

"All right." Alton half expected to hear a trumpet sound. Surely it was time for the rapture.

As Jensen backed out of the drive, Chase lifted his hand.

Jensen gave a curt nod.

After a moment's hesitation, the boy ran to the porch to wash up for dinner.

Alton stood still, ruminating the conversation with his brother. He hardly knew how to tell Mother. She was not going to believe this.

Connie found Judith packing clothes in her small brown suitcase. Ginger kept lying down on top of the folded clothes. Each time, Judith moved the cat back to the cot.

Connie laughed. "You silly cat. Come here." She picked the cat up and held it in her arms.

"I can't believe the summer's nearly over." Judith refolded a blouse before adding it to the suitcase. "It seems I've hardly had time to turn around, and I'm going home."

"We're sure going to miss you. And I know Joseph will miss his playmate."

"Don't make me cry, now. I know I'll see him once in a while, but he's growing so fast."

Still holding the cat, Connie plopped down on Momma's bed. "Oh, you'll be learning so many new things, and meeting so many new people, you'll barely have time to miss any of us."

Judith giggled. "You're probably right about that."

"Are you excited?"

"Oh, yes. I can't wait to get moved in to the dorm room and meet my roommate. But won't it be hard? Do you think I'll have any trouble?"

Connie laughed. "Not you, no. It's different, but I know you're a quick learner. And you're so outgoing, you'll blend right in and be settled in no time."

"I hope so. But I sure do wish I could be here to help you get ready for the wedding. I'm so glad y'all moved it up. It's so romantic."

Ginger jumped from Connie's arms to the cot, settling back down on top of the folded clothes.

Connie tugged Judith's pony tail. "You're going to

have to take that cat with you, I think."

"I wish I could." She stroked Ginger's fur. "But from the looks of it, she's going to multiply in a few weeks."

"What?" Connie glared at the cat. "Oh, no."

Judith nodded. "Yes, I think so. Probably about the time you get married."

"Oh, my goodness. Momma!"

Momma stuck her head in the door. "What is it?"

"Did you know Ginger is … in a family way?"

Momma covered her mouth. "Oh, dear. Well, it was only a matter of time, I expect."

All three jumped when a knock sounded at the door.

Momma turned to look. "I don't recognize that person, but he's holding a large box."

Connie jumped up from the bed and nearly rammed into Judith as they both made a beeline for the door.

"Hello? Anybody home?" The man called through the screen door.

Momma's excited voice rang out. "Yes, we're coming."

"I've got a delivery here for a Mrs. Connie Cross." He held up not one, but two boxes. One was a large flat, white box. The other was round, with vertical stripes.

Momma pushed the door open.

Connie stepped forward. "I'm Connie Cross."

The man handed her the boxes. She took them and turned to go back inside.

"Thank you," Momma said to the man.

He tugged the brim of his hat. "You have a real good day, ladies."

"What is it?" Momma and Judith asked in unison.

Connie laughed. "We'll know when I open them."

"It's from *Rosenbloom's*," Momma pointed to the name imprinted on the box. She looked at Connie. "You don't think—"

Connie fumbled with the lid, laid it aside, and folded back the tissue paper. She sucked in a breath. "Oh."

Judith grabbed Connie in a side hug. "Oh, it's so exciting."

"But who—?" Who had done this?

Momma touched her cheek. "I'm sure it was Miss Lillian. She told you she wanted to buy your dress."

Connie lifted the pale yellow jacket. It was so soft, so beautiful. And so dear. Could she really accept such an expensive gift?

"The other box is a hat, I'll bet." Judith reached out then drew her hands back. "Can I open it?"

Momma shook her head. "No, let Connie open it."

Connie laughed. "Go ahead, Judith. That way, I can watch."

Judith's hands shook a little as she carefully removed the lid, and spread wide the tissue paper. "Ooooh."

"It's lovely." Momma touched its satiny-smooth surface.

Connie picked up the pillbox hat with matching netting, the exact color of the suit. She stepped quickly to the mirror in the bedroom and tried it on.

Momma drew the netting down to just below the chin. "It's like a veil. Oh, and it smells like *Rosenbloom's* doesn't it?"

Connie grabbed at the hat as a sob formed in her throat. It was too much.

Momma took the hat from her and handed it off to Judith, who gently returned it to its wrappings.

"What is it, Pumpkin? Grab her a hanky, Judith."

Connie squeezed her eyes shut as tears ran down her cheeks. Why was she crying like this? Shouldn't she be happy? Or was she so overwhelmed with happiness, she didn't even recognize it?

Momma hugged her.

Judith pressed a hanky into her hand, and rubbed her back. "It's okay. It's just too beautiful, that's all."

"It's all happening so fast." Momma patted her hand. "Is that it, sweetheart?"

Connie nodded and blew her nose. "I think so. I'm not sure. I don't even know if I'm happy, or sad."

"I vote for happy," Judith said.

Connie giggled. In a moment, they were all laughing. And they were all wiping at moisture. The noise woke Joseph who gave a loud squeal. The sound sent them into more peals of laughter, especially when Judith noticed Ginger, standing just inside the room, eyes wide, back slightly arched.

Finally, the giggles subsided. Connie collapsed onto

the sofa. "Oh my, I don't know when I've laughed so hard."

Momma sat across from her, Joseph in her arms, happily clapping his hands.

Judith sat on the floor, still snickering. "I feel drunk."

Momma looked askance at her. "How do you know what that feels like?"

"I don't know it firsthand, just what I've seen in movies, and stuff."

Connie giggled. "It does feel good, doesn't it? Reminds me of that scripture, "A merry heart doeth good like a medicine."

Momma bounced Joseph on her lap. "A broken spirit dries up the bones. I believe it's in Proverbs."

"Seventeen-twenty-two," Judith said. "I had to memorize it for my Sunday School award." She giggled again.

"Oh my, let's not get that started." Momma handed Joseph to Connie. "Here, Mommy, take your boy. I'll get supper going." She pushed up from the sofa, and headed for the kitchen.

Judith picked at a loose button. "I sure wish we had a phone, so we could call Miss Lillian, see if she's the one that did this."

Momma glanced over her shoulder. "Oh, she's the one. I'm sure of it." She grinned at Connie before leaving the room. A moment later, she lifted her voice in song as she went about her work.

Judith got up. "Come on, Ginger, let's finish packing."

Connie sat back in the chair as Joseph began to nurse, her eyes on the two boxes sitting on the coffee table. In less than a month, she'd be Mrs. Alton Wade, living at Sutter's Landing. Joseph would have his own room, and Momma would be all alone. Tears pricked her eyes again. If anyone was strong enough to live on their own, it was Momma. But she wouldn't like it, Connie was fairly certain. Too bad she couldn't come live with them at Sutter's.

Or ... if Momma hadn't fallen out with Tom, she could marry him and live next door in a new house. One with a better view of the property. And she wouldn't be alone. Not only that, she'd have money. Connie suspected Tom did very well. After all, he could afford to build a new house. Yes, Momma could do much worse.

Except that thing about church attendance.

When Momma hit a crescendo, her voice cracked. Joseph rolled an eye toward his mother and smiled. When she sat him up, he gave a loud burp, bringing more giggles from Judith's room.

Momma stepped into the parlor, a potholder in one hand. "You know, you ought to start weaning him onto a bottle or a cup. You and Alton are going to want to go somewhere on your wedding night. I know Alton can't take much time away, but he might manage two or three days."

"You're right, I should." She patted Joseph's round tummy. "I think he's ready, don't you?"

Momma gave her a sideways grin and bobbed her head.

Connie peered into her baby's bright eyes. "So how do I do that?"

Chapter Twenty-Two

August 27, 1955

With a heavy heart, Annabelle kissed Judith goodbye. She waved her handkerchief until the car disappeared around the bend in the road. How she would miss that girl's bubbly good mornings. The bright sun warm on her back, Annabelle decided now would be a good time to walk over to the building site next door. She'd noticed the surveyors last week. Mac had seen Tom out there. She didn't want anyone to know, but her curiosity kept her feet moving forward. She ducked through the barbed-wire fence, looked all around to make sure no one was about, and strode quickly to the staked-out house.

An odd feeling—fleeting, but real—coursed through her. This could've been her house. She walked around the perimeter, wondering about the layout of the rooms. Would the kitchen window open to the meadow? Would there be a picture window? She'd always wanted one. Before anyone drove by and caught her, she slipped away, walking toward the back of the property where Alton had started on the new fence. Passing through the gap, she strode toward the garden, her heart and mind in turmoil.

If only Tom had waited another year or so before speaking of his love. Till the raw pain of loss subsides. But, maybe his strong feelings for her trumped common sense. What if she explained all this to him? She could try to make him understand. Try to convince him she needed more time. Maybe, just maybe …

But she'd be giving him hope. It may be false hope, setting him up for more hurt down the road if she never grew to love him as he should be loved. As more than a friend.

She bent to tug at a weed coming up at the garden's edge. As she tossed it aside, a new thought sprang to the surface. She brushed her hands together and gazed toward the east. Her lips curled into a smile as the pain in her heart eased. She closed her eyes. "Thank you, Lord, for giving me a glimpse of the future."

In the distance, Samson bayed. Connie's gaze searched the fields to the tree line. Somewhere over there, Alton, Chase, and Dad were setting up camp. Chase's happy summer was coming to an end. What a blessing he had turned out to be. Watching him with Alton, Connie had learned a few things about her future husband. Oh, she'd known he was a good man, but he'd proved himself a good father figure. He'd shown such patience as he taught the boy to whittle, tie knots in rope, and so many other things. She could well imagine him doing the same with her Joseph in a few years.

Glancing over her shoulder to the playpen in the shade, she smiled to see Joseph batting at a ball with his little fist. He'd had a rather fitful night. She hoped the fresh air would calm him. Momma found a slight swelling on his gums this morning and pronounced him teething. Connie figured it was a good thing she'd decided to wean him.

Her gaze returned to the field, where a slim, dark figure strode through the cotton. Willie's son, Anthony, crossed the plank bridge spanning the drainage ditch and headed toward the house. Connie picked up Joseph, and walked out to meet Anthony, wondering what news he carried.

He removed his hat at her approach. "Mornin', Miss Connie. Miz Wade sent me to ask if you and Miz Cross could come to dinner today. She said y'all need to make plans for the weddin'."

"You tell her we'd be happy to come."

Wasting no time, he turned, and headed back across the field.

Connie noticed Momma working in the garden, so she walked toward her. "Miss Lillian has invited us to dinner. She wants to make plans for the wedding."

Momma pushed at a stray curl dangling in front of her eyes.

Connie had seldom seen her outside without some type of head covering, a hat or bonnet. "I hope you don't mind. I told Anthony we'd be there."

"Well, I reckon it's a good time for it, with the men away overnight. We need to get the final preparations done." She examined her hands. "I better go in and get cleaned up first."

Just under an hour later, they set out across the old wagon road toward Sutter's Landing. Connie never tired of the view as the big, white house loomed ahead of them. With its wrap-around porches and large windows, it seemed friendly and inviting. When they stepped inside the kitchen door, she marveled at an odd sensation. As though it lived and breathed on its own, the house had welcomed her with open arms.

Miss Lillian turned from the sink, dried her hands on her apron just in time, as Joseph reached for her, a wide smile lighting his eyes. "That's what I like to see." She gave a loud smacking kiss on the baby's cheek. "Y'all come on in and sit down. I hope you don't mind eating in the kitchen. I've got a mess in the dining room. We'll talk about that after we eat."

Momma settled into the nearest chair. "We don't mind a bit. You know we always eat in the kitchen."

Miss Lillian spoke to Momma over Joseph's head. "Silly me. I forget you don't have a dining room. But y'all don't really need one. Your kitchen is a good size." She looked around her kitchen, as if searching for something. "Regina, where's that chair?"

Regina moved a high chair to the table.

Miss Lillian bounced Joseph on her lap. "I know he's not quite big enough to sit in it yet, but we thought you might like to see it. I had Anthony bring it down from the attic."

Connie ran a hand over the smooth, white painted wood. It was quite sturdy.

"My boys both used it, but as you can see, it's still in fine shape."

Connie bent to kiss Miss Lillian's cheek. "Thank you, you're always so thoughtful."

"Pshaw! It's just plain good sense to use what we have."

"While we're on the subject of gifts, I so appreciate what you sent from Rosenbloom's," Connie told her as she took a seat on the other side of the table.

Her lips set in a small smile, Miss Lillian raised her eyes to Connie's face. "Me? Oh, I would love to take credit, my dear, but I can't. It wasn't me."

A tremor ran through Connie. Had Alton done it—had he paid for her wedding outfit? Was that bad luck? Maybe not, as long as he hadn't seen it.

"No, your Daddy asked me what I thought he should get you as a wedding gift. I told him about that beautiful suit you tried on that day. We drove over to Jackson to see if they still had it. They did, along with a matching hat."

Moisture filled Connie's eyes. She covered her lips with her fingertips, struggling for control. It was from Dad. She'd considered asking him to buy her a dress, but just couldn't bring herself to do it.

"What a blessing," Momma echoed Connie's thoughts.

Miss Lillian nodded. "Yes, it is."

Regina poured iced tea before serving their meal. Thick, hot cornbread, fresh collard greens cooked with ham, creamed potatoes, and corn pudding. After serving the food, she gathered Joseph into her arms. "You come help me, little man, so your womenfolk can eat."

Miss Lillian gestured toward the food on the table. "I hope you don't mind all vegetables. We had ham yesterday. Regina loves to cook up a pot of greens with the leftovers."

Momma folded her hands in her lap. "This looks delicious."

They bowed their heads and Miss Lillian spoke the blessing. Afterward, she passed the potatoes to Connie. "Eat up, you're going to need your strength. We have a heap of planning to do this afternoon."

Dinner over, Connie followed Momma and Miss

Lillian into the dining room, while Regina's granddaughter, Pauletta, played with Joseph in a corner of the kitchen.

Miss Lillian hadn't been kidding about a mess. Piles of magazines, photo albums, and fabric topped the table. Connie's stomach roiled. This wasn't going to be easy.

Momma touched her shoulder. "It'll all work out, don't you worry."

"We'll have plenty of help available." Miss Lillian's crooked smile eased Connie's tension.

"You know, dear," she went on to say, "I was married right here—in the front parlor."

Connie drew back. "Were you?"

"I was, and it was beautiful. That intricately carved mantel served as a backdrop." She opened a photo album and pointed out a picture.

Connie gazed at the photo, taking in the lovely scene, especially the beautiful bride and handsome groom. She found features of Alton in both of them.

"I think we should plan on having the ceremony outdoors, with your garden in the background. Willie's working on an arch."

Momma crossed to the window and looked out. "What if the weather turns?"

Miss Lillian gave Connie a reassuring smile. "We'll have it in here. We can move all the furniture out to make plenty of room. I just think it's better to have it at Sutter's, rather than traveling in to church, returning to the house for the reception. Let's keep it simple. What do you think, dear?"

Connie agreed. "I like simple. Alton told me he'd spoken with Brother Nathan."

"Preacher said he's fine with whatever we decide." Miss Lillian closed the photo album and set it aside. "I don't know if you've considered it, but if we hold the ceremony out there, in the garden, some of your other friends will be able to attend."

"My other friends?"

Miss Lillian nodded toward the kitchen. "Regina and her family. Willie and Anthony, Miss Lucy and her lot."

Connie let that sink in. If they got married in the church, the colored folks could not attend? That didn't seem right. "They wouldn't come to church?"

Miss Lillian shook her head. "Oh, they could, and sit in the back. But if the sanctuary filled—and it probably will—there'd be no room. They'd have to move. You understand."

Connie did understand, all too well.

Momma turned from the window at the sound of a car in the drive.

Miss Lillian's face lit. "I believe the cavalry has arrived." She marched toward the door.

Connie glanced at Momma.

Car doors slammed, footsteps sounded on the porch, closely followed by feminine voices. The house quickly filled with Miss Lillian's friends, many of whom Connie recognized from church—even her Sunday school teacher. Bertha Tuley clapped her hands. "Let's get this wedding planned."

"Connie, what kind of wedding would you have in your native country?" Maggie's mother asked.

Behind Connie, Momma gave a quiet snicker. Connie looked at Mrs. Arnold. "It's really no different. Most native Hawaiians have taken the Christian faith." She folded an invitation and slid it into an envelope.

"Have they, really? I had no idea. I thought perhaps they'd have a luau or some such. Hula dancing, and all that." Mrs. Arnold swayed this way and that, possibly trying to emulate the dance.

Connie suppressed a smile, but realized the room had grown quiet. All eyes were upon her. "Well … some do have a traditional island celebration incorporated into their wedding. But the ceremony is usually held at their church. My family was not religious, so Joseph and I had a civil ceremony, but that was after I traveled to San Diego to meet him."

"I see," Mrs. Arnold said. "No pig roasting in a pit? My husband was really looking forward to that."

Miss Lillian set her glass down hard, and laughed out loud. "Oh, my land. Eliza, only your Arnie would say such a thing."

"Maggie is the one who brought it to our attention—" she paused, as though suddenly remembering something. Without a word, she returned to cutting tulle.

Connie could only imagine what Maggie had said about the wedding. Did she expect a heathen celebration? A human sacrifice at midnight?

Momma leaned close. "I don't expect to see her daughter there, do you?"

Connie laid a hand at the base of her throat. She supposed not, but it was too bad. If only she could figure out a way to patch things up.

With no one to drive them home, Connie and Annabelle made their weary way across the creek bed and walked up the old wagon road toward home. They'd just settled into a good stride when Samson galloped toward them, tongue lolling.

Connie glanced up, wondering if there was some sort of trouble, but her gaze landed on Alton's tall, lanky figure.

He strode up, a wide smile on his face.

She gave a little laugh. "Fancy meeting you here."

He held out his arms to Joseph, who went to him without a whimper. "I came over to check on the animals."

"Or maybe to get a break from all that guy talk,"

Momma chuckled under her breath.

Alton winked at Connie. "That, too."

Connie gave him a wide-eyed innocent look. "You didn't come just to see me?"

"No, I haven't missed you one bit." His grin widened, revealing the dimple.

Momma set a balled fist on her hip. "Alton Wade, that's an outright lie. Shame on you, and in front of an impressionable little one."

Joseph squealed and bounced in his arms.

Alton's guffaw echoed in the stillness of the late afternoon. "I've missed all of you. You both know that."

Momma covered her mouth and giggled.

Connie smiled as Alton blew raspberries on the baby's neck.

Joseph emitted a loud squeal and snuggled against Alton's chest.

"I believe Joseph wants to go back with me, and spend the rest of the evening with some manly men."

"Now that would be biting off more than you could chew." Momma cackled. "He's getting a tooth."

Alton looked at Joseph. "Is he? He'll soon be ready for venison." He brought his gaze back to Connie's. "By the way, Marla asked if she should plan for Joseph. Does he need anything special at dinner?"

In all the commotion, Connie had completely forgotten Sunday dinner at Jensen's.

"Maybe Thelma would like to take care of him,"

Momma said. "With him teething, he's likely to fuss. I'm not sure how Jensen would take that."

Connie agreed. "You're probably right. If she's not busy, I'm sure she'll be happy to do it. She's been asking."

Alton handed Joseph back to Connie. "Ok, I'll tell Marla he won't be there."

"I still can't believe Jensen invited all of us."

Momma sighed. "Maybe he's trying to do better."

Alton didn't say anything.

Connie tried to read his expression. His demeanor told her he wasn't convinced, and maybe didn't really trust Jensen. Her nerves danced a jig. She wasn't looking forward to Sunday dinner. In fact, she dreaded it, lest there be another confrontation. The memory of Alton slugging Jensen rose to the surface of her mind. Surely, they would behave themselves at a formal dinner.

Chapter Twenty-Three

"It is a mean gash." Tom dabbed away most of the coagulated blood on Billy Simpson's shin. He grabbed another bit of cotton, dipped it in peroxide and dripped the liquid into the wound.

The boy's mother peered at the wound. "It's not bubbling too awful bad. Is that a good sign?"

Tom nodded. "It bled a good bit and cleansed the wound." He wrapped the boy's shin with gauze and taped it. "You'll need to keep it clean and well covered for a few days till it scabs over." Finished with the bandage, he mussed the boy's hair. "Take it easy on that leg now. Let it heal up." He handed the boy a sucker.

Billy grabbed the sucker, but his mother caught his wrist. "What do you say, Billy Simpson?"

"Thank you, Mr. Tom."

Tom grinned. "You're welcome." He helped Billy down from the counter and led the way to the cash register.

"Fifty cents should cover it," he told Mrs. Simpson.

Her face relaxed into a smile. "God bless you, Tom." She dug in her pocketbook and pulled out the change.

Tom rang it up and waved to Billy as he held the door for his mother.

The door opened again and Bo entered, favoring his left knee. His face contorted in pain. "You get that delivery of BC powders, Tom?"

Tom nodded. "I think you might need to see the doc about that knee. Is there any swelling?"

"None to speak of." With a loud groan, he settled onto a stool at the counter. "Probably just a change coming in the weather."

With a nod, Tom stepped to the back counter for the BC powders.

Bo carried on the usual mischief with Arnie. "Don't give me none of that burnt coffee. Start a new batch. I can wait. You know I've got all day."

Tom set the box on the counter in front of Bo. "Here you go." He leaned against the counter. "Sometimes the cushion in your joint gets damaged, and the bones rest against one another. That's what causes the pain."

"Yep. That's exactly what it feels like—two bones grinding together. Hurts like the dickens sometimes."

"If it gets too bad, you're going to have to do something about it."

"Don't know what. Doc might want to cut on it, and you know what they'll do after that. An ole man like me, they'll slap me into that nursing home."

Arnie set a steaming cup of coffee in front of Bo.

Bo gave him a thumb's up and reached for the sugar. "I don't have anyone to help me, you know. And the kind of help I'd need if I couldn't get up and around, well … it'd be the nursing home for sure."

Tom had to admit that's probably what would happen. Bo had no family around to help him. He stepped to the register and added the powders to Bo's tab.

"You met the war hero yet?" Bo asked.

Tom glanced up from his paperwork. "What war hero?"

Bo held his coffee cup aloft. "I thought sure you'd be in the know. He's almost family, ain't he?"

Tom closed the register. What gibberish was the man talking? "I really don't know who you're referring to."

"I thought you were tight with the widow, Tom. I'm talking about Mackenzie Pruitt, the young Miz Cross's daddy. He's in town. All the way from Hawaii, for his daughter's weddin'."

Tom laid his hand on the marble top of the dairy bar. Was that the man he'd seen walking into church with Annabelle? He bit back a smile. So maybe she wasn't keeping time with someone else. "He's only in town for the wedding?"

Bo nodded. "'At's what I heard. Supposed to be a big write-up in the paper this week. Bentley interviewed him."

Tom scratched his head. "I've been so busy …" Once

again, his stubbornness had landed him in ignorance. He heaved a sigh. "Running the store, and the house."

"The word is, you're having a house built, right next door to the widow."

Bo's goofy chuckle usually irritated Tom, but his mind was racing ahead. If he got his work done and was ready to go at closing time, he could make it out to the building site before dark. If Annabelle was home, he just might get another invite to supper. That is, if she'd forgiven him for being such a dunce.

"You look like you could use a black cow, boss." Arnie held up a frosted glass.

Bo slapped his knee and cackled.

Tom shook his head. "I've got to get those orders finished."

On Friday afternoon, Connie left Joseph with Momma and walked to Sutter's Landing. Surely by now, the men would have returned from the camping trip. But as she drew near the creek bed, it was quiet, except the occasional lowing of cattle. No greeting from Samson. They had not yet returned.

The back door swung wide, and Miss Lillian stepped out. "You're just in time. Willie finished the arch. I was just going out to see it."

Connie waited as her future mother-in-law joined her near the side of the house. They walked around the old outdoor kitchen to the garden, where Willie stood.

He removed his hat as they approached.

Formed of thin slats of wood in a lattice pattern, the arch was painted white.

Willie set it in place.

Connie took in the scene. This is where she and Alton would stand, two weeks from tomorrow.

"You've done a wonderful job, Willie." Miss Lillian looked at Connie. "What do you think?"

"It's lovely."

"We'll weave in some vines, some blooms, and maybe some ribbon. Sally Rogers has a few ideas for it. She's a florist in town. It'll be real pretty."

The sound of an engine drew their attention to the barn as Alton's truck rolled beneath the overhang.

Willie set his hat on his head. "I best go help them unload."

Miss Lillian bent near the arch. "Look here, Connie. I want to show you something."

Connie wanted to excuse herself and run to the barn with Willie, but she supposed that would be rude. She moved closer, crouching to see what Miss Lillian pointed at—a round circle with a horse's head inside—very nicely carved.

"That right there is Willie's signature. He puts it on everything he creates. He could be a master carpenter, most anywhere. We're blessed to have him here."

"It's beautiful. He's an artist."

"Yes, he is." She straightened. "Have you ever heard him called by his surname?"

"I don't believe so." She rose, taking another long look at the excellent workmanship of the arch.

Miss Lillian crossed her arms at her waist and offered a satisfied smile. "It's Sutter—Willie Sutter."

Connie drew back. "Is he related?"

"In a way. He's a part of the original family, once owned by the Sutters. Many slaves took the name of their owners and kept it, even after they were freed."

"I feel I need to brush up on my history."

"You'll have plenty of opportunity for that." She raised her hand toward the house. "This place is filled with history."

They walked arm-in-arm through the breezeway that separated the outdoor kitchen from the main house. As they drew near the back porch, Alton drove the truck through the gap to the drive.

Anthony closed the gap and ran back to the barn.

Alton's strong gaze clamped on to Connie's. She gave him a welcoming smile, but from the looks of the trio in the truck, thought it best to maintain some distance.

Alton confirmed her opinion. "We all need a bath."

And a shave. She'd never seen him with a day's growth of beard. It highlighted his strong jaw.

Dad strode around the front of the truck and into her

line of vision. "We aren't fit for polite company."

Chase ran toward the horse trough, lying on its side. "Can I take my bath out here? One more time, please?"

Connie laughed to see such happiness shining from the boy's eyes. "I'll help him." She and Chase righted the trough. She picked up the hose and turned on the water.

Chase didn't waste any time. He peeled off his clothes till he stood in his undershorts and jumped in the trough. He laughed when Connie sprayed him with water.

When the water level in the trough reached a good height, she turned off the hose and settled on the back porch steps to watch. Samson loped over and sprawled at her feet. "I believe you wore Samson out." She bent to scratch the dog's head.

"We all got tired." Chase ducked beneath the water. When he came back up, he shook his head, sending droplets everywhere. "But we had so much fun, Miss Connie."

"Did you catch any fish?"

"Enough for our breakfast this morning. I wished we had more. I'm starving."

Smooth-faced and freshly bathed, Alton stepped onto the porch, a towel draped over his arm. He nodded at Connie before turning his attention to Chase. "Regina says half an hour before you need to get ready for supper." He draped the towel over the back of a chair.

Connie started to rise, but he held up his hand. "Stay put." He settled down next to her and smiled into her eyes.

"I saw you last night, but it seems like a week."

"Was it that bad?"

"Oh, no. We had a great time. Don't know if I could ask for better."

"Are you still thinking of doing this every year?" She nodded to Chase.

He looked toward the barn, then swept his gaze back to her. "I don't know. It would be naive to think there wouldn't be trouble. Not all boys are as well-behaved as this one."

"That's true."

"I need to pray on it some more."

She smiled into his eyes. "Good idea."

He took her hand and intertwined his fingers with hers. "You'll pray with me, won't you?"

"For the rest of my life."

The front porch rocking chair clicked and squeaked a merry tune as Annabelle fed little Joseph his bottle. He had taken to bottle-feeding right well as long as Connie wasn't anywhere to be seen. After he emptied it, she laid it aside, raised him up to a sitting position, and patted his back. He burped right away. She reckoned he was about old enough, he didn't need the help anymore.

With him snuggled into the curve of her arm, she

breathed in a deep draught of flower-scented air. The only interruption to the afternoon's peace and quiet was the occasional car or truck passing on the road, the drone of a bumblebee, the creak of her rocker. She looked down to find Joseph's eyes closed in slumber. He stayed asleep as she laid him in his bed.

Stopping by the stove, she stirred the soup, which she'd probably consume alone. She figured Connie would stay at Sutter's for supper. She'd urged her to, if they asked. But now, the quiet house haunted her. Loneliness clawed at her insides. No need in feeling sorry for herself, this would be her life, in just a couple of weeks.

She set to making cornbread to go with the soup. Before long, the smell of bread baking filled the small house. Annabelle set a bowl and spoon on the table and stepped to the refrigerator to get some ice.

"Anybody home?"

Tom's voice. She nearly dropped the ice tray. Setting it aside, she hurried to the kitchen door and spoke through the screen. "I'm in here."

He turned from looking through the other door to face her. "I see you are. I hope you don't mind, I was in the neighborhood, thought I'd stop by."

She held the door open. "Won't you come in? I was just about to have a lonely supper."

He gave a tremulous smile that set her heart to racing. Without hesitating, he strode forward. "Something smells mighty good."

"Nothing fancy, just soup and cornbread. I hope you'll join me."

He followed her inside. "You sure you don't mind giving up your lonely supper?"

Annabelle opened the oven and removed the skillet of cornbread. Good thing she had a chance to think about her answer. She almost told him there'd be plenty of lonely suppers to come, but he might say there didn't have to be. With a glance toward him, she set the pan on the stove. "I don't mind."

He pulled out a chair and perched on it. Just sat there, watching her. Not talking.

Annabelle poured tea, and set the food on the table. Tom shot up and pulled out a chair for her.

She settled in and bowed her head. Though tempted to pray over the man sitting next to her, she spoke a quick blessing, before ladling soup into their bowls.

"This is mighty tasty," Tom said, right away.

"Thank you, Tom." In between bites, she peeked at him. Time had certainly been kind to Tom. His hair was as thick as it had been in his youth. The gray at his temples made him look dignified. His white shirt was starched and professionally pressed. And he smelled good. Spicy. Heat crept into her cheeks. She shouldn't be thinking about these things.

Tom sat back in his chair. "I heard Miss Connie's father is in town."

"Yes, he's staying with Alton and Miss Lillian."

"Folks are saying he's a war hero."

"Pearl Harbor."

He set his spoon down. "Miss Annabelle, are you still upset with me?"

Annabelle sucked in a deep breath and exhaled slowly before meeting his gaze. "I'm not upset with you, Tom. But I do hope you understand. It's too soon."

He reached for her hand.

She didn't pull away, but allowed his fingers to curl around hers. Probably not the right thing to do. He might start thinking she'd softened toward him.

"Annabelle, I do understand. I've been thinking about it, and I realized I moved too fast. I just hope I didn't ruin our friendship."

Ignoring the sensations caused by his touch, she pushed her lips into a smile, hoping to reassure him. "I am fond of you, Tom. I'm just not sure …"

"It's okay—really. We don't have to talk about it."

She nodded. "More soup?"

He passed his bowl. "Yes, ma'am." While she took care of the refill, he helped himself to another slab of cornbread. "You're fond of me, huh?"

She smiled and handed him the soup.

His fingers brushed hers as he accepted the bowl. "I can live with that."

Try as she might, Annabelle couldn't suppress the thrill of his touch, or the warmth that crept into her cheeks.

Chapter Twenty-Four

Alton leaned a forearm against the kitchen door jamb and peered out at an apricot sky. The morning was almost too pretty for work. But he had no choice. Being away the last two days had set him back a bit. With the wedding coming up, it wouldn't do to get behind.

He pushed the screen open and headed for the barn. The clink of iron against iron echoed in the barn lot. What was Willie up to now?

But it wasn't Willie he found working on the tractor, it was Mac. Highly unusual. "What are you doing up so early?"

Mac paused to look up. "Couldn't sleep. Thought you probably wouldn't mind me tinkering with the tractor. You told me it needed a tune-up."

"A tune-up, yeah, not a beating," he offered with a smile.

Mac guffawed. "Well, this spark plug is welded in.

271

Any chance it was underwater?"

Alton stepped closer to see where Mac pointed. "Not underwater, but there was water all around us for days. It was like a monsoon."

"Ah, well, it's plumb rusted. I put oil on it. I guess it's best to let it sit a while." He grabbed a rag and wiped his hands, then cleaned the mallet handle.

If nothing else, the man was thorough and neat. Perhaps it came from his years as a chief petty officer. "You had your coffee yet?"

Mac sniffed. "No, I didn't want to disturb anyone. It was still dark when I wandered downstairs."

"Regina's in there now, making breakfast. I need to get the animals fed. I'll be in after that." He headed for the door, turning back when Mac spoke.

"Where's your little intern?" Mac grinned as he set the rag down and followed Alton.

"I let him sleep. He'll be back at school in a few days, and won't get much opportunity for rest."

It was good to have another man helping with the chores. They made short work of feeding the cattle and the workhorses. Willie milked the cows and had the pails ready to carry to the kitchen. Mac took one bucket and Alton the other. They were halfway back when Samson's yip broke the silence.

"Where've you been, boy?" Alton said when Samson ran up.

"You didn't know?" Mac asked. "He was sleeping at

the foot of Chase's bed."

Alton looked at Mac. "You're kidding."

Mac shook his head. "Big as life and snoring."

Alton was not surprised when Mother met them at the door.

"Do you know that animal of yours slept in the house overnight?" She barely stepped aside enough to allow them entry with their burdens.

Alton set his bucket on the sink and reached for Mac's. "Not until about two minutes ago, Mother."

"We're going to have to fumigate the place. I've looked Chase over head-to-toe, or at least as much as he would allow. If we send him home with a tick, his mother will have our hides."

Alton washed his hands at the sink. "Now, Mother, Chase would come as near to catching a tick as any dog. We just came in from camping in the woods. He runs wild, practically every place Samson does."

Mac held his hands out to Regina and asked what she had to get rid of grease. To Alton's surprise, she dropped everything and fetched him a spoonful of lard.

"Rub this in real good. Towel it off before you wash with soap. I'll get you a rag to use. If that don't get it, we have turpentine, but it'll shore rough up your hands."

Alton scratched his head. If he had asked for something, she'd frown and mutter. Which is why he never bothered.

A rumble on the stairs preceded Chase. His face was freshly washed, hair combed. Mother really had given him the once-over. Probably even scrubbed behind his ears.

"How you holding up, Chase?"

"I'm sorry I let Samson in the house, Uncle Alton. I didn't mean to break any rules, but he was whining. You think he knows I'm about to leave?"

Alton nodded. "I'm sure he does. He's a pretty smart dog."

"Y'all better set to. Food's getting cold," Regina set heaping platters on the kitchen table.

Alton noticed she'd found an extra-large mug for Mac's coffee. She still poured Mother's cup first, but Mac was next in line.

"I have a lot of work to do today, Chase, so you're on your own." He glanced at Mother. "Unless your grandmother has something for you to do."

"I want to help you, Uncle Alton."

Alton nodded. "All right, you can help me." He took a big bite of scrambled eggs and chewed slowly. Something was different. What was it? He glanced around the table. No one else seemed to notice. He took another bite. They weren't bad, just different. Alton wasn't used to different.

"Excellent breakfast," Mac announced, patting his stomach. "Thank you, Regina."

Regina beamed. "You're most welcome, Mr. Mac. I'm glad you liked it. I made it just the way you told me."

"What do you think of the eggs, son?" Mother's eyes held a flicker of mischief.

"They're good."

Mac flashed a smile. "Cheddar. Just a sprinkling. Adds an extra layer of flavor."

The man was a cook, too? Was there anything he couldn't do?

Connie gazed down the length of the clothesline and marveled at the number of diapers in today's wash. She shook out another one and pinned it to the line. Poor little guy was up most of the night with a tummy ache. Momma still thought it was the tooth, but Connie suspected it was the milk.

At the sound of someone whistling a tune, she turned to see Dad striding up the drive.

He crossed the yard and joined her at the clothesline. "Morning, Daughter."

"Good morning, Dad. You're in a good mood."

"Happy to be alive this fine morning. How about you? Do I see shadows beneath your eyes—little one keep you awake?"

She told him about her night as he followed her inside.

Momma met them at the door. "Good morning, Mac. You're just in time to hold your grandson. He's wide awake now." Joseph punctuated her declaration with a loud squall.

Mac didn't hesitate. He strode to the bedroom. Connie smiled at Momma as they listened to the interaction between the two. Mac reappeared, with Joseph in his arms.

Momma held up an empty cup. "Coffee?"

He nodded. "Yes, thank you."

They sat around the table.

Connie loved watching her dad with Joseph. The little boy would never remember these moments, but she would. "I'll be right back." She returned a moment later with the camera, and snapped a few photos. At first, Joseph recoiled at the flash bulb. But his curious nature soon won out. He grinned and clapped his hands with the next shot.

Dad suggested they walk outside and get a couple of pictures in the sunshine.

Momma stopped by the mirror to check her hair. "I'll take one of you and your dad, too."

"Thanks," Connie passed the camera to Momma.

Outside, they stood near the porch steps, with Momma's flowers in the background. Even in black and white, the flowers would provide a lovely backdrop.

After snapping a couple of photos, Momma handed the camera back to Connie.

She focused on Dad and Joseph, with Momma at their side. "I hope all these turn out," she told them. "They'll make wonderful memories for our album. Her gaze fell on

Dad's face. "I'll send you some copies."

"That'd be wonderful, kid." He climbed the steps, eased into a rocking chair, and settled Joseph on one knee. "I want to talk to you about tomorrow."

Momma pointed Connie to the other rocker. "I'll grab a chair."

"You mean church, or dinner at Jensen and Marla's?"

Momma returned with a chair and sat down.

Mac cleared his throat. "Alton and I had a long talk last night. He told me a bit of what they've been through with Jensen. I got to wondering if there's some reason why he's invited all of us over. Maybe he thinks he can appeal to me to keep you two apart."

Connie shook her head. Even though Jensen had put on that show a few weeks back, tried to convince her that Alton was a hothead she shouldn't consider marrying, Connie chose not to share this with her dad. She'd made a personal commitment to pray for the man every time she was tempted to be angry or think badly of him. "I don't think that's it, Dad. I think he wants to make a show of welcoming you."

Momma chimed in. "He's got something up his sleeve, all right."

Dad looked at Connie. "I guess we better be on our best behavior, daughter. We can exhibit good island manners. Should I take anything, like a gift, or something? What do you think, Miss Annabelle?"

"I don't know what it would be, they have everything."

"Well, I'll think about it." He bounced Joseph once more before handing him to his mother. "I best head on back. I didn't sleep much last night either. Your mother used to blame it on the full moon." He rose from his chair.

Connie got up and settled Joseph on her hip. "I'll walk with you a ways." She looked at Momma. "Do you want to go, too?"

"I don't believe so. I need to get a few things done, so we can be gone all day tomorrow."

Connie took her time walking back. She'd enjoyed the pleasant conversation with Dad. He and Alton had also talked about a future trip to the islands, possibly as soon as next year. Maybe for as long as a month. She looked at the baby. "Wouldn't that be grand?"

His mouth turned up in a toothless grin, he gazed at her with large, expectant eyes, reminding her so much of his father.

She'd dreamed of Joe last night. He'd been excited about something. He wanted to tell her, but each time he came close to speak the words, little Joseph woke up, fussing.

As she trudged up the drive, she asked herself the question, had it been a warning? Was Dad right in assuming Jensen still planned to cause trouble?

Sunday morning's chores behind him, Alton ambled across the pasture, taking in the view. The weathered barn and tall house sat on a rise among fields where ears of corn dried on the stalks and cotton bolls neared to bursting open. Any other time, his heart would swell with gratitude. But today, a heavy weight lay upon his shoulders.

Even Samson loped along, barely taking time to sniff the air. The dog always knew when something was up.

Chase was leaving. His bag packed, he sat at the kitchen table, waiting for Uncle Alton so they could eat breakfast. Alton noted the obvious signs of Mother's intervention in the boy's appearance. Starched collar buttoned up to his chin. Clip-on neck tie perfectly straight. Hair combed and glued into place. Face scrubbed. His fingernails were even clean. Mother hadn't lost her touch.

Chase brightened as Alton entered. "Morning, Uncle Alton."

Alton returned the boy's greeting with as warm a smile as he could muster.

Mac entered from the other side of the house, dressed in a brown suit, a white rosebud tucked into his lapel. The man was determined to impress Chase's parents today. He'd talked of little else last evening.

Mother spoke from her place at the table. "I thought it might be nice if we held hands for our prayer this morning."

Alton glanced at her. Dampness rimmed her eyes. She'd miss the boy, too. He offered thanks to the Lord and prayed for the Father's will and favor over the boy as he set out on life's journey.

Chase didn't speak till nearly halfway through the meal. "I wish it wasn't over."

"What'll you miss the most?" Mac asked.

Chase thought a moment. "Samson. And not being ordered around and called bad names."

Alton set his fork down. He'd told himself he wouldn't get angry if the boy ever confided in him, so he clamped his jaw and held his tongue till his ire cooled.

"What sort of names?" Mother asked. She kept a calm countenance, but Alton guessed the truth. She was as shaken as he.

Chase cast a glance toward Alton. "I can't say."

"That bad, huh?" Mac asked.

Chase nodded. "And they accused me of being a … of thinking too highly of colored folks, like Edris and Hero."

Alton could guess the name they'd called him. He'd heard it all his life, even from his brother.

Mac made eye contact with Alton and Mother as he spoke to Chase. "It's a military thing, son. You have to dodge those words like bullets. When you know they're headed toward you, start thinking about the best day of your life, or something you like. You can think of Samson. I won't say it'll work every time, but it sure helps. And those times when you know you deserve to be chewed out, show your respect. Look the man in the eye and say, 'Yes, sir.'"

Chase nodded. "Yes, sir."

Mac grinned. "You got it."

"Thank you, Mac." Mother pressed her napkin to her lips, keeping her eyes averted.

"I couldn't have said it better," Alton told him. "We're sure going to miss you, Chase. But we'll write to you often. How's that? And maybe when you're home for the holidays, your parents will allow you to come stay with us a bit."

Chase's eyes widened. "That sounds keen, Uncle Alton. I'd like that. And I'll write to you, too." He faced Mac. "Mr. Mac, do you think you could write to me? It would be so neat if I was to get a letter all the way from Hawaii."

Mac beamed. "I'd be honored, son."

Alton slid his chair back. "Well, I'd better get ready for church."

"Big day today." Mac pushed away from the table.

Mother laid her fork down. "Don't remind me."

Alton glanced over his shoulder as he headed for the stairs. Her expression told him she was worried. Sometimes he despised the influence his brother carried, even when he wasn't present. Over the years, Jensen's bitterness had worn a hole in their peaceful existence. Seems like they'd be used to it, but maybe it was something they weren't supposed to accept. Who knows—maybe it was a cry for help. Was Jensen as miserable on the inside as he made everyone else around him?

Chapter Twenty-Five

"Is that the only dress she owns?" Maggie's raspy comment echoed in the quiet Sunday school room.

Connie wore the pale blue dress with the matching sweater. She fingered her pearl necklace as she sank into a vacant chair on the opposite side of the room from Miss Cranky-pants.

This was her best dress. It would have to do, and besides, Momma spent an entire hour ironing the crinoline underskirt. Maggie's rudeness was only a symptom of her need for attention. Connie had learned to expect such behavior from primary grade children.

Bertha began the lesson, but the story of Caleb and Joshua failed to capture Connie's attention. All she could think about was what would happen later.

After Bertha dismissed them, several of her friends surrounded Connie, blocking her exit.

"Don't forget, Thursday evening at Matilda's," Julie

said. "Do you need a ride?"

She shook her head. "No, Alton said he'd bring me."

Matilda touched her arm. "Six-thirty. And try to have fun today. We'll say a prayer for you."

The other girls nodded in unison.

"I appreciate that." Connie blew out a breath. Fun— ha. As if she could relax long enough to enjoy herself. Sliding by a group of teen girls in the hall, she made her way to the sanctuary. As she took her seat beside Momma, Connie's eyes lit on a new face on the other side of the room. A young man, she'd guess in his early twenties, sharply dressed. He stood near Jensen and Marla. He bent down to make eye contact with Chase, touched the boy's shoulder and smiled. Maybe he was a relation of the Wades?

She leaned toward Momma. "Do you know that man?"

Momma shook her head. "No, but he came in with Jensen. Maybe he'll be at dinner."

Connie sat back, her mind returning to the upcoming visit. By the time Alton and Dad sat down, the contents of her stomach had soured due to tension. She drew a breath and eased it out.

Alton touched her hand. "Okay?"

She gave him a reassuring smile, but it was a lie. She was not okay. She wouldn't be okay until this day ended.

As she sang the words to the Doxology, her nerves calmed a little, but the hymns that followed were a blur. She mouthed the words, pushing through ever-mounting anxiety.

Pastor Nathan stood and opened his Bible. "Please turn to Philippians 4:6."

The whisper of pages softly turning was the only sound in the sanctuary.

Pastor cleared his throat before reading, "Be careful for nothing ..." He explained this meant you shouldn't worry. "Don't be afraid. Pray. Give it to God. Thank Him for the answer. Verse seven goes on to say, 'And the peace of God, which passeth all understanding, shall keep your hearts and minds through Christ Jesus.' The mere thought should give you comfort."

Connie closed her eyes, focused her mind. When she opened them again, she found Alton watching her, his gaze questioning. She smiled again, and gave a slight nod. Her stomach still churned, but she was working on that.

The service ended, Connie started toward the nursery.

Thelma bustled forward. "Let me go and get him. If he sees you, he may fuss." She brushed Connie's cheek with a motherly kiss. "He'll be just fine."

"Thank you, I know you'll take good care of him."

Connie turned to find Dad waiting for her. "Time to go, daughter. Are you ready for this?"

Déjà vu—he'd said that before, but when? "I'm as ready as I'll ever be."

"It'll be okay. At least you don't have to do it alone."

"Where's Alton?"

"Outside. He's pulling the car around."

"It's only two blocks to their house."

"Well, we don't want to walk back over here to get the car, now do we?"

"I suppose not." She followed him outside. Momma and Miss Lillian were already getting into the car. This was really happening. They were going to dinner at Jensen and Marla's. A lump the size of a tennis ball clogged her throat. At least it seemed that big. She slid into the seat beside Alton.

"I can't wait for you to meet Edris. She's going to love you."

She'd heard all about Edris, wonderful cook, housekeeper, and nanny to Alton and Jensen when they were growing up.

They pulled into the drive a couple of minutes later. Connie remembered the day Momma showed her this house. "I was born here," she'd said. What if Charles Wade senior had not kicked Momma and her mother out of the house after his son's death? Connie might not be here today.

But she was here, getting ready to go inside that great house. She waited for Alton, but before he had time to walk around the car, a young colored boy ran up and opened her door.

Alton strode up behind him. "Connie, this is Hero, Edris' grandson."

Connie almost stuck out her hand, but caught herself just in time. What if Jensen was watching? Why should it matter? She chose the safe route and smiled instead. "Hello, Hero, I'm so pleased to meet you."

He gave a polite nod, and stood aside so Alton could help her out of the car.

Alton tucked her hand in the crook of his arm and drew her near, as if to protect her.

If only she could stay so close to him throughout the afternoon.

Annabelle stood for a moment, gazing up at the stately white columns of the front porch. The Wade Mansion—she'd never expected to return there. Beside her, Miss Lillian paused, too. After a moment, Annabelle linked arms with her friend, as the two of them climbed the wide front steps.

Edris opened the door and greeted them with a smile. "Miz Wade, you come on in," she whispered. "Bless the Lord, for He is good."

"Yes, He is, and it is truly a blessing to see you again," Miss Lillian answered, stepping past Edris.

Annabelle followed close behind.

Mac stepped through the door, but stopped to admire his surroundings. "Impressive."

Annabelle suppressed a giggle. Why did everyone feel the need to whisper?

She looked back just in time to catch Connie's expression. Annabelle could almost read the girl's thoughts. The two-story foyer, shiny white marble floor, elegant chandelier, curved, mahogany staircase—oh, it was grand. But almost overwhelming. And here she was, wearing a plain old blue dress. Yes, when Alton let go of Connie's arm for a moment to hug Edris, Connie smoothed the front of her dress. It's what she did when she was feeling self-conscious about her appearance. Which was a real shame, because the girl was a beauty.

"Geez, Louise," Mac mumbled as he stepped into the formal parlor. He gave a soft whistle under his breath and turned to gaze at Annabelle. He quirked a brow.

She wanted to remind him of the things money couldn't buy, but Marla chose that moment to enter.

Talk about your finery. The girl wore a trim white skirt topped with a creamy silk blouse. Diamonds sparkled at her wrist. Every inch of her screamed money, right up to her expertly wrapped French twist hairdo.

"Welcome, everyone, if you'll step into the parlor—make yourselves comfortable."

Connie drew up beside Annabelle. "Not possible."

"Anything is possible," Alton murmured, giving Annabelle a wink.

Mac stepped forward. "You have a beautiful home."

"Why thank you, Mr. Pruitt," Marla answered.

Annabelle watched the woman, wondering who she was. The Marla she knew had never acted in so civil a manner, not in her company, anyway. Had Alton's kindness to Chase made such a difference?

Once they were all seated, Marla advised them her husband was in a short conference with a colleague. "They'll only be a few minutes, then we'll have dinner. I hope you'll excuse me a moment, I have a couple of things to tend to."

As she left the room, Edris entered, tray in hand.

Annabelle scrutinized the finger food on the tray. It was almost too pretty to eat. No one else seemed reluctant, however, and the tidbits soon disappeared.

Edris returned with small glasses of lemonade, which everyone sipped quietly.

Their hunger postponed by the refreshments, the group began to relax.

"So, you grew up in this house," Mac said to Alton.

Alton nodded. "Yes, I did."

"We were very happy here." Miss Lillian's voice held a wistful tone.

Annabelle's gaze snapped to Miss Lillian's face. What was the woman remembering? Maybe she didn't want to tell Mac the real story.

A soft rustle from the foyer brought Annabelle's attention to a small face capped with blond hair, near the bottom of the staircase.

Miss Lillian held out her hand.

Assured of his welcome, Landers jogged into the room. He waited until all eyes were upon him before speaking. "Hello, Uncle Alton. Hello, Grandmother." He paused to scan the other faces in the room. "Hello, other people."

Alton introduced Landers to each one, saving the best till last. "And this is my fiancée, Mrs. Connie Cross."

Landers moved to stand in front of Connie. He stood for a moment, gazing into her eyes. "Chase told me you were real pretty."

Alton frowned. "You don't agree?"

The boy glanced from Alton to Connie. "I prefer blondes."

Alton's laughter seemed to please Landers.

Mac slapped his knee and chuckled.

When Jensen appeared, he was not amused. "Landers, your mother's looking for you."

"Yes, sir." Without a backward look, he left the room, nearly colliding with the well-dressed young man they'd seen at church.

Jensen waved him into the room. "Folks, this is John Tyler Woodruff. He's working at the courthouse for a while, and he's agreed to help me with a project. I'll tell y'all more about that later."

Before he could continue, Mac spoke. "Well, I'll be. Good to see you again, John."

John stepped forward to grip Mac's hand. "Mac, good to see you, too." He greeted each one as Jensen introduced them. "Mac and I met on the train out of Dallas. We had quite a conversation." By now, he stood before Connie. "I feel I know you already, Princess Connie."

She blushed and bit her lip.

Annabelle eyed both of them. What was up with that?

Jensen rubbed his hands together. "Y'all come on in to the dining room. I expect dinner's ready by now."

Alton hung back, keeping a close eye on Jensen. He didn't trust his brother as far as he could throw him. He'd never seen him so polite, and couldn't figure out why. The atmosphere in the room held energy. And Jensen's overall pleasant attitude led Alton to suspect his brother had been drinking.

Across the room, John Tyler Woodruff told Connie his parents owned *Carriage's Department Store* in Jackson. Alton tried to read her expression. What did she think about that, after the way their clerk had treated her?

Marla directed everyone to a chair.

Alton and Mac assisted the ladies before taking their places.

Interesting seating arrangement. Alton scanned the guests, beginning with his brother at the head of the table. John sat at Jensen's left, beside Connie, and Mac next to her. Marla occupied the chair at the other end of the table. Annabelle sat between her and Alton. Mother sat on his other side. Her placement next to Jensen puzzled Alton no end.

His eyes on Alton, Jensen spoke. "Would you ask the blessing, brother?"

A dozen thoughts filled his mind right now, but he kept his prayer short and thankful. Dinner smelled mighty good.

Edris and another young woman began to serve the food. He smiled to note Edris had prepared his favorite— roast beef and popovers. Her roast beef held layers of flavor and melted in your mouth. She served him a healthy slab.

After everyone had been served, Jensen looked around. "Just as I always suspected," he paused a moment, probably for dramatic effect. "Edris favors Alton. Look at that great heap of meat on his plate." He followed the statement with a hearty laugh.

Everyone reacted in kind, but Alton noticed the uncertainty on their faces. Like peons in the presence of the king. If he laughed, they laughed, or they lost their heads. He chuckled at the thought as he dug into the meat.

"Well, Mac," Jensen said, "I hope you'll regale us with a couple of those stories you shared with John on the trip. He's talked of little else since he arrived. I'm especially interested to hear how you earned that Medal of Honor."

Mac finished chewing a bite of food and blotted his lips with a napkin. "Well, sir—in my opinion—everyone there should've won a Medal of Honor. We were surrounded by heroism that day. Even the injured threw in and did their part—if they weren't too badly disabled. Seeing that, and being a part of it, well, it was a greater honor than receiving any medal." He sipped his tea.

A frown creased Jensen's brow. "Are you saying you'd give it back?"

Never taking his eyes from Jensen's face, Mac stirred his tea. "No sir, I would not. Being singled out like that made me a bit uncomfortable, but mighty proud. The fact is, I couldn't have done it alone."

"You did just that, from what I understand," Jensen sucked his teeth.

Alton watched his brother through narrowed eyes. What was he up to? Maybe just the lawyer coming out, questioning and testing his witness.

"Only in the beginning. I put my leadership training to good use, organized a small army of islanders. We scrounged up every boat we could find and headed to Pearl. We had no idea what we were going into."

Jensen seemed enthralled. "If you had known, would you still have gone?"

Mac tilted his head forward. "In a heartbeat."

Jensen leaned back, hooking his thumbs in his belt. "That's courage. That's the reason you were singled out. How many of those islanders would've gone and done that without leadership?"

Mac smiled and nodded. "I see what you're saying. Most of them would've hidden in caves with their families. And I have to admit, some didn't make it. There was still an active battle raging all around us. But, something compelled me to get as many out of there as I could."

"You made a real impression on my boy. I thank you for sharing your stories with him."

Alton met Connie's gaze. Was Mac to get all the honor for the good done in Chase's life?

"He's a fine boy," Mac said. "And he'll make a good soldier."

Jensen sat forward, resting an arm on the table's edge. "I appreciate that. Earlier this summer, I wouldn't have agreed with you, but …" He shot a glance toward Marla. "My brother saw something I couldn't see, spent some needed time with the boy. The good Lord knows, if I'd had the time, I'd a done it myself." He eyeballed Alton. "You know what a busy man I am."

Alton buttered a bite of popover. "Indeed, I do."

Jensen ruminated on that a moment. He laid his knife and fork across his empty plate and sat back. "Fine meal, Edris." Looking at Connie, he pursed his lips. "You know she's all set to bake you a wedding cake."

Connie gave a polite nod. "So I heard. I'm sure it'll be wonderful."

"Oh, it will be spectacular. After dinner, Marla will show you the photos of our wedding. Of course, your cake won't have to be quite so fancy, or so big. Half the county showed up at our shindig."

Marla interrupted. "If everyone has finished their dinner, perhaps the ladies would like to go with me? I'm certain the men have no interest in looking at our wedding album."

Alton observed her with interest. Though Marla's words were meant for the females at the table, her eyes remained on Jensen. Something was definitely up.

Chapter Twenty-Six

Connie followed Momma, who followed Miss Lillian into the much smaller back parlor. Marla called it her study. It looked a bit like an office, with bookshelves and a small writing desk on one end, and seating on the other. The furnishings provided more finery than comfort. Delicately carved settees, and wing-backed chairs in muted mauves and blues. Heavy brocade drapes all but hid the tall windows, allowing only a glimpse of their beauty behind lace sheers.

Marla crossed to the desk and picked up a large album. "Please make yourselves comfortable. Would anyone like coffee?"

Miss Lillian said she'd love some, and Momma agreed.

Connie's stomach was so full. No room for another ounce of anything. Would it be impolite to say so? "I'd love a cup." She cringed at the lie, but no one else seemed to notice. Marla held their attention.

She opened the album and set it on the coffee table. "Here are the pictures. I'll be right back."

Miss Lillian turned the pages and pointed out items of interest. "Look at the decor. Isn't it beautiful? The church was done up so well, I hardly recognized it." She turned another page.

Connie drew in a quick breath at the sight of Marla in her wedding dress.

Momma poked her arm. "It is spectacular, isn't it?"

"It's elegant."

"The best money could buy." Marla had entered so quietly, Connie hadn't noticed. "That's what Father said, anyway. In my opinion, it was much too extravagant for a dress I'd wear only once, but I have to admit, it felt wonderful on."

"You were stunning." Miss Lillian's tight smile didn't quite make it to her eyes.

Marla turned the pages past several photos of herself with Jensen. "Here's the cake."

Connie stared at the tower of pastry. A close-up photo showed some of the intricate detail. "Beautiful. It must have taken hours to construct such a wonderful cake."

"Three days," Marla stepped back and folded her hands. "The first attempt failed. But I insisted Edris try again, and she accomplished it."

Momma shook her head. "Five layers. Are those doves on top?"

"Yes, and each layer a different flavor," Miss Lillian said.

Marla sighed. "Of course, your cake won't be quite that elegant, or time consuming. We can't really spare Edris for so long. But she can do a perfectly nice one in a few hours. And of course, she'll want to attend. She practically raised those boys."

Miss Lillian settled back in her chair. "Yes, she did."

Connie glanced at her face. Was she offended by the remark?

"Well," Marla closed the photo album. "Enough of that. Here's the coffee. Set it on the table, Minnie."

The young woman set the tray where Marla indicated.

Marla handed her the album. "I'll pour the coffee. Return this to my desk."

After setting the book on the desk, Minnie left the room.

"Is she new?" Miss Lillian asked.

"She is. Edris can't go on forever."

Miss Lillian raised her eyebrows. "True."

Momma and Miss Lillian conversed quietly while Marla poured the coffee and passed the cups.

Connie sipped the steaming liquid. It was delicious. She aimed her gaze at Marla. She should probably make polite conversation. It would be good practice for later, after she became the mistress of Sutter's Landing. She bit back a smile at the ridiculous thought. "Thank you for inviting us. Dinner was wonderful."

Marla's glance slid across Connie's face before sliding down her front, probably taking in the shabbiness of her appearance. "It was my pleasure. We are to be family, after all." She stirred her coffee, and set the spoon aside.

The tone of her voice sent a chill through Connie. "Yes, we are."

Marla drew a breath as though to speak, but hesitated. Her voice barely audible, she said, "I'm not good at friendship. And I'm sure you're aware of our … differences. I tend to stay to my social circles, so I hope you won't be offended by my … reticence."

Arrogance? Coldness? Haughtiness? Connie supplied a few more definitive words, but she had to admit, the woman's honesty was refreshing. She nodded her understanding.

Moments of silence passed. Connie checked on Momma and Miss Lillian. Had they fallen asleep? Both gazed out the window.

"I hear you're a teacher." Though Marla directed her question to Connie, her gaze remained on the coffee tray.

"Well, yes, I have a degree. I haven't held a teaching position yet."

"She graduated with honors," Momma said, with her usual enthusiasm.

Marla drew in a breath, apparently unimpressed by Momma's statement. "Have you ever met with anyone who can't learn to read?"

Connie searched the woman's face. Was she speaking

of herself, or perhaps her younger son? She'd heard Chase read, so it wasn't him. "There are cases of difficulty learning the alphabet. It's called dyslexia, and is more common in boys. We studied it in college."

"Dyslexia? So, it is a thing? I mean—it's real?"

Miss Lillian set her cup down. "I've heard of that."

"Yes, it's real," Connie said. "The individual sees figures backwards. It has something to do with the brain. But it's not as uncommon as one might think."

Marla smoothed her hem, avoiding eye contact. "Is there treatment for it?"

"No treatment, just retraining the student to identify what he sees. There has been some success. I attended a seminar during my final semester. In the past, it was treated as a medical condition, but it's easier to remedy the situation with various training techniques. I found it interesting, but it's quite challenging."

"You have some experience with this … dyslexia?"

Her curiosity piqued, Connie wanted to answer with the question, *who are we discussing*, but she held off, didn't want to appear pushy. "Only a little. I do have contacts, however. I could get the information for you, if you're interested."

Marla set her cup and saucer on the tray. "No, not me. I … was merely asking. I thought perhaps you could help someone."

"I'd be happy to try."

Marla nodded. "It's Hero—Edris' grandson. He's a

perfectly fine boy, but he struggles in school. Edris is afraid he'll get into trouble. The other children make fun of him."

Connie looked at Marla, who held her gaze for a millisecond. Was she hearing correctly? Marla was concerned for the grandchild of a servant? A colored boy? Perhaps there was hope for this woman after all. "I … could work with him."

Miss Lillian touched Connie's hand and gave her a reassuring smile. "His mother lives near Sutter's."

"Yes," Marla said, glancing out the window. "After you're settled, of course. I'm sure you'll be much too busy before the wedding."

"Well, yes, and I'll need to write to the foundation I spoke of earlier. I'll see about getting some information and the materials I'd need."

"We'll pay you, of course," Marla said, "for your time, and whatever materials you require."

"Oh, no need for that," Connie told her. "I could use the experience, and the training those materials would provide."

"Yes, well, let me know what you come up with. Regina can send word to Edris."

"Of course. I hope I can help him."

"So do I. Children can be so cruel."

Was she only thinking of Hero, or did she speak from recent experience, with her own boy? Alton had told Connie what Chase confided. She'd almost decided to ask about him, when loud laughter sounded from the dining room.

Marla sat forward. "I imagine the men are ready for their dessert. Edris has prepared one of her specialties— pecan pie."

"Oh, my," Miss Lillian said. "Annabelle, you are in for a treat."

Alton suppressed another yawn. The day dragged on as they lingered over pie and coffee. Mac and John could pretty much talk the hair off a donkey. Jensen looked as though he enjoyed every moment. When they finally rose to leave, he followed Alton outside.

"I know it's asking a lot, after all you've done, But Marla and I wondered if you'd like to take Chase to school on Wednesday." He leaned against the car, arms crossed over his chest.

In the background, Mac said something and John laughed out loud.

Alton looked at his brother. "To Columbia? Well, I don't know. Are there any restrictions?"

Jensen quirked a brow. "Restrictions?"

"On who can go along?"

Jensen scoffed. "You say that as if you kept your word last time."

Alton shrugged.

"No restrictions. I meant what I said in there. John thinks it's best."

"I'd be happy to take Chase. I'm sure Mac would like to see the hill country."

"That's right. Take him to Nashville." He reached for his wallet. "Have dinner on me."

Alton held up his hand, but Jensen insisted.

"No, you're spending gas money, and giving more of your time. You take it. Go someplace nice." He handed Alton a fifty-dollar bill. As Alton accepted it, Jensen added, "And buy your wife-to-be some clothes. She looks like a moppet, for heaven's sake."

Alton narrowed his eyes, but before he could come up with a response, Jensen held up his hand.

"I apologize."

Alton turned toward the car. "When should I pick him up?"

"We usually leave around seven. They just need to be there by noon."

Of course, Jensen would drop him off early, anxious to be rid of him. "We'll be here at seven."

"I appreciate it."

Tom stepped out of the store and locked the door as the Wades passed by in Miss Lillian's automobile. Alton tapped the horn and everyone waved. Tom's nerves kinked into knots as he waited until they'd turned the corner. He stood still another moment, gazing down the street toward the Baptist Church. What had possessed him to make this appointment? Checking his watch, he started walking down the street, keeping a sharp lookout for anyone who might recognize him.

Gossipers, one thing this town was not short on, and not just those of the female persuasion. Satisfied no one was about, he crossed the street and hotfooted it to the side door of the church.

After his eyes adjusted to the cool dimness of the sanctuary, he looked around. How long since he'd been in here? Too long. Not long enough. It seemed just the same. Sunlight streamed through the lighter panes of stained glass. Outside, a gust of wind whistled in the eaves. No, it hadn't changed.

He turned and walked toward Pastor's office.

"Hello, Tom," Pastor called out.

"Pastor, thank you for taking time out of your Sunday to talk with me."

He gripped Tom's hand. "Sunday's a work day for both of us, I believe."

Tom nodded. "I only work a few hours, mostly organizing things."

"I understand. Won't you have a seat?"

Tom sat in the chair Pastor indicated. He laid his hat on a small round table and faced forward.

Pastor Nathan returned to his chair and eased into it. "What can I do for you?"

Tom sucked in a deep breath and blew it out. "I need to talk, and I'm hoping you can maybe advise on a certain issue."

"I'll do my best."

Talking wasn't exactly his strong suit, so he took his time, didn't rush. "I know you weren't here during all that ruckus after my Uncle Jeb died. But I'm sure you've heard all about it."

Pastor nodded, but didn't say a word.

"My family left the church and vowed they'd never come back. I reckon that meant as long as Jensen Wade was a part of this church. Of course, that was before he apologized and stepped down from head deacon. I don't reckon anyone of my family expected to see that happen." He steepled his fingers. "I'm honest enough to tell you, I've been perfectly happy reading the Bible and praying on my own. I felt no need of church." He ducked his head. "Until Annabelle Cross returned a widow."

He peeked at Pastor and found him much the same as before. His expression had not changed. "She took every opportunity to invite me to church, knowing full well I'd say no."

Pastor chuckled and shook his head. "That's Annabelle. She's a good woman."

"Yes, she is. I have to go back a bit, and tell you, I was in love with Annabelle throughout high school. Maybe even before that. I lost her to Ray Cross, partly because I never told her how I felt about her, and partly … well, Ray was a whole lot better looking than me. And he had something else going for him—he was from California— far away from Trenton, Tennessee.

"So now she's back and I can't stop thinking about her. But she refuses to allow me to call on her—to court her— unless I'll go to church with her." He stretched his back and settled in the chair. Maybe he was squirming, like he always did when he was fighting his conscience.

"Pastor, I don't want to come back to church under false pretenses. And, I don't want to lie to Miss Annabelle—come to church just so she'll go out with me. My cousin Riley did that. I reckon you know how he is."

"I do. He's not alone."

"I know, but that's not me. I can't be duplicitous—" He glanced at Pastor. "Is that the correct use of the word?"

Pastor nodded. "Yes, it is."

Tom grinned. "It was in the crossword puzzle this morning." He drummed his fingertips together. "Well, the fact is, I love Annabelle. I'd do anything for her, but this church attendance thing is tearing me apart."

After a long pause, Pastor sat forward, elbows on his desktop, fingers intertwined. "You said you lost her once because you didn't tell her how you felt. Does she know now?"

Tom nodded. "I told her, but it was too soon. She wasn't ready for that. She promised herself she'd never marry another man that wouldn't go to church. Ray didn't go either."

"I see." Pastor picked up a pencil and began to scribble on a piece of paper. "Just making notes. It helps me think."

Tom rubbed the back of his neck, hoping to loosen the tension. What he wouldn't give to be out on the river right now, casting a line.

"Regarding what happened with your family, have you forgiven those responsible?"

"If you mean Jensen, I've had dealings with him. I try to be friendly, though he doesn't really reciprocate."

Pastor nodded. "Doesn't matter."

"No, I don't reckon I ever have."

"Well, the Bible says in several instances, that we should forgive others so we can be forgiven."

"That's in the Lord's Prayer."

"Yes, but there are other verses where Jesus repeated that. In fact, he told a parable about a master who wanted to settle his accounts. He called for the man who owed him the most money and demanded payment. The man didn't have the money, so the master condemned him to prison and commanded his family be sold to pay the debt. When the man begged for mercy, the master gave it, and pardoned his entire debt."

Tom scratched his chin. "I remember that one. The man went out and found one of his friends that owed him money. When his friend couldn't pay, he had him thrown into jail. When the master learned of it, he put the debt back on that man and threw him into jail."

"So, you understand the principle of forgiveness."

"I believe so. I reckon it's something I need to do."

"I'm going to say something else that may surprise you." Pastor laid his pencil down and leaned forward. "Though I would love to have you in our church, don't feel this is the only church. If you'd be more comfortable elsewhere, by all means, go. I'd rather you were in church somewhere, if you could see your way clear to go."

"I can't imagine attending anywhere else. I mean, this has always been my church. I guess that sounds funny, since I haven't been here. But I grew up in this church. These folks are my neighbors, my customers, my family."

Pastor gave him a knowing smile. "I reckon you have some soul searching to do, Tom. What's important to you? Do you love this woman enough to make a sacrifice of praise for her? We're talking about an hour a week at the least. And who knows, you might enjoy it."

He sat back again, and picked up the pencil. "Miss Annabelle knows her own mind. She won't back down. We both know it. That's pure gold, Tom. A strong woman like that might be worth an hour a week. But it's your decision to make. I won't think less of you, if you decide not to."

Tom met his gaze. "I'll give it some thought. Thanks for allowing me to talk it out." He stood and picked up his hat.

Pastor rose and walked with him to the door. "We still on for lunch Thursday?"

"Yes, sir, we are."

"Good. I love those ham sandwiches."

Tom stopped just short of the door. "One thing, Pastor. If you were to look up from your pulpit one Sunday morning and see me coming in, or already seated, please don't make a big deal."

Pastor grinned. "So, no public greeting?"

Tom shook his head.

"You've got a deal." He stuck out his hand.

Tom shook on it before he stepped outside. An odd feeling set up a whirl in his chest, like something leaving. A great weight rolling off his shoulders. He set his hat on his head and pressed it down. Didn't bother to check if anyone was watching. He really didn't care.

Chapter Twenty-Seven

Connie snuggled her baby boy as Alton drove them home from Jensen and Marla's. The day hadn't gone horribly, though doubts still hung in the air. Alton promised to talk about it after they'd stopped to pick up Joseph.

As Trenton's city limits faded behind them, she looked at him. "So, what did Jensen say?"

The murmur of talk in the backseat stilled as everyone's attention turned to Alton.

"Well," he glanced in the rear-view mirror as he tightened his grip on the steering wheel. "Jensen is running for City Council."

Miss Lillian sucked in a breath. "What?"

Alton nodded. "Yep. According to him, that's just the beginning. He plans to start with councilman and move up. He's got grand aspirations."

Connie greeted the grin on his face with doubt.

"You're not serious?"

Momma asked if he was thinking of running for president.

"Not that grand," Dad said. "He's thinking senate, or maybe state representative."

Connie still couldn't believe it. Would people vote for him?

Alton must have read her thoughts. "So, that's why he's taken up with John. He worked in the Eisenhower campaign and knows politics. Now, he's advising Jensen. You can all thank him for our being invited to dinner today, and for our warm reception there."

Warm reception … Connie remembered Marla's confession that she had no wish or intention to be Connie's friend. However, she did show compassion for Hero. This was a complicated woman.

"It all started on the train from Dallas," Dad said. "Or maybe it really started with a letter."

Connie smiled at her dad's silly laugh. He sat directly behind her, so she couldn't see his face, but she knew how it shone with glee when he laughed like that.

Alton stared straight ahead. "It was the right thing to do."

"But you went a step farther." Dad had entered storytelling mode. "You didn't have to look into my past. If you hadn't done that, I can promise you, I wouldn't be here today. You did what you did. I went to Kansas, took the train to Dallas. It was the first available, which was fine with me. I'd always wanted to see Texas. Found myself seated across from a young man with the same exact destination in mind. He heard my story. The rest is … well, history, as they say." He patted Connie's shoulder.

She laid her hand on his.

"The Lord works in mysterious ways," Momma said.

Miss Lillian finished her quote. "His wonders to perform."

"Speaking of performing," Alton said. "Jensen has asked me to take Chase back to school on Wednesday morning." He glanced in the mirror. "Mac, I thought you might like to go along, see a bit more of our fine state." He smiled toward Connie. "I hoped you'd go, too."

Miss Lillian leaned forward. "Wonderful plan. Annabelle and I can keep Joseph with us at the house. We'll get an idea of how that's going to work when you two go off on your honeymoon." She grinned at Connie.

"I agree," Momma said. "He needs to get used to his new room. It's coming at us full speed ahead, isn't it?"

Alton slowed to turn into the drive at Sutter's. "Yes, ma'am, it is."

The broad smile on his face warmed Connie's heart.

For Alton's way of thinking, time was passing too slowly. But Wednesday arrived and with it a mad rush to get everyone situated. Still, he pulled into the drive in front of the Wade Mansion with five minutes to spare.

Minnie brought a couple of suitcases out to the car, which Alton stowed in the trunk.

After Chase said goodbye, Marla didn't leave the porch, but stood watching as Alton backed out of the drive.

Chase was so quiet, Alton glanced over his shoulder to check on him. The boy was curled up, fast asleep, even though his seatmate talked nonstop. Mac talked for about an hour before he dozed off, too.

Alton draped his arm across Connie's shoulders. She slid closer, keeping an eye on the scenery. They'd left the cotton fields and flat vistas behind and were now climbing hills and traversing sharp curves.

"I love this part of the state," he told her. "You'll notice a lot of dairy farms as we get closer to Columbia."

And road construction. He'd already found two detours.

Alton pointed out a massive work site—a connection to the new interstate system. "Interstate 65 passes through here and one of these days, will end at the Gulf of Mexico. Interstate 40 is east to west, and I'm not sure where it'll end. Maybe all the way to California."

"It looks like a blight on the landscape," Connie observed. "And don't they already have a perfectly good east-west highway? We came across Route 66 last year."

"But it's only two lanes, and traffic gets snarled in the cities."

Connie sighed. "It's bad for all those small towns along the two-lanes—they're sure to lose business."

They'd end up ghost towns, like the old mining towns Alton had seen. All in the name of progress. Of course, he didn't mind easier travel.

Columbia was a picturesque town, another county seat with a beautiful courthouse and town square. Stately mansions sat along quiet, tree-lined streets.

The gates were open at the Academy. Uniformed young men stood guard. When Alton told them they were dropping off, a pleasant young cadet waved them forward.

Chase jumped out as though anxious to be away, but his movements slowed as he lifted one of his suitcases out of the trunk. A moment later, he threw himself at Alton and hugged him around the waist.

Alton patted his back, but found words difficult.

Mac put his hand on the boy's shoulder.

Chase let go of Alton and turned to face the older man.

"Remember what I told you, son. When times get bad, you know what to do."

"Yes, sir," Chase reverted to the little soldier. He stood straight and saluted Mac, who saluted in return.

Connie's eyes brimmed with moisture. Her lips trembled as Chase held out his hand to her.

"Goodbye, Aunt Connie."

"Goodbye, Chase." Her eyes met Alton's before she turned away, no doubt touched by the boy's endearment. It was the first time he'd called her that.

Determined not to dwell on it, Alton grabbed the other suitcase and followed Chase inside.

"He'll be fine," Dad slipped his arm around Connie's waist. "That boy's level-headed. I'm not sure where he got it, but it must be in the family, since Alton's pretty smart, too."

Connie smiled through damp eyes. "Here I was thinking you'd taken a liking to the family. You seemed to get along well with them on Sunday."

"I can get along with most anyone, daughter. But I saw right through that act Mr. Jensen put on. He's a big bag of wind, that one." He chuckled. "Which will probably serve him well in politics."

He stepped aside, taking in their surroundings. "This seems a nice enough place. A lot of history here, I imagine. Wonder how much it sets them back, sending Chase here?"

Alton rejoined them, his face a blank.

One thing Connie had learned about Alton—he didn't like to show emotion.

He opened her door. "Ready to roll?"

"Where to now?" Dad asked.

"We're less than an hour from Nashville, depending on traffic. I thought you'd like to see the state capitol."

"I absolutely would. Is that where there's a replica of

the Parthenon?"

Alton closed Connie's door. "Sure is."

Dad picked up his camera. "I'd love some pictures."

"Well, let's go."

On the way out of town, Alton pointed out the Polk house where the former president James K. Polk had lived, and a neon light factory, apparently a famous one.

"What Columbia is most known for is Mule Days," he told them.

"What is that, a gathering of mules? A stubborn conference?" Dad snickered at his silly joke.

Connie groaned.

Alton smiled. "Mule owners come here from all over. There's a parade, competitions, and a sale. It's a big deal."

Connie watched the scenery. They were still in hill country, winding through back roads as Alton avoided the congestion of the main highway. She enjoyed the drive so much, it seemed only a few minutes had passed before they crossed the Cumberland River and Nashville lay before them.

"A city on a hill," she said.

Alton agreed. "I'd never really thought about it, but it is." He pulled into a parking space near the Parthenon. "Here we are."

After a short walk around, Dad snapped a few photos. Alton led them down the street to what looked like a small cafe with a neon sign shaped like a guitar. The sign read, *On Cue*. When he opened the door, music filled the air as someone strummed a guitar and sang a soulful tune.

They found a table with a view of the performer, a slim young man with black hair combed into the latest style.

Dad elbowed Connie. "He's wearing one of them DA hairstyles."

"Dad," she tried to quiet him, but too late. He'd already said the words to Alton, who smiled and shook his head.

"It does kind of look like a duck's behind." Alton winked at Connie.

She giggled. In an effort to change the subject, she grabbed a menu. "What's good here?"

"Barbecue," Alton said. "But they have good burgers, too, if you prefer."

The music quieted as the singer left for a break. The waitress took their orders and disappeared.

"It's a good time to eat here," Alton told them. "Later at night, you can't get near this place."

When the music started back up, Connie recognized it from the radio, *That's All Right*. Her curiosity piqued, she watched the performer. As recognition dawned, she leaned toward Alton. "I think that's—"

He nodded. "It is."

"Who?" Dad asked.

"Elvis Presley. He's making some pretty big ripples in the music industry. Older folks are complaining about it, but the youth love it. I kind of like it, myself." He grinned at Connie.

Dad nodded, his attention on the performer. "It's got good rhythm. I can see why the fogies don't like it. Wonder if he'll pose for a picture later?"

Connie looked at Dad. Oh, no. He was probably going to embarrass them.

Thank goodness, the food arrived. Maybe he'd forget. Or perhaps Elvis would take another break, or finish and leave.

After a delicious cheeseburger, Connie excused herself and slipped away in search of the ladies' room. When she left the restroom, the music had stopped. Please let him be on break, not interrupted by Dad.

In the semidarkness of the hallway, she ran into someone. A man, who grabbed her arms and kept her from stumbling. She couldn't see his face, but apologized for her clumsiness. "Oh, excuse me."

"Don't worry about it, they keep it pretty dark in here." He turned and escorted her back to the dining room. Once they were in the light, she looked up at him and her heart nearly stopped. He was taller than he seemed on stage, and quite handsome.

He let go of her arms and took a step back. "Are you all right now?"

His crooked smile and quiet, polite manner impressed Connie. She smiled and nodded. "Yes, thank you."

Alton appeared at his shoulder. "Connie, are you okay?"

Dad almost fell over chairs trying to get to them.

"Would you have a minute for a photograph, Mr. Presley?" he asked, bold as ever.

Elvis smiled. "I'd be honored."

Dad barked out orders. "Connie, stand closer to him. Alton, you stand by Connie—now squeeze together a little more—say cheese!"

Connie suppressed a groan. Her dad.

Alton extended his hand toward Elvis. "Alton Wade." While they shook hands, he introduced Connie as his fiancée.

"Congratulations, you're a mighty lucky man." He smiled and winked at Connie. He shook Dad's hand, then walked with him to the platform.

Dad snapped a couple more photos of Elvis with his guitar. "He's a real gentleman," he told them as he slid into his seat.

Elvis began speaking into the microphone. "I'd like to dedicate this next song to some brand new friends who'll be getting married next week." He nodded toward them as he strummed the opening chords to *I Love You Because.*

Alton reached for her hand and squeezed it, while gazing into her eyes.

She would've been embarrassed if her dad's attention had not been glued to the stage. He was on cloud nine, from the looks of it. Dad loved all kinds of music.

When the song ended, Alton stood. "We better get on the road. It'll be dark before we get home."

Dad raised his hand to Elvis, who nodded in return.

"He seems real nice," he said on the way out of the cafe. "Thank you, Alton. I enjoyed that."

Alton grinned. "You can thank my brother for the meal." He paid for the fuel and told me take you someplace nice. I don't imagine this was what he had in mind, but I knew how well you liked barbecue."

Dad rubbed his belly. "Yes, sir. That was some prime 'cue."

On the ride home, Connie snuggled up next to Alton and leaned her head against his shoulder. As she drifted off to sleep, Dad was still talking about Elvis and wondering if those photos would be worth money someday.

Mother and Miss Annabelle were sitting on the front porch when Alton pulled into the drive. The sun had nearly disappeared. The evening star was rising. Soon the mosquitoes would chase everyone inside.

"About time y'all got back." Mother fanned herself in slow motion, no doubt hoping to keep the bugs at bay.

Connie climbed the steps to the porch. "I hope Joseph is all right."

"Oh, yes. He's sound asleep. In for the night. We kept him so busy all day, he fell asleep in his supper." Miss Annabelle hugged Connie.

Mother rose to greet Alton. "We were just worried you

may have had engine trouble. That car hasn't taken a long trip in years."

"The car was fine." Alton gave his mother a side hug.

Mac rubbed his hands together. "Guess who we met? And I got pictures."

Connie looked at Alton, a smile on her face. "Dad, they're not going to guess. They won't know who he is."

"Elvis Presley," Mac said.

"Who?" Mother raised her brows at Alton.

"Elvis Presley," Alton repeated. "He's a singer. Really popular among the younger set. I'm surprised we found him at such a small cafe. He's already been on tour, I believe."

"Oh, well." He could tell Mother was not really impressed by their find. "We have leftovers from supper, if you're hungry."

Mac patted his stomach. "I could eat."

Alton smiled as he held the door for everyone to enter. He caught Connie's hand and pulled her back outside and into his arms.

She leaned against him, smiling into his eyes. "You're shameless."

He touched her nose. "I'm a man in need of a kiss." He kissed her deeply, till she melded against him. Until his mother called out.

"Alton, where'd you go? Food's ready."

They sneaked through the door, where Connie tiptoed up the stairs, to go and check on Joseph.

Alton considered waiting for her, till Mother appeared at the door to the kitchen, hands on her hips. "What're you doing? Where's Connie?"

"She went upstairs to peek at the baby. I thought I'd wait for her."

At that moment, Connie came back down the steps. "Sorry to keep you waiting, I just had to see him."

Alton grabbed her hand and led her to kitchen, tempted to steal another kiss behind his mother's back.

Chapter Twenty-Eight

Annabelle read the letter again. Jensen Wade requested her presence at a meeting in his office on Tuesday morning. This could not be good. She chewed her lower lip and gazed into the distance.

It had to be about the property … unless … would he try to do something to delay the wedding, this close to the day? Why would that thought even enter her head? She still found it difficult to trust the man.

Tuesday morning—how was she going to even get there? She had no car, Jensen knew that. She gazed toward the highway. There was a bus stop about a mile up the road.

She scanned the letter once more before heading into the house.

Connie stood at the stove, stirring a pot of something savory. She turned, spoon in hand, her other hand palm up beneath it. "Here, taste this. I think it's missing something."

"It smells wonderful." Annabelle leaned forward for the taste. The rich flavor caught her by surprise. "It's delicious. But I see what you mean. There is something." She crossed to the Hoosier cabinet and shuffled through the spice shelf. "Here it is."

"Nutmeg? Really?"

Annabelle nodded. "Just a smidgen. Use the side of the grater with the smallest holes."

She found the grater and handed it to Connie, watching as the girl sent a couple of scrapes into the stew. Connie stirred it and was about to taste again when Annabelle stopped her. "Let it simmer a bit, then taste it."

She set the spoon down and faced Annabelle. "Did you get something in the mail?"

Annabelle handed her the letter.

As she read it, her brow creased. She raised her eyes to Annabelle's. "What is this?"

"I don't know. But I guess I'll find out."

"I'll ask Alton to drive you in."

"I don't want you to do that. He's a busy man, getting ready for the wedding and all."

"He's going to want to know about this."

"Well, you can tell him, but don't worry about asking him to drive me in. I'll take the bus."

Connie arched her brows. "Okay."

Joseph's hungry cry pierced the air.

Annabelle smiled "Love's calling."

Matilda Grace's cottage-style house exuded a welcoming warmth as Connie entered. Most of her friends had already arrived. The cozy living room seemed ready to burst. Surely there was no room for her.

Matilda greeted Connie with her usual bubbly excitement. "Sit here and make yourself comfortable. We're almost ready to begin." She scampered into a side room, possibly the kitchen.

Connie sat in a large, overstuffed chair in the middle of the room, a tight circle of mostly occupied chairs surrounding her. She almost laughed as that radio show Momma used to love—*Queen for a Day*—popped into her mind. Everyone smiled back at her, though they had no way of knowing the reason for her expression. A buzz of polite conversation filled the void.

Julie entered, a laden tray in her hands, and headed straight for Connie. She had to turn sideways to pass through the circle of chairs, but didn't seem to mind. "It's going to be so much fun."

Connie doubted that. She'd been to her share of showers. They usually played goofy games and gossiped. But when Matilda settled into the chair beside her, a hush fell over the room.

"I thought it would be nice if we started with prayer."

Connie bowed her head. She had never attended a

Southern Baptist shower. Maybe it would be different.

"Lord, we thank you for this time we have together. Help us to be a blessing …"

After Matilda said amen, Connie opened her eyes and looked around the room. By this time, her entire class had assembled—even Maggie—she tried not stare, but couldn't help the amazement. Must be an obligatory event, or maybe some of the others had inflicted guilt on her.

They played one game to see who could come up with the most words from "bridal shower." They offered advice to the bride. Some of it was useful.

Matilda spoke again. "We know you'll be moving into a well-equipped home, but we wanted you to have some things of your own."

The gifts were lovely. Things like towels, embroidered pillowcases, handmade doilies, and even a silver tray for her dresser. Afterward, Matilda and Julie served refreshments while everyone fellowshipped.

Connie stepped into the kitchen for a drink of water, and nearly ran into Maggie. Was she hiding? "Thank you for coming, Maggie."

Maggie murmured something unintelligible.

Connie almost turned and left her there, but she hesitated. It was now, or never. "Maggie, I … I know you had hoped to marry Alton."

Color flooded Maggie's cheeks. Her eyes flashed. "I don't know what you're talking about."

Connie ignored her clipped denial, and gave her a soft

smile. "I've often wondered why, because you're so young and pretty. Surely you could have anyone—"

"You really don't know what you're talking about," she rasped, keeping her voice low. "In case you haven't noticed, we live in a small town. We don't have an abundant supply of eligible bachelors."

Connie nodded. "I know that. But Alton's ... a farmer."

"He's a landowner."

"Yes, a landowner who loves farming. He'll always be a farmer. I can't see you living out there, a farmer's wife. You belong in town. You are parties and concerts and plays."

Maggie turned her face away, but didn't comment.

An idea popped into Connie's head. Should she mention it? She drew a breath. "Have you met John Woodruff yet?"

Maggie faced Connie, her dark eyes piercing, one brow arched. "Who?"

"He's new in town, working at the courthouse. I could introduce you." Storm clouds descended over Maggie again, but before she could open her mouth, Connie continued. "His family's from Jackson. They own *Carriage's Department Store*."

Alton stood looking out the window. Here and there, bits of white appeared among the green leaves of the cotton. Some of the bolls were popping. It wouldn't be long now. By the time he returned from his honeymoon—their honeymoon—the idea sent a thrill through his body. Head to toe. He couldn't even finish his thoughts about the cotton.

After last night's bridal shower, he took the long way home, just for a few more minutes alone with Connie. Parting with her had become more difficult with each passing day.

He moved away from the window, his mind filling up with tasks he needed to complete before the wedding.

One of them was on the way up the stairs. Alton watched Anthony's ascent from the landing.

"Hey, Mr. Alton, we got it ready in plenty of time." He carried a couple of boards under his right arm. "Where does it go?"

Alton stepped to the master bedroom and swung the door open. "In here."

Willie climbed the stairs, with more lengths of wood. "Morning, Mr. Alton."

"Morning, Willie. You know where it goes."

"Yes, sir, I shore do. I can't wait to see it all set up."

Alton agreed, but he held back. "Do you need help carrying the rest?"

"No, me and Anthony can get it," He headed back down the stairs.

The screen door slammed. It opened again as the men carried a large headboard up the stairs. The sheen of the amber wood caught the light. He followed the men into the bedroom this time. He couldn't help himself, he had to see it.

"It's a work of art, Willie."

"I'm happy you think so, Mr. Alton."

The clock downstairs chimed. He blew out a breath. "I need to go. When you're finished, leave the door open to air out the room." He paused at the door. "It's amazing, Willie. Thank you."

Willie grinned and nodded. "You're most welcome, sir."

Downstairs, Alton wished Mother a good day and headed out the door.

Samson jumped into the truck and Alton followed. "You're going to have to ride in the back on the return trip, and you better not complain."

Connie and Joseph were staying with Mac and Mother while Alton took Miss Annabelle to town. After the meeting with Jensen, Miss Annabelle had a shopping list to complete.

Samson danced around them as the ladies climbed in with the baby. Next, he jumped into the truck bed and sat down. Eying his master, the dog's face radiated something akin to pride, as though he'd herded his flock into the truck.

Alton shook his head and chuckled. "Good boy."

A few minutes later, he left Connie, Joseph, and one

happy dog at Sutter's Landing.

Miss Annabelle rode in silence. Highly unusual. Alton glanced at her from time to time. She tended to hide her feelings, but he could plainly see the lines furrowing her brow. "You all right?"

"I'm fine. I just don't like not knowing."

Alton nodded. "I'm the same way."

He parked in front of his brother's law office, got out, and helped Annabelle climb down. "I'll be across the street."

"All right. Thanks again for the ride."

He waited until she entered Jensen's office before he crossed to the drugstore. The bell tinkled as he entered. A fan whirred over the dairy bar. Folks sat at the counter, drinking coffee. Several of them smiled greetings.

"Morning, Alton," Tom called from the pharmacy desk.

Alton waved to Tom, found a stool, and sat. "Coffee, please, Freddie."

After ringing up a customer, Tom sidled over to the counter and stood beside Alton. "Business in town, today?" He grinned. "Maybe a license or some such?"

Alton stirred sugar into his coffee. "We did that the other day. All set on that front. I brought Annabelle in for a meeting with my brother."

A muscle in Tom's jaw flinched at the mention of Annabelle's name.

Alton suppressed a grin by sipping his coffee.

Tom slid onto a vacant stool and propped his elbow on the counter. He didn't ask about Annabelle's meeting with Jensen, but the question hung in the air all the same.

"Good coffee," Alton said to Freddie.

Tom still didn't speak.

A customer got up from the counter. "See ya, Tom, Mr. Alton."

"See ya, Bud. Come again," Tom said.

Alton nodded to the man.

The door opened and shut.

"I don't know what it's about." Alton kept his voice low. "She got a letter from Jensen."

Tom rubbed his brow. "Hmm. That could be something about the land."

"Could be."

"Well, I guess if it's something I'm supposed to know, I'll hear about it."

Alton nodded. "Most likely."

Tom looked as though he might say something else, but he changed his mind. Probably too many people in the place. When the phone rang, he went to answer it.

Alton picked up a newspaper and flipped through the pages. It was the Jackson Sun. Wonder who left that here?

Forty minutes or so ticked away on the clock before the door opened again, and Annabelle entered. With a glance to the back, she headed to the counter and sat beside Alton.

"Morning, Miss Annabelle," Freddie called out.

Bo Anderson gave a nod. "Howdy-do, Miss Annabelle."

She greeted them then looked straight ahead.

Alton observed her calm, which settled him somewhat, but when she didn't speak, his curiosity grew. "Almost finished. You want something?"

Her lips tight, she shook her head.

Tom almost fell over the phone cord trying to get back up front. His eyes latched onto Annabelle and didn't let go. "Morning, Miss Annabelle."

"Morning, Tom."

Tom glanced at Alton before refocusing on Annabelle's face. "You all right?"

"I'm just fine, Tom." Her smile wavered.

Alton scratched his eyebrow. Whatever happened in Jensen's office, it had rendered her pretty much speechless.

He rose. "I guess we better be on our way."

Annabelle stepped down from the stool.

Tom looked crestfallen. Like a man in love.

Alton held out his hand. "Good day to you, Tom."

Tom gripped his hand. "Alton."

Surely the silence would break in the truck. After all, they still had an errand to run in Jackson, and he didn't want to spend the entire time dancing around this thing.

As he settled into his seat, she turned to him. "Jensen asked me not to say anything to Tom. He's decided to relax his stance on selling that land."

Alton backed out of the parking spot. "What's that

mean?"

"In light of everything that's happening with the two families, he thinks it's time. He's gonna sign the permits and whatnot to get the land divided up so Tom can buy it outright. Except for the mineral rights, of course. It'll still be deed restricted."

"In light of … are those his words?"

She nodded. "He said Tom came to his office and told him he forgave him for everything that happened."

Alton glanced at her then back at the road. Her eyes held moisture, like they might overflow at any minute. He hoped not.

"He did, huh? How about that."

"Well, that young John Woodruff was there when it happened, and he thought it would be good for Jensen to clear the air. So, he had me sign the preliminary papers. He plans to have Tom in as soon as the plat is done, so he can get it filed at the courthouse."

Alton hated to ask, but he couldn't help himself. "Did you read everything thoroughly?"

She glared at him. "Every jot and tittle."

He held up his hand. "Just checking. So, Tom will own the property. How do you feel about that?"

Annabelle patted her purse. "Like a woman of substance."

Alton glanced at her and found a smile on her face.

"God is good."

Alton laughed. "Yes, He is."

Chapter Twenty-Nine

Connie wore her yellow suit, only she couldn't seem to get the skirt seam just right, and the hat kept coming loose from her hair.

The music started. Frustrated, she applied her lipstick, then hurried to the staircase, where she glanced down to find sneakers on her feet. Good grief!

She ran back to her room, but couldn't find her shoes. Wait a minute—she was in her room—not Miss Lillian's. This was all wrong. Why was she still home? Had they changed the venue at the last moment?

The music outside grew louder. Ah!

Taking the stairs two at a time, she glanced about for Dad. Where was he? After all this, had he gone back to Hawaii before the wedding? Panic sent her heart into wild beats. She had no choice, she'd have to walk the aisle alone.

People waited, their backs to her. Maybe they

wouldn't notice she was wearing her sneakers. Only Maggie turned to glare at her, as Connie made her way up the garden path.

"Is that the only pair of shoes she has?" Maggie hissed.

Jensen scowled at her. "Think about what you're doing."

"I will never be your friend." Marla shook a finger at her. "You're just not good enough for our family."

Connie swallowed back tears. She couldn't let anything spoil this day. Poor Alton, it would break his heart. He'd waited too long. She looked for him. There he stood, with his back to her as he faced Pastor Nathan.

Why didn't he turn? She wanted to see his face, to know what he thought of her, dressed in the wedding outfit.

Maybe he'd changed his mind.

She reached his side, gripped his arm and pulled. He turned … but it wasn't Alton.

It was Joseph.

Connie gasped for breath and woke from the dream, damp with sweat. Tears burned her eyes. She stuffed a knuckle between her lips to keep from sobbing. Why had she dreamed such a thing?

Was it still guilt? Hadn't she conquered that? Joseph would want someone to take care of her and his son. And he'd be honored that it was Alton. Assurance washed over her.

It was true. It had to be true.

She sat up and swung her feet over the side of the bed.

Getting up, she tiptoed into the kitchen for a drink of water. Her hands shook as she reached for a glass and turned on the spigot. As she sipped the water, she moved to the window. Bright moonlight bathed the landscape. It almost looked white with snow.

She set her glass down, and turned from the window, but didn't want to go back to bed. In the moonlight, she easily found her way to the sofa, where she sat with her knees drawn up beneath her chin. It was probably normal to experience anxiety and nerves a week ahead of one's wedding. She hadn't had any fear the first time, but she'd been so young. She never used to worry about anything. She just went headlong into life.

Alton was the most amazing man she'd ever known. In some ways, he and her late husband were alike, but in other ways, not at all. Alton was mature. More serious than Joseph, though lately … a thrill ran down her spine at the memory of the stolen kisses. The secret smiles. The light in his eyes.

She sucked in a deep breath and blew it out, before taking another sip of water.

It had to be anxiety. After a few minutes, she leaned back on the sofa and allowed herself to relax. She'd loved two amazing men in her life. Did she deserve such an honor? Maybe not, but she'd take it.

She sent up a prayer, and let her mind drift. Alton's face lit her thoughts. Was he awake, too? Or was he sleeping, dreaming of her?

Annabelle assembled the gifts she'd purchased for Connie. With Lillian's help, she'd made a list of the articles Connie needed. The money Lillian gave her stretched even farther with the end of season sale going on at *Rosenbloom's*. Annabelle had even found a dress she could afford from her ever dwindling savings. Knowing she had money coming in from the sale of the property, she'd splurged a bit for a matching hat. Wouldn't Connie be surprised when she saw her Momma dressed up fine for the wedding?

"What's this?" Connie peeked over her shoulder as Annabelle tucked a small, white box into the shopping bag.

"None of your beeswax." She tried to keep a straight face, but couldn't.

Connie giggled. "I miss Emily, don't you?"

The beeswax remark was one of Emily's favorite sayings. "I sure do. I don't understand why we haven't heard from her. I hope she's all right."

"I'm sure she's just busy with that new baby."

"I suppose."

Connie folded her arms. "So, you're not going to tell me what's in that enormous shopping bag filled with boxes?"

"Nope."

She shrugged. "Okay, have it your way. Are you about ready to walk over to Sutter's?"

"Well, maybe in a minute. I need one more thing, so shoo!"

"I'm not one of your chickens. You have to ask politely." She faked a scowl.

Annabelle laughed it off. "So, *please* wait in the other room? By the time you get Joseph, I'll be ready to go."

"I think the stress of this wedding is starting to get to you," Connie tossed over her shoulder as she walked away.

Annabelle mumbled to herself as she stuffed the last box into the bag. Now she had to find a spot for it, where Connie wouldn't be tempted to peek. She stepped to the other side of the bed. At least it would be out of sight. When she set the bag down, she heard a soft noise. Was that a mouse? She'd hate for mice to get into the packages.

"Ginger must not be keeping up with her work." Poor girl had gotten so large, she could barely move. She mostly laid around these days.

Annabelle lifted the bag and looked under it. Nothing there. She got down on her knees, lifted the bedspread, and peered beneath. A pair of large, yellow eyes greeted her. Ginger meowed.

"Oh, it's just you. Are you hiding under there to have your babies, huh?" In answer, there came a softer mewing sound, like little birds peeping. "Kittens."

She pushed up from her knees and stood beside the bed. She couldn't leave the bag there, so she stuffed it in the corner near the chifforobe.

"Connie, the kittens are here."

Connie entered, carrying Joseph.

A moment later, all of them lay on the floor looking at the kitties.

A knock sounded at the door.

Annabelle got up and dusted herself off. "Who could that be?"

Connie rolled over, gathered Joseph and got up.

Mac stood looking through the screen door. "Morning, Miss Annabelle, Connie. I was hoping I hadn't missed you. I drove the car over to pick you up, so you don't have to walk. Looks like it might rain."

"I'll be right out," Annabelle told Mac, waving him on.

He turned to help Connie with Joseph.

Annabelle hurried to the bedroom. If they were going by car, she could take the gifts. She grabbed the bag, and scurried from the room. "We'll be back later, Ginger. Hold down the fort."

Connie followed Dad to the car, settling in beside him in the front seat. "Where's Alton this morning?"

"He's busy with something at the barn."

Momma opened the back door and got in.

Connie glanced over the back of the seat. "There's room for you up front, Momma."

"I'm just fine right here." She and Dad exchanged a glance that ignited Connie's curiosity. Those two were planning something. Did it involve that large shopping bag?

When they reached Sutter's, Momma got out of the car and headed straight inside, bag in hand.

Connie watched her go, then looked at Joseph. "What's your grandma up to?"

Joseph gurgled and clapped his hands.

Alton held the back door open. "Good morning, darling. Come on in."

Warmth and a wonderful aroma greeted them in the kitchen.

Regina stirred something on the stove. She nodded toward the dining room door. "I believe they've gone upstairs."

Laughter echoed in the stairwell. "I think we found them," Connie walked toward the stairs. "What are they doing up there?"

"I've been told it's for womenfolk only, so I'll wait down here." Alton reached for Joseph, kissed her forehead, and gazed into her eyes. "See you at dinner."

Connie followed the chatter to Miss Lillian's room. She pushed open the door. "Am I invited to the party?"

Miss Lillian turned. "Honey, you are the party. Come on in."

Momma looked like she'd stolen the last cookie.

Connie stepped to Miss Lillian's side. "What are we doing?"

"Well, I was thinking, since you can't see Alton before the wedding, you can use this room to get ready. Mac's going to pick you up on Saturday morning. You can come straight up here, and make yourself at home." She stepped around the room as if giving a tour. "This is the second largest of the bedrooms, and there's a direct view of the garden, so you'll have an idea when to go down."

"But this is your room, Miss Lillian."

"I can get ready anywhere, and besides, I'll be busy. You can put your things in here." She opened the closet door and tugged at a hanger. "Let's move this, it's just in the way. Here, you hold it."

She handed a dress to Connie—a deep, rose pink, in a beautiful style. Connie held it up to the light. "Oh, Miss Lillian, this is lovely."

"I'm glad you like it. I bought it for your wedding trip. The color is perfect for you. What do you think, Annabelle?"

Connie glanced from one to the other. This is what they'd been up to. And there was more in that bag Momma brought, unless she missed her guess. They knew she wouldn't spend money on herself, so they'd done it for her. "You shouldn't have, but I'm glad you did. It's lovely."

"Well, that's not all. Annabelle had all kinds of fun shopping for you. That suitcase over there is filled and ready to go."

"What?" She looked at the suitcase at the foot of the bed.

"Go ahead, you can open it, but don't mess it up. We've got everything in there, perfectly folded. All you'll need are your toiletries."

Tears stung her eyes as Connie opened the suitcase. She touched the beautiful white silk undergarments, a stylish cotton blouse. How had they done all this without her knowing? She looked at Momma. "When did you have time?"

Momma's chin came up. "The other day after my meeting with Jensen, Alton carried me to Jackson. *Rosenbloom's* already had all your sizes, so it was easy as pie. I had a ball."

"Oh, Momma. But you need clothes, too."

"Pumpkin, I have all I need, don't you worry. You won't be ashamed of me, come Saturday."

Connie shook her head. "I would never be ashamed of you."

"It's just a saying."

But Connie read the doubt in Momma's eyes. Did it have something to do with losing her to Alton and Miss Lillian? No one could ever take her place in Connie's life, surely Momma knew that by now.

Miss Lillian stepped to her dresser and pulled out a small drawer. She returned and held out her hand to reveal a charming pendant necklace set with a pale blue stone. "It belonged to my mother."

"It's beautiful—so delicate."

"It's aquamarine, mother's birthstone. I want you to wear it on Saturday. I reckon it'll do for something old, something borrowed, something blue."

"Oh, Miss Lillian, I don't know what to say."

"Thank you does well enough." She placed the pendant back in the drawer. "It'll be right here when you need it."

"Dinner," Regina called up the stairs.

Momma sighed. "Just in time. All this subterfuge made me hungry."

Miss Lillian chortled. "You're a card, Annabelle. We're going to have so much fun together—just like old times." She linked arms with her as they started toward the stairs.

Connie couldn't resist teasing them. "Just don't forget about Joseph, while y'all are having all that fun."

Momma chuckled and waved her hand. "Oh, don't worry about the baby. He's gonna have two doting grandmas to look after him."

Chapter Thirty

Friday showed up with an overcast sky. Not to be deterred, Connie washed diapers, and hung them on the line. Now if only the rain held off, they'd dry quickly. She and Momma needed to be at Sutter's for dinner. Pastor and Mrs. Nathan had also been invited, so they could rehearse the wedding.

Momma stepped outside, Joseph on her hip. "I never expected to feel sad about washing diapers."

Connie glanced at her. "I know. There'll be a lot of last times today." She stepped near Momma to put an arm around her waist. "But I don't want you to be sad, Momma. It's a new beginning for both of us."

Momma straightened her back. "You're right, it is." She kissed Joseph's pudgy cheek. "I know you won't be far away. I can come over as often as I want." Her attempt to smile failed.

"But you've never been alone, I know." Connie went

back to the wash, and hung the last two diapers. "You may be surprised how much you like it. Besides, you'll have a houseful of kittens."

Momma laughed. "Not for long, I won't. I intend to give them away. The calico has already been claimed."

A black pick-up pulled into the old wagon road and stopped. A couple of men got out and stepped around to the back of the truck.

Momma's brow furrowed. "Wonder who that is?"

One man carried a satchel over his shoulder and what looked like straight sticks in his hand.

Connie watched the men for a moment. "Surveyors, I think. Didn't Jensen say they'd be out?"

"Yes. I didn't expect them this soon, is all."

"Have you heard from Tom?"

Momma shook her head and fumbled to hold on to Joseph, who struggled to get down. She set him in the empty laundry basket.

Connie handed him a clothes peg to play with as she and Momma watched the men set up their equipment. "Soon, I guess they'll be digging the foundation, and starting on the house." She looked at Momma. "Maybe you won't be so lonely, after all. You can bake them cookies."

Momma cackled. "You always look on the bright side, don't you?" She walked along the line and checked to see if any of the diapers were dry. "Did Lillian tell you she plans to go to her sister's after y'all get back home?"

Connie scanned her mother-in-law's expression. "No.

Is her sister ill again?"

"She just wants to give you a chance to settle in, get used to the place on your own. 'Course, you won't really be alone. Regina will be there most days."

"I hope Miss Lillian doesn't feel … obligated … or uncomfortable. I don't want to push her out of her own home."

Momma had found several dry cloths, which she draped over her arm, dropping the pins into the bag. "I don't think she feels compelled to go, she wants to. You know she goes over to Bells every once in a while. It gives her sister's girl a rest."

Connie nodded as she crouched beside Joseph and smoothed his silky hair. She'd considered telling Momma about the dream. Just talking about it might help ease the anxiety that still stung her emotions, but she hesitated. Would it cause Momma pain?

Hearing voices, Connie rose and looked to the place where the men were working. When she noticed Dad standing with them, she almost laughed out loud. Of course, he had to go see what they were doing.

Masculine laughter drifted their way.

Momma sniffed. "Your daddy surprised me."

Connie pulled her gaze from the men and latched onto Momma. "In what way?"

"The way he treated you when you left home—I saw how it hurt you—and Joseph. But I suppose he was just reacting."

"He has apologized for that."

Momma draped another dry cloth over her arm. "I know, he apologized to me, too."

"Did he?"

"Ladies, I've come to offer my assistance," Mac called from just inside the barbed-wire fence. He ducked between the two top wires, to join them at the clothesline. "Alton said to tell you, he'll bring you back home this afternoon in the truck, and haul back anything that needs to go over to Sutter's.

Anxiety twisted a knot in Connie's stomach. She'd been halfhearted about packing. She needed to get everything ready so there'd be no delay tomorrow.

Dad touched her shoulder. "You okay, daughter?"

"Yes. There's still so much to do, I'm a little overwhelmed, I guess."

He gazed down his nose at her. "Just so it's not cold feet."

Determination rose within her, pushing back the memory of the dream. She couldn't let it spoil the excitement and pleasure of the next twenty-four hours. Forcing her lips into an upturn, she bent to pick up Joseph. "It's not."

"There's still so much to do is all." Momma met Connie's eyes. "And maybe being hit with reality all of a sudden."

Mac nodded. "I understand. It's a big life change. Moving to a new house, learning to live with new folks."

"Learning to boss servants around." A mischievous grin transformed Momma's face.

Connie glared at her. "You mean learning to submit to Regina. She's the boss of their kitchen, and I'm perfectly fine with that."

As soon as he could get away, Alton left the kitchen and headed to the barn. For nearly twenty minutes, he'd been subjected to Regina's and Mother's plans for the reception. He'd about had all he could stand. The only thing that interested him was having the wedding over and done.

He'd nearly made it to the gap when Jensen's car pulled into the drive. He tilted his head back and gazed heavenward. No. Why today?

Samson ran ahead of him back to the house, raising a ruckus.

"Samson, heel," Alton commanded, but his heart wasn't really in it.

The dog stopped barking, trotted over, and sat.

Jensen got out of the car. "Morning, Alton."

"Good morning."

"I was over talking to the surveyors and thought I'd stop by."

Alton brushed his hands together. "Work's started,

huh?"

"This morning. I still don't like it, but I figure if everything works out as it should, the property may not leave the family after all." He made an odd noise that sounded like a giggle.

Alton figured he'd misheard. "How's that?"

Jensen leaned a fist against the car. "I don't make a habit of listening to gossip. Except when it helps me win a case, of course." He sucked his teeth. "I heard Tom Franklin has a thing for Annabelle."

Alton raised a brow, but didn't comment.

"So, I put two and two together, and got four. In this case that means the Wades win."

Alton shook his head. "I'm still not quite following you."

Jensen held up his right forefinger. "Tom buys the property from Annabelle," he held up two fingers. "Annabelle marries Tom." Three fingers. "The property goes to Annabelle if she outlives him, or to her heirs, who will eventually inherit anyway." Four fingers. "And there you go."

Looking at his brother's self-satisfied smile, Alton wanted to turn around and continue his journey to the barn. But he held his ground. There were any number of things that could happen with Jensen's perceived scenario, including Tom outliving Annabelle. Perhaps it would occur after his brother had met his own demise. And no one would care who ended up with the property.

"Do you want to come in, Jensen?"

"What? No. I don't have time for socializing." His chest expanded as he drew a deep breath, reminding Alton of a rooster about to crow. "I'm happy, Alton. Can't you see that? I just wanted to share it with you, so you'd know I'm okay with all that's happening right now."

He narrowed his eyes at Alton, scolding. "I still don't really like the fact that your choice of a bride carries a bit of color, but I've decided not to make an issue of it. I could have—but I'm not going to. I'm taking the high road." He opened the door and climbed in. With a wave of his hand, he backed around and headed down the drive.

Taking the high road? Alton had seldom seen Jensen so jovial. He wanted to trust him—wanted to believe his brother had really changed—but history gave him pause. After the elections, then what? Would he go back to his old ways? While Alton processed these thoughts, his conscience bothered him. As a Christian, it's always preferable and good to believe the best.

He just didn't want to get burned again.

At quarter till six, Alton, Mac, and Connie gathered in the parlor with Pastor Nathan and his wife, Ilene.

"I thought we might do a run-through after supper, if that's all right with you," Pastor said.

Alton looked to Connie.

"I like that idea."

Pastor pulled a small notepad and pencil from his jacket pocket. "Also, I need your proper names—what you want me to say in the vows."

"Alton Ezekiel Wade."

"Nice name." Pastor jotted it down. "I like that." He leveled his gaze at Connie.

She drew a breath. "Constance Leilani Cross … er … Pruitt …" she bit down on her lower lip. "I don't know. How should we do that?"

Ilene Nathan spoke up. "Leilani—that's beautiful. What does it mean?"

Mac supplied the answer. "Bird of heaven. Each one of our daughters has a traditional American name, and a traditional Hawaiian name."

"How wonderful," Ilene turned to her husband. "What should she do about the surname?"

He tilted his head to the side. "It's entirely up to you, Connie. We can use both, if you'd like to honor your father and Miss Annabelle."

Alton caught sight of Miss Annabelle standing in the doorway, as though she waited to hear what Connie had to say.

Connie rested her hands in her lap. "If it's not too much, maybe we could use it all?" She glanced at Alton.

He gave her a nod.

Annabelle's expression relaxed into a smile.

"All right, but I'll need to know how to spell Leilani."

Connie spelled it for him.

His lips moved as he wrote. "Constance Leilani Pruitt Cross." He glanced up at her. "Bird of heaven. I like it."

Connie laughed as Pastor finished another of his hilarious adventures. He had led such an interesting life. No wonder his sermons were always so riveting.

Ilene impressed her as well. She'd always thought the pastor's wife so straight-laced and reticent. Far from it. She was truly funny, but respectful, a woman who knew her place and held it well.

After the meal, they wandered out to the garden. Ilene loved what they'd done.

"This is wonderful. You're going to have a showplace when this fills in. And I hope you intend to leave the arch. Climbing roses, or wisteria would look beautiful there."

After the mini-tour, Pastor walked them through the entire wedding.

"It's so informal, we don't really need a full rehearsal. Bull Reynolds told me you'd agreed to *All Things Bright and Beautiful* for the bridal march. He loves that hymn. It'll give you chills the way he plays it on that fiddle."

Connie nodded. "I'd never heard it, so he played it for us. It was very touching."

The men wandered off, talking cotton.

Ilene and Connie sat with Momma and Miss Lillian on the front porch. The women talked of days gone by while Joseph lay on a blanket, playing with a few toys.

Connie couldn't help but look at this as a small sampling of what her life would be like. Sutter's Landing had wrapped her in its arms and welcomed her.

Earlier in the day, she'd stood in the master bedroom, struck by the beauty of the bedstead Willie made. She found his signature—an intricate horse's head in a circle, centered near the bottom of the headboard.

She'd looked up to find Alton leaning against the door jamb, his eyes burning holes in her.

Ignoring him was difficult at this stage, so she'd concentrated on the room, feeling the gift of it all.

Afterward, she wandered the upstairs hall and landing, gazing at the many photographs. The history of the place and its family intrigued her.

Samson announced the return of the men and brought Connie back to the present. While she'd daydreamed, Joseph had fallen asleep clutching a toy car.

Ilene rose from her chair. "I reckon we'd best be going. It's getting late, and some of us have a big day coming up." She winked at Connie.

"Yes, we do." Pastor gripped Alton's shoulder. "This time tomorrow you'll be an old married man."

Lillian brought Ilene's purse. "Y'all come over whenever you're ready in the morning."

As Alton walked them to their car, Dad put his arm around Connie. "So, tomorrow's the big day."

"Yes, and I'm glad. I don't think I could take much more of these preparations."

Dad chuckled. "Well, I'll hang around till you and Alton get back from your honeymoon. I thought it might be good for the ladies to have a driver in the house, in case of emergency."

"Thank you for that." She sighed. "I hate to see you go, Dad."

"It's time though. I miss the ocean. You're going to love my new place. I can't wait to show it to you, especially to Alton. He's never seen anything like it, so it'll all be new."

"Won't that be fun for you?" Dad would be like a kid with a new toy. He loved giving tours around the islands. "Maybe you should consider hosting tours."

He grinned. "I have thought about that."

Alton walked up. "I need to check on the beasts of the field. I'll be back in a bit."

Dad bent near her ear. "Why don't you go with him? I'll keep an eye on the little one."

Connie didn't wait, but jogged to catch up with Alton. They met at the gap. His expression brightened when he caught sight of her.

"Hello, beautiful."

The timbre of his voice sent a thrill through her. She moved into his open arms.

He sighed. "I needed a hug."

When she tilted her head back to look at him, he kissed her till her knees gave out. She clung to him, breathless, but happy. One more day.

After seeing that all the critters in the barn were in for the night, Alton strolled to the house hand-in-hand with Connie. Surely Heaven had come down, and he was walking in it.

They were about halfway back when Samson took off toward the drive. A black car rolled to a stop near the front.

Before he could speak, Connie gave a little hop.

Her face alight, she raised her arm and waved. "Judith!"

Judith jumped up and down, much like a small child excited with a new toy. "I've come to spend the night and help you get ready for your wedding."

Alton watched as the two women embraced. A moment later, Judith hugged him, too. He was going to like having a large family.

Chapter Thirty-One

September 17, 1955

After a restless night, Connie got up and made her bed. Joseph's soft snore assured her he still slept, so she crept into the kitchen, where Momma stood at the stove.

"Good morning. It's your wedding day," Momma smiled over her shoulder, while bacon sizzled in the pan. She turned the slices with a fork. "Coffee's ready."

Connie set the cups on the table. "Looks like a nice day, anyway."

"Crystal-clear, and gonna stay that way, according to Bitsy."

Connie giggled. "You and your chickens. How could they know what the weather's going to do?"

"Oh, they know." She moved the crispy slices of bacon to a plate and turned the heat down on the skillet. "Can you eat a couple of eggs?"

Connie swallowed a sip of coffee. "I don't know, my stomach's so full of flutters."

Momma turned to press a kiss to Connie's brow. "This is a big day. Flutters are completely normal. I'll just fix you one egg. Try and eat, to keep up your strength."

She hummed *Abide With Me* while cracking eggs into the skillet.

Judith entered, looking a bit worse for wear. They'd sat up way too late, packing and talking, and playing with the kittens. "You're mighty chipper this morning, Aunt Annabelle."

"Someone has to keep this party going. How many eggs you want?"

Judith grinned at Connie. "Two—I'm famished. I hope y'all didn't drink all the coffee."

Connie poured her a cup. "Here you go. I'm so glad you were able to take time off for the wedding."

"My boss is really keen. I have a lot of studying to do, but I can catch up on Sunday."

The food on the table, they sat down and waited as Momma prepared to say a blessing. After a very long, quiet moment, Connie peeked at her.

"Are you okay?"

Momma sucked in a breath. "I just realized this is our last—" her voice broke.

Connie covered her mouth as tears filled her eyes.

Judith jumped up, hugged Momma's shoulders, and kissed her cheek. "It's all right, Aunt Annabelle."

"I know," Momma dabbed at her nose with a hanky.

"I'll visit often. And I'm sure you'll be over at Sutter's

every chance you get."

"I'm sorry I'm blubbering like this."

"You don't have to apologize. I'll miss all our sweet times, just us two living in this cozy little house."

Momma chuckled. "You didn't always think it was such a cozy little place. Remember that first visit?"

Connie grimaced. "Oh, my goodness, it was a dump. No doubt about it. But you made it a home, Momma."

"It wasn't just me. All those folks from church, and you, and … little Joseph."

Judith straightened. "Don't start on that, you'll have us all blubbering. I plan to come out and spend weekends with you whenever I can. And besides, you'll never be really alone."

Momma drew a breath. "You're right. The Good Lord is always with me."

Joseph chose that moment to call out.

"Sounds like someone wants to join the party," Connie stepped into the bedroom and found Joseph standing in his crib.

"You better come see this."

Judith and Momma bustled into the room.

Momma pressed her hands together. "Well, I'll be, look at our big boy."

His chubby legs gave out.

Connie lifted him and held him close. "As if today needed anything more to make it special."

The closeness of Lillian's room, with so many of Connie's friends inside it pressed in on Annabelle. She left to go downstairs, but only made it as far as the landing. She held onto the banister, and forced a deep breath and slow exhale.

Back in the bedroom, the girls tittered and giggled, having a good old time. While Matilda worked on the bride's manicure, Julie fashioned Connie's hair into a French twist. Annabelle didn't want to spoil their fun, but she didn't feel right—hadn't felt quite right all morning.

Dizziness rolled over her, leaving her weak in the knees. She glanced around, looking for a chair. Not finding one, she crept into the nearest bedroom and sat on the bed. Judging from the articles strewn about, she figured it was the guest room, where Mac stayed.

A few minutes passed. Steady enough to stand, she headed for the landing and looked down. Had those stairs always been so steep? Her heart raced, her face flushed. What was happening to her?

A prayer on her lips, she made it down the steps, no problem. But when the side door swung open, she nearly lost her balance again.

Mac stepped inside. Seeing her, his brow furrowed. "Miss Annabelle—you all right?"

She drew another deep breath. "I'm just breathless

from the stairs, I reckon."

He grabbed a straight-backed chair. "Here, sit down. I'll get you a glass of water."

Mac returned almost before Annabelle knew he was gone. He set the glass on the table beside her.

Miss Lillian appeared in the doorway. "What's going on?"

Mac patted Annabelle's shoulder. "She got out of breath."

Lillian bent in front of Annabelle. "You're white as a sheet. Mac, help me move her to the sofa, where she can get her feet up."

"No need to fuss." Annabelle tried to resist, but she was soundly ignored. Too tired to care, she allowed them to help her up. Her stomach lurched. The room went black.

Hearing the commotion, Alton entered the front parlor in time to help Mac lower Annabelle's inert form to the sofa.

Mother rushed to the kitchen to get a damp rag.

Mac patted Annabelle's hand. "Annabelle? Annabelle, can you hear me?"

Alton knelt beside her. "Reckon I ought to call the doctor?"

"Yes." Mother bustled in to apply the cool rag to

Annabelle's forehead. "Could be her heart. We don't want to take any chances."

Alton rushed to the phone, and made the call. While waiting for the connection, he glanced up the stairs. Connie would want to know. She'd want to be here. But … he wasn't supposed to see her.

Mother's voice rang out. "Someone should go up and get Connie."

"I'm not supposed to see her."

"That doesn't matter now."

"I'll get her," Mac's quick steps sounded on the stairs.

Alton spoke to the doctor's receptionist. As he hung up, the noise increased. They must be coming down. Should he make himself scarce?

He stood like a deer in the headlights, uncertainty keeping him grounded to the spot.

Annabelle stirred and groaned.

Mother leaned over her. "Don't move, Annabelle. We've called the doctor."

Dressed in a pale blue robe, Connie ran into the room.

Her frightened eyes made him want to go to her, but he held back.

She raced to the sofa, and knelt beside it. "Momma, what is it?"

"She fainted." Mother put an arm around her. "We've called the doctor."

Connie nodded. "Dad told me."

Annabelle tried to sit up. "No. No doctor."

Mother pressed her fingers against Annabelle's chest. "Stay right where you are. We will have a doctor come look at you. We need to make sure you're all right."

"I'm fine. Just tired. Too much going on." Annabelle's voice sounded far away, as though she might faint again.

Alton moved forward. "Rest yourself, Miss Annabelle. Don't worry about anything."

She took Connie's hand. "The wedding—I don't want to delay the wedding."

"Don't you worry about it." Connie patted her hand. She looked up at Alton with calmer eyes than before.

He wanted to comfort her, reassure her. But he wasn't sure himself. Had Annabelle suffered a heart attack?

"Sheriff's coming," Matilda called from the doorway.

Alton had forgotten about Matilda and Julie. He strode toward the door and looked out.

The sheriff cut the siren as he pulled into the drive, but the light atop the car still flashed. Another car pulled in behind the sheriff's. Dr. Kestle rushed forward, bag in hand.

Alton held the door open. "She's in here, Doc." He remained at the door to talk to Sheriff Jordan. "I appreciate you doing that."

Jordan hooked his thumbs in his belt. "Doc said it was an emergency. Thought I'd wait around just in case she needs an ambulance, or something."

Alton nodded. Most likely, the sheriff didn't have anything else to do. "Can I get you anything?"

"No, you go on back inside. I'll wait out here."

Alton returned to the parlor just in time to be asked to leave. Doctor shooed everyone out so he could examine Annabelle. Mother sent Connie and the girls to the dining room. She laid her hand on Alton's arm. "Why don't you and Mac go sit on the porch?"

"Good idea. Sheriff's out there, anyway." He led the way to the porch.

"So, it's your wedding day." Sheriff took a seat as Alton and Mac settled into chairs.

Alton nodded. "Yep."

"Bad luck to see your bride on the wedding day."

Alton bit his lip and concentrated. How should he answer that?

Mac dismissed it with a wave of his hand. "Old wives' tale."

Sheriff chuckled. "Could be. Women stuff, anyway. Hope this doesn't delay the wedding too much."

Mac leaned close to Alton. "Annabelle said to go on ahead with it. I think she's going to be all right."

The sheriff looked from one to the other. "Maybe too much excitement. All that work getting ready, you know."

"Most likely." Alton kept his attention on the door. How long would it take?

Sheriff sat forward, leaning on his elbows. "The garden looks beautiful. One wouldn't even know the shanties had ever been there."

Mac rubbed the back of his neck. "The ladies have

been working on it, spiffing it up for the wedding."

Alton peered at his hands, checking his nails again. Wouldn't do to get married with dirt under his fingernails.

Mother pushed the screen open. "You can come back in."

Sheriff kept his seat. "I'll just wait out here."

Alton held the door open for Mac.

Dr. Kestle cleared his throat. "Seems to be anxiety. She's a bit dehydrated, blood pressure's high. Let her rest, drink plenty of fluids, and a light lunch. I believe she'll be just fine in time for the wedding. I do want to see her one day next week, though, for a thorough examination." He directed his attention to Mother. "Call the office Monday morning and set an appointment."

Mother nodded. "Will do."

The doctor shook Alton's hand on the way out the door. "Congratulations on your wedding, Alton. I hope you'll be very happy."

"Thank you, Doctor." Outside, he also thanked the sheriff. After both cars had completely disappeared, he returned inside. Though nothing would please him more than another long look at his soon-to-be bride, those women were set on keeping them apart for the rest of the day. He may as well cooperate.

"Bad luck," he heard repeated several times.

Alton didn't believe it, not for a second. With the Lord on your side, what need had you for luck?

While Momma relaxed on the sofa, sipping iced tea, Connie headed back upstairs.

Judith joined them with Joseph, fresh from his nap.

The minutes on the clock ticked away. Judith enjoyed a light snack, but Connie couldn't eat anything. Her nerves had completely taken possession of her appetite.

Judith handed her a glass of iced tea. "You should at least sip some tea, or we'll have another dehydration on our hands."

Connie loved Judith, but she'd give anything for a few moments alone. What a day it had been.

When the time finally came for her to don her dress, she fumbled badly.

Judith took over. "Here, let me help with that."

"Won't be long now. It's filling up fast."

Connie's stomach did a somersault at the thought of so many people watching as she repeated her vows. "My shoes! Where are my shoes?"

"Right here," Judith held the red heels. "Don't panic."

Connie slipped them on her feet, determined to keep them in her sight. She sucked in a breath and blew it out.

"Okay," Judith said. "Sit in the chair so I can get your hat in place."

Connie sat, taking care not to wrinkle her skirt. Maybe they should have done the hat before putting on the skirt?

No, it would have to go over her head, so that wouldn't work, either.

Maybe she should hum like Momma did when she was nervous, or troubled. But Connie couldn't think of a single tune. Not even one. She fiddled with the doily on the dressing table.

The necklace. "Wait." She jumped up and retrieved it from the small drawer in Miss Lillian's dresser.

Judith took it and draped it around her neck. "Oh, how lovely."

Connie told her what Miss Lillian had said.

"That's so sweet of her."

Judith picked up the hat and was just about to set it on Connie's head when they heard someone shouting. "Oh no, now what?" She stepped to the open window.

Women squealed. Samson barked.

Connie rushed forward, but Judith waved her away. "Oh no, you don't. What if someone sees you?"

"What if it's Momma?"

"It's not," Judith pushed the window higher and leaned out. "Oh, my gracious, folks are running about like there's a fire."

Connie's heart raced as panic filled her. "Judith, what's happening?"

"There's my brother." Judith leaned out the window. "What is it?"

He answered, but Connie couldn't make out what he said. She heard the laughter, though. Her panic eased a little as Judith erupted into giggles.

"A skunk."

Connie gazed at the ceiling. What else could go wrong?

Connie wrinkled her nose. "Aren't they nocturnal?"

"Usually, unless you startle them." Judith covered her nose. "Whew, I just got a whiff of it. Better shut the window."

Connie sat back down. "It's all so surreal."

"You're not kidding. I'll take the baby downstairs. I'm sure Pauletta's here to take care of him." She held him near enough so Connie could nuzzle his cheek and kiss him.

"Thanks, Judith." Relief rushed in. Finally, a few minutes alone to gather her thoughts and--

A soft knock sounded.

Now what? "Yes?" Connie caught Dad's reflection in the mirror.

"Don't you look a picture?" He sighed and shook his head. "There'll be a slight delay. I guess you heard the ruckus."

"Yes, it was a skunk."

"No, it was Samson. He'd met with a skunk. He ran all around, trying to get away from the odor, I guess. Folks scattered, and jumped back in their cars." He gave that goofy laugh and grinned ear-to-ear.

"Oh no, poor Samson."

Dad stepped into the room, his hands outstretched. "Stand up and let me look at you."

She stood, smoothed her skirt, and straightened her shoulders. Were those tears in his eyes?

His chest expanded with a deep breath. "You know, I was feeling sad that I never got to see you in bride white. But honey, I can't imagine you looking any better than you do right now."

Tears stung, but she forced them back. "Oh, Dad, thanks."

"I mean it, kid. You could be a movie star. Which reminds me, the newspaper's here. I mean, there's a reporter down there, with a camera. I guess this is big news."

"He'll have a good story, what with the skunk and all."

Dad cackled. "He sure will. Anything else will be the cherry on top. That means the pressure's off you, daughter."

Chapter Thirty-Two

Alton needed a headache powder. He rubbed the back of his neck, kneading his tight muscles. Could anything else go wrong? He didn't believe in bad luck, but this was ridiculous. Poor Samson hadn't meant to disrupt everything. Boy, had he made a mess. The scent still hung heavy in the air.

Pastor walked in the door, smiling and shaking his head. "Can you believe it? We're all set now, though. Here's what I was thinking—I'll go out and quiet everyone down, say a prayer over the whole situation. After that, I'll signal the music. That'll be your cue to come join me."

Alton's pain left, taking the stress with it. "Sounds good, Pastor."

He stood just inside the door, as Pastor called upon the saints to pray.

"Lord, as we gather together, we ask that You bless this day. Sweep over this beautiful garden, cleanse the air, and settle our hearts and minds."

As the pastor spoke, a cool breeze kicked up from the east, blew through a nearby stand of pine trees and cleansed the air.

Even the guests remarked on it.

Alton drew a deep breath and slowly exhaled. "Thank you, Lord."

As Bull Reynolds began to play the fiddle, Alton ignored a sudden attack of nerves, and stepped off the side porch. His lungs filled with pine-scented air, he joined Pastor Nathan beneath the arch.

Dad held out his hand. "Time to go, daughter. Are you ready for this?"

Connie turned from the window to face him. She'd heard those words before. Déjà vu—could a person sense the future? Did God foreshadow events to come?

She gazed at Dad, who seemed almost as nervous as she. Her heart constricted painfully, with the knowledge that he'd be leaving soon.

Don't start, she cautioned herself. Tears are permitted, but only a few. No floods, no gushes. It would ruin Judith's beautiful makeup job.

She stepped forward. "Yes, Dad, I'm ready."

He planted a kiss on her cheek. "Your mom would

weep for sure."

"And blow kisses," Connie spoke through trembling lips.

Dad laughed. "Yes, she would."

"I just wish my sisters could be here."

"I'll take lots of pictures. And it won't be long till you come. We'll all be together." He bit his lip. "Most of us, that is."

At the bottom of the stairs, Judith handed Connie her bouquet of sweet white rose buds. "You look amazing."

The roses trembled a little as Connie stepped to the door, giving away the nerves she felt.

The fiddler began to play *All Things Bright and Beautiful.*

Judith set off down the path.

Dad shielded Connie until Judith stood at the front. Only then did he step aside and guide her down the porch steps, and along the path.

The day was warm and the sun beat down, but beneath the tall oak trees, it was probably ten degrees cooler. Odd, the things that pass through one's mind in moments like these. Connie struggled to keep her nerves in check as she smiled at their guests. So many folks had gathered to witness the vows. Many more than she'd expected.

Instead of standing with their backs to Connie, they turned to face her. She breathed a sigh of relief. It was nothing like the dream. Maggie almost smiled. Jensen and Marla kept a very proper stone face, which mattered … not at all.

Finally, Alton came into view. He looked so tall and fine, standing beside the preacher. The expression of his face answered all her fears and settled her heart.

As Connie approached, Alton stood at attention, amazed that such a beautiful woman would soon be his wife. From the moment their eyes met, he couldn't look away. He almost had to remind himself to breathe.

When she came alongside him, he gazed into those guileless eyes that had so arrested him the first time they met.

The music stopped. Pastor asked who was giving this woman.

Mac squared his shoulders. "I am."

As Alton closed his fingers over her small hand, a tremor of nerves, or possibly excitement coursed through him.

His attention left Connie, but only for a moment, as he faced Pastor Nathan.

Somehow, he made all the right responses, repeated the vows with no major mistakes. Placed the ring on her finger. Received his ring.

"I now pronounce you man and wife."

Alton glanced at Pastor.

He nodded. "You may kiss your bride."

"My bride." After a proper Baptist kiss, he drew back, still holding her hand, cherishing the moment. He'd been given the gift of a lifetime. Energy coursed through him. He wanted to sweep her off her feet, dance around, and shout how much he loved her.

But of course, he did none of those things.

Pastor stepped forward. "Ladies and gentleman, I am pleased to introduce you to Mr. and Mrs. Alton Wade."

Annabelle dried her damp cheeks. As Connie and Alton walked back down the aisle, husband and wife, only happiness filled her heart.

"It's time to go." Lillian linked arms with her as they followed the bride and groom.

So many folks had turned out. Annabelle reckoned they had almost as many as had attended Jensen and Marla's wedding. Some had even brought their own chairs, apparently.

Miss Lucy and her family sat in a cluster on the ground beneath a burnished maple tree. Annabelle smiled and waved her hanky in their direction. It was good they'd come.

When she turned back to the main group, her eyes met Tom's. She tried to remain cool, but it was too late.

Warmth rushed into her cheeks and filled her heart. Truth is, she wanted him here. She even hoped he'd speak to her before the day was over—about the property, of course.

The wedding photographer worked quickly.

After he'd turned them loose to mingle, Lillian held onto her. "You're going to go sit in the shade, and I'll see you get some of that lovely punch."

"Yes, ma'am." Annabelle shook her head, but did as Lillian commanded. "Don't know if I can take several days of you ordering me around."

"It's gonna be the best thing for you, Annabelle, and you know it. No moping about over there by your lonesome. You need looking after for a bit. I'm just the one to do it. Now you sit still, and I'll be right back with the punch."

While Annabelle waited, she scanned the crowd. Everyone seemed to be having a good time. Well, maybe not everyone. Jensen's face held strain. While she watched, he led Marla to the car. They were leaving without even saying goodbye. Well, at least they'd put in an appearance.

Not five minutes later, Tom stood over her, holding two cups. "Miss Lillian asked me to bring you some punch."

Annabelle examined his face, and found concern in his eyes. Yes, he'd probably already heard what had happened to her. She took the cup and sipped. The sweetness of the liquid almost overwhelmed, but she didn't let on.

He grabbed a chair and brought it near, taking

advantage of everyone's preoccupation with the cake and punch. "Are you all right, Miss Annabelle?"

She drew a breath and slowly exhaled. "I'm good, Tom."

"I couldn't believe it when Doc Kestle told me what happened. I hope you're planning to take it easy for a few days."

"I can now, I believe, with the wedding over and all."

"And you'll have Miss Lillian to take care of you. Will you need someone to drive you to town?"

Annabelle met his gaze. He knew about the doctor appointment, too?

He shrugged. "Doc Kestle stopped in. He ordered your prescription." He nodded toward the house. "I left it in the kitchen."

"Y'all discuss cases?"

"It was professional, Annabelle. There's always a follow-up when it involves … the heart."

A slow smile lit his eyes and warmed her insides. Oh, she was in trouble. Must be the weakness of her condition, for she could not remember why she had rejected him in the past. "Thank you, Tom. I appreciate your thoughtfulness."

"I told you I'd take care of you, and I meant it, Annabelle. I'm here for you—as your friend—and I'm not going anywhere."

As your friend. She sighed. Just when she was beginning to feel there could be more.

They sat in companionable silence, watching the crowds mill about. A warm glow, a healing balm, filled Annabelle's chest. She smiled, completely at ease. She almost dozed off, till someone behind her spoke.

"Would you look at that? I believe Miss Annabelle has a beau."

Annabelle swiveled around, trying to see who had spoken, but there were too many folks standing about. Impossible to tell.

"What is it, Annabelle?" Tom asked.

She looked at him. "Oh, nothing. I was just wondering about Connie and Alton."

A song played over and over in Connie's mind as she and Alton visited with their guests. *I Love You Because.* She wasn't just remembering that day in Nashville. The girls sang it while they helped her get ready. Now, she couldn't get it out of her head.

John Woodruff approached them, a big smile on his face. "Congratulations, you two."

"Thanks," Alton clasped John's hand. "How's the new job?"

While the two men talked, Connie looked for Maggie. It'd be great if she could introduce them right now.

As if Maggie read her mind, she moved into view.

Connie waved.

Maggie hurried over.

"Thank you so much for coming to the wedding."

Maggie gave a shrug. "It's the social event of the season." She eyed John. "Is that him?"

Connie took her hand and started forward.

Maggie hesitated. "My name is Margaret."

Margaret in tow, Connie approached John.

He smiled into Connie's eyes as she spoke.

"John, this is my friend, Margaret Arnold. She also attends our church."

His brows arched as his lips quirked into an admiring smile. "I'm pleased to meet you, Miss Arnold."

Alton caught Connie's eye and mouthed, "Margaret?"

She bit her lip, then held out her hand to him. "If you'll excuse us, John and Margaret, we need to greet some of our other guests."

"No problem." John quirked a grin.

Maggie's expression told Connie all was forgiven. For the moment.

"That was a major coup," Alton whispered in Connie's ear.

"I know, wouldn't it be wonderful?"

"Hmm … I don't know. I'm really having a hard time thinking of anyone else right now."

When Miss Lillian waved from the back porch, Alton led Connie through the throng to meet her.

"Regina has the cake ready for our friends over there,"

she indicated the black families assembled in the side yard.

Connie and Alton accompanied Regina as she carried the two-layer sheet cake.

Alton helped her set it on the table beneath the maple trees. He reached for Connie's hand. "Thanks, all of you, for coming and helping to make this day special for Connie and me."

Miss Lucy stepped forward. "Thank you, for allowing us to have a part, Mr. Alton. We wouldn't have missed it for the world."

For one fleeting moment, Connie felt almost like royalty. It was something reflected in the eyes of several of her friends, now standing before her. She had worked as one of them—was it only last fall? Now, she was Mrs. Alton Wade. On a whim, she pressed her fingers against her lips and blew them a kiss.

Her spur-of-the-moment gesture was greeted with cheers and laughter.

The noise died down as Miss Lucy began to sing *Amazing Grace*. The rest of her family joined in. Many of the other guests stopped talking to listen.

Bull Reynolds took up his fiddle and played.

Alton squeezed Connie's hand and smiled into her eyes. "Happy?"

"Oh, yes. What a perfect ending to the day."

Joseph snuggled in one arm, Connie hugged Momma with the other. "I'm going to miss you."

Momma gave her a warm look. "I hope you don't, sweet girl. I hope you're so blissfully happy, you don't think of me at all."

"I just want you to know how much I love you. You're still my momma. Not just my former mother-in-law. What we went through, it binds us together. I can't forget that."

Momma reached for her hanky and dabbed at her eyes. "Sometimes it seems so long ago, other times, it seems like yesterday." She shifted in her chair before continuing.

"They say time heals. I don't know. I think it's kind of like leaving a place you love to go on a long trip. You watch till it disappears over the horizon. Or maybe it's more like driving up a mountain. You circle around till you can't see what's behind you. Come back around, and there it is, but it's farther away. You can't see it as well. You can't make out the little things anymore. That's what it's like for me right now. But hope is shining up ahead. I can almost grasp it. I don't want to lose it."

Connie passed the baby to her. "Here's hope, Momma."

"Oh, sweet girl, I love this boy with all my heart." She caressed Connie's cheek. "I love you for carrying him, for giving birth to him. Yes, I lost my boys—my babies—but you mean more to me than seven sons."

About the Author

Her writing credits include a 20's era romance, Amelia's Legacy (2014), Carlotta's Legacy (2016) Books 1 & 2, Legacy Series from Write Integrity Press (WIP), and the Grace-Award-winning Annabelle's Ruth (2015), and Sutter's Landing (2017), Books 1 & 2, Kinsman Redeemer Series, also from WIP. She has two fantasy-adventure novels, The Lady of the Haven and A Gathering of Eagles, in a second edition published by Sign of the Whale Books™, an imprint of Olivia Kimbrell Press™.

Amazon Author Page
www.BettyThomasonOwens.com
Twitter: @BATOwens

Facebook.com/betty.owens.author

Pinterest.com/btowens

writingpromptsthoughtsideas.wordpress.com

Acknowledgements

I am not alone. I'm surrounded by a community of writing friends who know and understand the daily angst of the writing journey. Their help and encouragement keeps me moving forward. To my hard-working ACFW Scribes team—sorry about the rush at the end! Thanks, Nike Chillemi, Patricia Reece Krugel, Karen Harrison, and Celeste Charlene. Your catches and suggestions sent me deeper into the story and made me work a little harder. I'd also like to thank Louisville ACFW friends, Harriet Michael, Karen Richardson, and Ralene Burke for your friendship and encouragement. And a big thank you to one of my closest writing buddies, Jennifer Dison Hallmark, who always has an encouraging word for me.

To my editor, Julie Hausmann, and publisher Marji Laine Clubine at Write Integrity Press—so many thanks! You made my writing better and helped bring my vision of a story into reality.

I have to also thank a group of women who have become very important in my life—the women in my Bible study group at Trinity World Outreach Center—my champions and prayer warriors. You are blessed and highly favored!

Thanks, with all my love to my husband Bob, for putting up with me when I'm in my story world, and allowing me the time and space to bring my vision to life. To my family—all my love and thanks for your encouragement and sometimes, just for being there.

To the strong women in my life, to whom this book is dedicated, the late Aunt Jen and Aunt Fran, who loved beyond measure, and laid a beautiful foundation of love and humor in my life. And Aunt Edna and Mom, still very present and shining love's light in the face of daily struggles. Just knowing you're there makes my life better.

Most importantly, thank you, Heavenly Father for your gift of life and inspiration.

Other Books by Betty

Available at
Amazon

Books
1 & 2

in the
Legacy
Series

Book 1 of the Kinsman Redeemer Series shares the original trials of Connie and Annabelle. Follow them through desperate grief and a treacherous journey, and enjoy their initial introduction with Alton.

Annabelle's Ruth is a 2015 winner of The Grace Award and is available from Amazon.

Recent Releases by Write Integrity Press

A contemporary reimagining of the biblical character of Bathsheba.

Literally a starving artist, Hope must depend on a doctor whose sister died from Hope's mistakes.

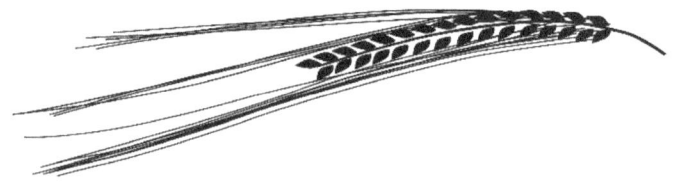

We hope you enjoyed reading
SUTTER'S LANDING.
If you did, please consider returning to the
Amazon page and leaving
a review for the author.
And watch for Book 3 of
The Kinsman Redeemer Series.

Thank you
for reading our books!

Look for other books
published by

Write Integrity Press
www.WriteIntegrity.com